THE FRONTIER

THE FRONTIER

by

PETER E. S. KING

Stethoscope Publishing
105/2 Clarke St, Crows Nest, NSW 2065 Australia

First published in 2025 by Stethoscope Publishing

Text © Peter E. S. King
Cover artworks by Ted Lewis
Design by BKA+D

Typeset in Adobe Garamont Pro

Printed and bound by Ingram Spark

ISBN 978-0-6455059-8-6 (paperback)
ISBN 978-0-6455059-9-3 (eBook)

The Frontier, King, Peter E. S.

A catalogue record for this
book is available from the
National Library of Australia

CAST OF CHARACTERS

(in order of appearance)

Ian Percy – *mounted policeman*

Bill Todd – *mounted policeman*

Cedric Hall – *gold panner (former clerk)*

Nancy Hall – *school teacher*

Alice and Alfred Hall – *Cedric and Nancy's six year old twins*

John Hale – *mounted policeman*

Ma Shell – *proprietor of Hill Top food tent*

Sergeant Norman Green – *Sergeant of Hill Top*

George Nash – *mounted policeman*

Mr Wickham – *merchant in Hill Top*

Gary and Bessie Holt – *landowners*

Bob Pringle – *mounted policeman*

Sergeant Greg Knox – *Sergeant of Sunny Flat*

Mr. Hunt – *carrier (former school teacher)*

Betsy Hunt – *daughter of Mr. Hunt, runs a food tent in Sunny Flat*

Dick and Tom Hunt – *sons of Mr. Hunt, carriers*

Jason Hunt – *runs a shop in Sunny Flat*

Jack May – *mounted policeman*

Fred Hall – *city detective*

Sergeant Rich – *city Sergeant*

Ben Holt – *city Constable*

Charley – *city Constable*

Sid – *city Constable*

Alex – *city Constable*

Kevin – *city Constable*

Mr. and Mrs. Allan Lake - *landowners*

Albie Jones – *gold buyer*

Andrew Hade – *eldest son of Sam Hade*

Shaun, Patrick and Toby Hade – *Andrew's brothers*

Senior Sergeant Shaw – *city policeman*

Sam Hade – *landowner (former army doctor)*

Elizabeth Hade – *Sam's wife (trained nurse)*

Dan – *old shepherd on the Hade property*

Betty Thorne – *15 year old daughter of Alf Thorne*

Angus Thorne – *five year son of Alf Thorne*

Dennis Stone – *criminal*

Jenny and Jane Hade – *daughters of Sam and Elizabeth*

Alf Thorne – *landowner*

Jeff Hake - *landowner*

Jim Thorne – *brother of Alf Thorne*

James Wade – *new mounted policeman (former stockman)*

Sally Pearson – *old acquaintance of Ian Percy*

Bernie Sharp – *patrol policeman*

Barry Hodge – *patrol policeman*

Harry Elms – *gold panner*

Chapter One

A lone horseman rode over a high ridge on an early summer's afternoon into a beautiful valley. Surrounded by hills, a stream and gum trees were nestled in the valley flats. As always, he was delighted at the superb virgin country set out below.

He couldn't see any movement and there were no squatters in the valley. Further down the slope were a few kangaroos sitting up looking at him. He began the descent towards the valley floor.

Most valleys had waterholes of one kind or another between the hills, though, in summer, many dried out under the hot sun. This country was so different from England or India. In these wide open spaces, he could ride a very long distance and not see another human being.

He was aware that he was not alone. Black shadows moved rapidly behind trees – watching. His rations were on the light side when he made camp in an open area near some rocks close to a waterhole. He preferred to camp with views in all directions. His horse was hobbled and able reach water and good grass nearby, happy to remain near his sleeping master.

*

The next morning, after a light meal and making sure the fire was out, he removed all evidence of his camp, mounted his horse and continued to ride up the valley and over the other side, keeping out of the thick, low trees on the crest of the hill.

All day he rode through this barren countryside, devoid of white settlers. The goldmining areas were back behind him. He was on the lookout for squatters on land they were not entitled to – though he could understand their desire for this virgin country.

He loved this country. In the distance he could see a blue range of hills covered in trees. These were to be avoided – the terrain too uncomfortable for his horse. Also there were steep gullies with much dead timber. A wildfire had not been here for a long time.

He had learnt the hard way about being very careful of the dry summer storms with their great flashes of lightning and bone-dry grass. The thought of being caught out in such a thing was unsettling, to put it mildly. It was a matter of sitting still, feeling the direction of the wind, then galloping to safety in the opposite direction.

Now it was late in the day, and he saw in the distance, the rising column of blue smoke. This needed investigation. It was still too early for a camp – it felt about four in the afternoon.

He descended the hill using a native animal track. The smoke rose above a creek. He put his hand into his saddlebag and took out a small brass telescope he had bought in India.

There was nothing threatening to see, but no way he could approach without being seen, so he rode across the flat ground in full sight.

He rode closer. Suddenly, a uniformed police officer stood up in surprise.

He had discovered a long time ago that not all police were friendly. Yet those who could meld together became good friends.

The man watched the stranger's approach as he alighted and walked forward, leading his horse by the reins with one hand and holding out the other.

"I'm Ian Percy, also on patrol."

"G'day, Bill Todd," the other stepped forward, shaking hands.

Both did a quick assessment of the other as men do at a first meeting. Each was in their twenties, over six feet tall, with wide shoulders and slim waists. They were dressed in skin-tight white pantaloons which needed a wash. They wore tall black boots ending just below their knees, blue shirts, and straw hats. Both were tanned by long days in the saddle. Ian had brown hair and Bill's was black. Both had short beards – fit and healthy physiques.

Ian was curious.

"I saw the smoke from your fire and wondered…" His voice faltered.

Bill smiled, "I managed to kill a couple of ducks and decided to cook them in clay."

"Clay? I don't understand?"

Bill seemed amused. "There's a gully running into this waterhole a bit further along, back down that direction," he indicated with his hand. "On the bank, clay was exposed and I thought I'd cook dinner." He gave a big smile as he looked at Ian. "Now I'm going to have company."

Ian felt a warmth towards Bill. Feeling he ought to make a contribution, he asked, "Where did you find the ducks?"

"Further down at that other waterhole, a couple of hundred yards from here. Do you want to see if you can get another two, which would give you food for a couple of days?"

"Yes, I'd like to have a go. Cooking them in your clay'd be something different."

"Good. You get them, and I'll dig out some more clay," Bill encouraged him.

Ian mounted his horse and rode down the creek until he saw ducks in the distance on the bank. Generally, he liked watching birds, but today he needed food. He lined up two ducks side by side, and with two quick shots, bagged both of them. The other ducks took instant flight.

Alighting from his horse, Ian retrieved his catch, quite pleased with himself. It was not always easy to get one duck, let alone two. Often he had gone hungry.

Back at the camp, Bill looked up in surprise.

"I'm impressed. Thought you'd be lucky to get one. They're not easy to catch."

"When I was home, my dad took me on duck shoots. It wasn't for food… It was such a waste of lovely birdlife," Ian said quietly.

"I did the same when I was younger. Didn't value wildlife," Bill agreed.

Ian led his horse to an area with shade and put the hobbles on. He gutted the two ducks and watched as a few black magpies flew down to eat what he had discarded nearby on the grass. Using the hot water, he plucked the birds. Taking note of what Bill was doing, he wrapped the clay around them, but not too thickly.

"Why haven't you put them in the fire?" Ian was puzzled.

Bill played with the coals, didn't answer for a moment or two.

"You can't see it, but before I made the fire, I dug a hole that was bigger than I needed it to be. Irritating… but with your birds it will be just right."

The coals were red – a perfect bush oven. Bill used a piece of wood to move the coals so he could place the four ducks side by side. Covering them with the coals, they were deeply buried.

"How long does it take?" Ian asked.

"It depends upon how you like your meat cooked."

"Cooked well – no blood." Ian was definite.

"I reckon I like well-done, too. Ought to be ready before dark," Bill answered with a smile.

The camp site was a little way from the creek, out in the open, away from the big trees. No risk of branches falling on their small swags overnight. They had a good view of the surrounding countryside.

It was unlikely anyone would creep up on them, except, of course, the black shadows. But neither were worried. None had been in sight the last few days.

They bent down at the creek bank to wash and fill their quart pots. They murmured about fishing, watching the swirl and shimmer of silver perch.

Each man knew what the other was thinking – what could they use to catch perch?

Patrols required silence. Shooting was unwise if a senior officer was within earshot, so better on the distant frontier like this, a long way from known habitation.

There is something about a campfire which creates good fellowship. Both men were feeling comfortable with each other.

It was early evening – the sun sinking behind the hills, when Bill announced, "I think the ducks are cooked now."

He began scraping the hot coals out of the way.

"Can you move that stick and raise the ducks as I move the fire out of the way?" he winked at Ian.

Soon they were eating with relish. Ian was so pleased he had investigated that plume of smoke.

"Keep some of the fish for tomorrow night, and we can have a light breakfast in the morning," Bill suggested later in the evening after the pair had cleaned up.

Ian agreed.

Bill added a couple more logs to the fire before rolling out his swag at a safe distance. Ian did the same in the opposite direction as a rough sort of camp protection. The pair talked very quietly for a short time before dropping off into silence.

When the day had ended and talking had ceased, it was not quiet in the bush. The out-of-sight rustlings were amplified, as animals seemed to creep all around the camp. A different world making its own lullaby.

*

The camp was quiet in the morning as the men rolled up their swags, checked their horses, packed the remainder of the ducks away in the saddle bags, and made the first tea of the day. They put out the fire, covered the coals with water and soil, removing all evidence of the campsite.

Both men had saddled their horses. "Bill, I don't see why we shouldn't continue our patrol together," Ian offered.

"Yup, I agree, we'll make a good team."

With the decision made, the two mounted police rode on down the valley beside the creek.

"What was that black and white bird flew into our camp last night to eat?" Ian asked.

"I thought you knew." Bill was incredulous. Then remembered that this might be a new landscape to his mate. "Magpies – the ones singing early this morning. Didn't you hear them?"

"Yes, I did, and I loved the sound," Ian admitted.

"There were lots where I grew up on the other side of the Blue Mountains."

Ian continued to talk about the birds he'd seen in the colony. Bill helped him with names when he could identify them from Ian's description. The blue wren was their favourite.

"Were you born in this country?" Ian changed the subject.

"I was born just over the mountains, near a big river called the Nepean. Mum and Dad have a small orchard, and our house sits on high ground well away from the floods after heavy rain."

"It must have been a good childhood. Whatever made you leave and join the police?"

"There are those born free and those sent as convicts, or their people were convicts. These do their best to keep it a secret, particularly if they are doing well," Bill replied cryptically.

"So how do you fit into this?" Ian persisted.

"I keep the secret of my parents' convict past. Growing up isn't easy. There are always people who know and taunt those who try and move forward. I too hate thieves – a plague in this country."

"I experienced the caste system in India, and it's very hard to escape from it," Ian offered.

"So that is your accent?"

"Partly. I was born in England. My parents were not rich but were determined to give me a good education. I was sent to a good boarding school until I was sixteen. Then my father admitted there was not enough money for my upkeep. He arranged for a cadetship in the Bombay Army – he had a cousin in the Honourable East India Company, so I found myself in a very foreign country."

"My parents were also keen for me to be educated, but I left school at fifteen and went to work in a brick kiln for four years," Bill countered.

"What came next?"

"I managed to get a shop job and learnt about money – very important as it's hard to keep."

"Particularly when the currency is foreign and it has to stretch," Ian laughed.

Suddenly almost at the hooves of the horses, a flock of birds rose as one, taking to the air in an instant. The horses shied away. It took a few moments to settle them as Ian commented on the bright pink feathers.

"They're lovely birds, what are they?" he asked.

"Galahs, they're everywhere all over the land. If one gets killed, the other will mourn for it; they mate for life."

They had been riding for some time along this creek which wound itself around the tall hills, some quite steep. The pair had to cross to continue along the opposite bank. This was part of their patrol – where there was water was the most likely place to find squatters. It wasn't always easy for the horses. There was lots of debris washed up by the floods on each bank. So they rode slowly, picking their way.

Each wanted another night on this creek. There was never a plan made in the morning of where they'd be at the going down of the sun. The patrol could take them anywhere.

"Ian, can you swim?" asked Bill, as the temperature rose and the air thickened with flies.

"I learnt to swim in India and loved playing in the water. Can you?"

"Yes, when we were kids we spent hours in the water. With a river nearby we had to learn – otherwise it would have been too dangerous," Bill explained.

Ian looked up at the sky, noting the position of the sun.

"I could do with a wash. In this weather, we could wash some clothes and get them dry before nightfall. What do you think?"

Sometimes it wasn't possible, but they had been in the saddle for over two weeks, and a wash was one of the luxuries of bush life.

"Let's do it," Bill grinned. "We ought to be quite safe."

The creek lay between two hills with a split in them. Facing north, this spot would give them sunshine into the late afternoon.

It didn't take long to hobble the horses, and remove the saddles and saddlebags. Their swags put aside, both men stripped naked and were soon in the water.

"You're not English-bred?" Bill asked in surprise, staring at Ian's coffee-coloured torso, legs and butt.

"No, I have a great, great grandmother who was Spanish. I don't suffer from the sun, nor do I get sunburnt. And I love the heat."

Ian turned to Bill, who really did look surprised.

"Do you mind that I'm not your colour?"

Constantly outdoors, Bill's arms and face were almost as tanned as Ian's. Now he felt awkward. He'd spoken without thinking. He really liked Ian.

"No, I don't mind. In fact, I'm jealous because I get sunburnt before I get a good tan."

After a moment or two, Bill added reflectively, "No one would know unless they saw you as you are now."

Ian accepted that Bill had not meant to not offend in any way. He wanted this friendship, and it was progressing too well to allow this minor matter of a Spanish lady to interfere.

Soon their clothes were washed and hanging on branches and shrubs nearby – away from where the horses were feeding, otherwise they'd be on the ground again.

"How did you get into the police?" Bill asked, as they lay naked in the sun waiting for their clothes to dry.

"I was in England in fifty-three to see my father, who was very ill and died while I was with him. At the time, New South Wales had requested to the Colonial Office to find men from England and Ireland with at least three years' experience of policing and send them to the colony. I had three years in the Indian police and was not looking forward to returning."

"So that's how you ended up here."

"I qualified and came out on the first available ship, pleased to get away from India. There was trouble brewing in the northwest frontier and I liked the Indian people. The Honourable East India Company is not all that good in dealing with people. They were closer to thieves as I saw it."

"The earlier police were taken from the army, and it wasn't successful –

they were more of a problem than peacekeepers," Bill explained. "There was corruption. No standards in the work."

*

At last, their clothes were dry enough to put on. The rather-squashed ducks were again put into some clay to heat up for the evening meal.

"Why do you avoid walking or camping under the old gum trees?" Ian asked.

"These old trees have a nasty habit of dropping their branches at any time without warning, and bad luck for anyone underneath. You can't afford to break anything so far from help," Bill warned.

"Last night I saw how you positioned your swag. I did likewise with the intention of asking you why you did so."

"Now you know!"

"I also noticed that you dug a hole before you put your swag down," Ian persisted.

"To make my sleep comfortable for my hip, so it was not flat on the ground which I don't like at all."

"So much to learn. I'm glad I met you Bill."

"We have to keep learning, Ian, every day."

"You were born in this land, and it's in your blood, you're part of the land."

"You're here now, Ian, and it will be your country, too."

"Bill, I'm a foreigner and this land is very strange, with animals so different from the rest of the world."

"As you say, I'm born here. Even so, this frontier is foreign to me, too. This is an ancient land with a story that we may never understand."

They talked while the campfire slowly died down. The night gradually closed in and only sounds of the unseen were heard. As last they wished each other a good sleep and silence reigned in the camp.

Chapter Two

The next morning, the pair quietly packed everything away in their swags and saddle bags, and prepared for the day. They had checked this district. Now they needed to locate a goldmining camp believed to be somewhere a little east. Gold was the draw to lure men and women from home and into unknown country.

Bill began to look around this way and that way as if there was something wrong and he couldn't locate it.

"I can smell smoke."

Ian was thinking of the long, dead grass they were riding through after beginning to climb the hill, which had a gentle slope to the top. Near the crest, the terrain became rough on the horses due to the quantity of sharp stones strewn about.

"What kind of smoke?" Ian asked.

"I'd say wood smoke."

"Which direction?"

"I'm not sure except it's ahead of us – it's a very faint scent in the wind. All of us near the mountains know summer storms and the sudden lightning strikes that cause grass fires."

They continued riding through the trees.

"Let's keep going along the top of this hill until we get to that bare area away from the trees. We just might be able to see what lies ahead," Bill suggested.

Ian was happy to let Bill ride ahead. "Lead on and find that smoke."

"I assure you we are quite safe, wood smoke means people," Bill replied, turning in his saddle.

"I've learnt the hard way to be very careful of bushfires."

They rode in and out of the trees, over logs, and the beginning of a gully going down the hill, at last reaching an area of ground without growth of any kind.

"Ian, how about using that brass telescope?"

Taking it out of his saddle bag, Ian looked in all directions.

"Bill, take it and look down there," Ian pointed to a distant valley. "I can see blue smoke rising, almost curling through those tall trees."

Bill took the telescope and looked in the direction indicated.

"I'd say that's the mining camp we're meant to find."

Bill and Ian knew the object of their search was within half a day's ride. They decided to make camp at a convenient place, closer to the gold seekers.

"We're fairly low on food. It'd be good if we could bag some more game while we're still away from people," Ian said.

"Alright, we'll go down to that valley ahead and see what we can find in the water?"

As they rode carefully down the slope, the pair thought about the distant miners' camp and what they might find.

"If this is the mining camp, it's important that we're a reasonable distance from it. They are bound to be poor and all the thieves in the world are in these camps," Bill speculated.

They shot two young ducks without much trouble, put them in the saddle bags, and continued to ride closer to the camp, before pitching their own swags in the next valley. They cooked the ducks in clay and discussed the next day's job.

"Do you ever think about acquiring extra money on the job?" Bill asked after the meal as they settled down in their swags.

Ian thought for a moment or two as he listened to his horse munching on grass nearby.

"It was when I was in the Indian army. We were instructed if, at the end of a conflict, we found any jewels – which Indians inevitably wore in battle – we were to hand them to officers. Such valuables belonged to the State. I did hand in some lovely jewels, and a couple of weeks later I saw them being worn by an officer's wife. So the next time, I kept them. From then onwards I'd pick them up, sometimes all bloody. I sold them quietly in the bazaars."

It was quiet while Ian recalled, "Jewels would not have been missed – the gulf between very rich and the poor was vast."

"Would you do it here?"

"No. Best locate the owners."

There was silence as Ian remembered India, and Bill considered Ian's words. Ian wondered why Bill had asked.

"Do you worry about how you got your few pounds?" Ian asked.

"Now I'm a policeman, it's difficult sometimes to draw a line between what's right and wrong. I picked up extra cash by running errands for a man in a gambling business. He paid well for silence and for the work I did. When he was drunk, he gave me more money. For a time it did not occur to me what he wanted. I found out the hard way, and from then onwards I kept out of his way when he'd been drinking."

Ian winced. "I had a similar experience as a boy going out to India on the ship. There'll always be men who'll prey on…"

"Why didn't our families warn us?" Bill asked.

"We have to learn about life ourselves, make our decisions, decide what we will or won't do. I grew up with an honour code, like not cheating at cards, things my father didn't approve of. I have to decide what code I live by. In this job, it won't be easy."

"My dad used to tell me if I could look into a mirror in the morning when I was doing my hair and not feel guilty about something, I was doing okay. He said when I couldn't look at myself in the mirror, then I was in trouble," Bill explained quietly.

"I like that image. It's very true. It's good for boys, but we're men and we have to make some hard decisions. For instance, we have needs. Maybe we rely on girls who work in the trade – not easy in this job."

"Codes of behaviour are fine, but there are issues close to our wellbeing – food while on patrol for instance." Bill was just warming up.

"This is part of the decisions we make. When meat is our need, if I find a person killing a beast, I'll ask for some, providing they don't have a large family. You have to be fair as I'll very likely be seeing them again. You want the people to stay friendly – some will, but probably most people try and avoid us."

"If asked to join a squatter for a feed, do you accept or make an excuse to move on?" Bill wondered.

"You make a decision at the time, but never camp in their hut or anywhere near it for obvious reasons. You have to be careful about those who might use us to their own advantage. If anyone offers food though, I take it even if not required. You can always pass it on to someone else."

The full darkness of the night had come and sleep crept towards each man, as they thought about work and a code of behaviour. The only subject left alone was girls. Those in the trade would be their clients or at least available if needed.

*

The next day after leaving camp, they travelled through some very rough country and steep hills following the scent of wood smoke where, at last, they walked the horses down a steep incline to the water. The nearby men panning for that precious metal, looked up in surprise. No words were spoken for a few moments.

"Have you found any gold this morning?" Bill asked.

"I've just started," grunted the panner closest to Bill.

It was obvious he was afraid of the police. It would be unwise to admit to any gold. The hopeful miner was young, though it was hard to tell because of his long and unkempt hair.

As the policemen had not ridden on, he stood and looked up from his pan.

"We heard two shots yesterday and worried it might be someone comin' to demand our property. We treat all newcomers with caution," the miner warned.

"Point taken. In future, we will be more considerate near the goldfields," Bill replied.

"I wasn't having a go at you," the fellow countered quickly, now flustered.

Ian had been watching the play of emotions on the man's face.

"Goldmining is a dangerous occupation. There are lots of crooks only too happy to relieve you of your hard-earned find. We also have to find food in this wilderness."

The troopers rode on down the opposite side of the creek, much to the man's relief. As they rode, the pair counted about fifty people panning for gold in the areas where the water flowed over tiny rapids before entering the large waterholes. The men were a mixture of ages – from quite young to old grey-haired men.

"Up ahead that could be a family," Bill nodded and arched a finger forward.

There was a long waterhole and a pile of logs in the water, left behind by the last flood. A young man was panning beside the stones running into the next waterhole. As they approached, he stood up and waited. A woman also stopped what she was doing beside the fire. Two faired-haired children left their fishing lines, moved closer to their mother and waited.

"Found a good return?" Bill called out.

"Does anyone?" the man countered, smiling.

Ian thought this man was not a usual miner. He leant forward on his horse's neck.

"You're not a miner by normal work, are you?" he asked.

"I thought I looked the part very well!" he laughed, looking surprised, before adding, "We're about to stop for a break. Would you join us?"

The woman looked surprised at his words but quickly covered it up with a smile. Bill and Ian alighted from their horses and tied the reins to a nearby tree away from the camp.

"I'm Bill Todd, and this wise young man is Ian Percy."

"Bill is too young to comprehend wisdom, hence his misuse of the word!" Ian smiled.

The woman laughed and continued with the introductions, "I'm Nancy. This is my husband Cedric, and these are our twins, Alice and Alfred. You are right, Mr. Percy. I was a school teacher until the school was burnt down. My husband was a clerk until his business folded."

Cedric, who had completed washing his hands in the creek and drying them on a rag, now walked to the fire and sat down on a log opposite the two policemen, who had found their own log seating.

"Do we have any tea left?" Cedric asked his wife.

"Sorry, we're out of tea, but I've got some herbs which make a good brew?"

Ian looked at Bill and made a gesture with his head.

"We have tea for your billy," Bill said generously.

"Yes please, we ran out of tea some weeks ago, and I put together a herbal concoction, which is not the same, but it's better than nothing in hot water." Cedric and Nancy now wore big smiles.

While she was speaking, Bill had gone to his saddle bag and taken out a small bag of tea, walked back to the fire and dropped a couple of spoonfuls into the billy, to the delight of Cedric and Nancy.

"Thank you. Herbs are all very well but there is no substitute for tea," Cedric spoke quietly.

"Caught any fish today?" Ian asked Alfred, looking across the fire at the children.

"No, Mr. Percy, not this morning but we did yesterday and swapped it for some meat from one of the other men down the creek."

"We swap whatever we can. Also, Nancy is able to teach some of the children in the camp to read and write – it brings in a little money," Cedric explained.

"We have no paper or slates, so I use a patch of sand further down the creek and a sharp stick to draw. The children have no problems," Nancy said.

"Mr. Percy, what do you do?" Alice asked, who had been quiet and just listening.

"Alice, he's a mounted policeman," Cedric said, looking at his daughter.

"I know he's a mounted policeman, but I want to know what he does?" said Alice looking at her father.

The six-year-old child showed some irritation.

"Alice, Mr. Todd and I ride long distances to check on the welfare of people like you and your parents. This is a very vast land with all kinds of people. Some are not very nice and are a danger to good people, and we do our best to protect those who need help," Ian smiled.

"So that's what you do? We have some of those people here."

"Alice, we have spoken about this matter before today. You really must mind your tongue," Cedric said to Alice quickly. "Those miners must never hear you say those words, it would put us all in danger. Alfred, you must explain to your sister."

"Sometimes it is difficult to get her to understand," Alfred shrugged.

"It's difficult for everyone the way we are living. After we lost our jobs, we decided to try to find enough gold to buy land somewhere, to create a better life," Nancy changed the subject.

Alfred and Alice lost interest in the adults and went back to fishing.

"Dad, I've got a fish, come and help me," Alfred called out, feeling a tug on his line.

While the family assisted Alfred, Ian and Bill went to their horses and mounted.

"We've enjoyed meeting you both and hope to see you again one day. You will always be welcome at our fire," Cedric farewelled them.

They called out a cheerio and rode away from the miners' camp, up the steep hill overlooking the settlement of Gold Creek at the base of a narrow valley.

"You know Bill, you smelt the smoke so far away, and then we found it quite near at hand. I've begun to notice that the last two valleys are very narrow ones, not at all like those ones which were several miles wide which we took a long time to cross a few days ago," Ian commented.

"We're getting closer to the big hills and the valleys are becoming smaller. What about returning to barracks to give a report? We are almost out of supplies."

"I'm happy to do that. Do you think they'll let us go out again together? I'm happier working with you."

"Same here, the horses will be glad of a rest too," Bill replied.

Both men were looking forward to meeting fellow troopers and hearing about their activities. The spread of settlement seemed small compared to the vastness of the bush. Official settlement was confined to a number of counties outside of which government had not yet allowed land sales – only leases.

Ian and Bill's patrol was in the leased settlements and goldmining areas. The barracks had recently been established in a place called Hill Top which had rapidly grown in size. The number of new dwellings had exploded. With the open cesspits, the usual stink was an unpleasant reality.

Chapter Three

They rode into what appeared to be the main street and followed this rather muddy track to the other side of Hill Top. The patrol office was beside the barracks and the stables were further away down towards the creek. It was well away from the flood level, and the horse paddock was now full. They were all government purchased, so perhaps not the best stock, but good horses for the police.

It was late afternoon by the time they had unsaddled their horses and let them go into the paddock and stowed their gear in the stables. Carrying the swags and saddlebags, they walked up to the barracks and deposited them on their respective trunks beside their beds. Then both went to the office to give a verbal report.

The office was run by a Sergeant who had his own ideas about the job based mostly on what he had experienced as a young police officer. Change wasn't part of his agenda. If it works, don't change it. So he was quite happy to allow Ian and Bill to patrol together.

"Two heads might be better than one in solving problems. On your next patrol, I want you to go down in the southern area amongst the settlers. We've heard a whisper of something disturbing, but exactly what we don't know. So we want you to find out what the problem is."

The pair walked out of the office in a thoughtful mood.

"Bill, we've only got a very short time here so let's forget about work for tonight and enjoy what the place has to offer," Ian suggested.

"Okay, first of all, a wash in hot water, then food we don't have to cook, and then we'll find out what's new in that grog shop."

In the washroom, Ian and Bill met up with John Hale, another mounted man. He was a well-built, strong young man with a cheerful personality and popular with his colleagues.

"What have you been doing since we last saw you, John?" Bill asked him.

"I was sent to a small community where a number of young women were being harassed by a man when they went down to the river to wash their clothes."

"Did you get him?"

"Yes, I did, and the magistrate ordered a good whipping."

"That ought to stop him?" Ian commented.

"I hope so," John commented, although he was not so sure.

"Depends upon whether he is strongly tempted again. These communities are so isolated. He may well think the police won't catch him," Bill added.

They continued washing themselves and swapped tales about their colleagues.

"I did hear a few interesting words about Ma Shell, where you get some extra food in that tent at the end of the street," Bill said to John.

"What are you referring to?" John replied cheerfully, wiping soap away from his face as water dripped down from a trimmed black beard.

"I heard she was speaking about her man while fully tanked at the top of her voice."

"What did she say?"

"It was in response to her man saying in a loud voice, 'If you have balls, show them!' in the grog shop, and Ma is reputed to have said, 'That's all very well, he rolls on to me and off again and I often wonder if I've been visited at all!' She then added, amongst the loud laughter and his obvious discomfort, 'Just because he's got 'em, it doesn't mean he knows what to do with 'em'!"

The men chuckled.

"Where did you hear that story?" John asked.

"From one of the men present on the night. It was too good not to share!"

"Any other news since we've been away the last couple of weeks?" Ian asked.

"The Sergeant, Norm Green, wants to retire as soon as they can find a replacement as he's getting on in years. We'd rather he stayed. He's so knowledgeable about frontier conditions."

"Too much sitting down, he's put on a lot of weight. What is he going to do?" Bill asked.

"He has a nice slab house, and his wife is a good housekeeper. I suppose he'll continue to grow his vegetables."

At last, they finished washing and, for the night, decided not to wear their uniforms.

"Until people recognise us as police, we can move in the settlement and people will still talk to us," John said.

"What have you in mind for tonight after we have a meal?" Bill asked him.

"There're lots of new girls at the grog shop halfway down the main street. These girls are very accommodating, if you have that particular need."

"We'll follow you John, and for your sake I hope they are pretty!" Bill said.

As they walked out of the washroom another mounted man, George Nash, who was just inside the door, said, "You're kidding yourself, John, if you think these people won't recognise you. Those eagle eyes would know every one of us the moment we rode down the street towards these barracks." He looked straight at John before adding, "We're just less threatening out of uniform, but they'd know."

"I know you're right, George. All the same, for that brief time we can pretend at being just like everyone else."

George walked over to a jug and basin on a bench, while the others walked back to their trunks, left their towels on a hook above their beds and proceeded to the shed where the food was being cooked. Tonight it was a meat stew, with vegetables and freshly cooked damper, the kind of meal they dreamed of on wet nights out on patrol.

For a few minutes they ate in silence, and then John asked, "Did anything interesting happen to you fellows on your recent trip north?"

Ian looked at Bill and suggested, "What about our conversation with the miner who said we ought to be more considerate at shooting ducks near the goldminers?"

John looked very surprised, and said almost in disbelief, "Did he really say that?"

"I could see his point with so many crooks around the goldminers, that shot would make me nervous too," Ian replied.

Bill, equally thoughtful, had been thinking about it. "Perhaps we should organise our food a bit better and shoot our game further from the gold areas?"

"I know a mounted man who, if a miner dared to say those words to him, would have no hesitation in riding over him and his camp," admitted John, looking at Ian and Bill in surprise. He added carefully, "You're right, if we want people to trust us, we must make an effort to not unduly irritate them."

"That's our thinking. We can do without the arrogance in some situations – it's important to build a degree of trust," Ian said.

"Once we put on the uniform it does not give us the right to act contrary to how we would behave in ordinary clothes. We have a power over people, but how we use it is the core of the matter," Bill mused.

Soon they finished their meal and were looking forward to a good night's amusement. They walked out of the barracks into a side street, headed in a roundabout way to the grog shanty, on a street filled mainly with tents and a couple of slab dwellings. The shanty was a combination of tents and one slab building with nothing permanent about it. These places moved with the population, they sold a type of beer, which was mostly safe, and spirits, which you drank at your own risk.

The men walked into a room full of smoke and loud laughter. There was a stench of cheap, stale tobacco. Sawdust on the floor did not cover things best not seen. Poor quality oil in the lamps gave off a black smoke. Well-intoxicated people threw themselves around to the music of an old piano in the corner of the room. Tables and chairs were spread in one section of the establishment. It was to the tables that the men went to sit and view the young girls who were dressed to find customers. At the back were doorways with curtains.

"This place will get closed down as the respectable population grows," Bill said quietly.

"It will just go underground for those of us who need it," Ian countered.

"What about when you all become respectable married men?" John said with a laugh.

"That's another matter, we're not there yet!"

Being early in the evening the place wasn't full yet, so they had a good choice of the girls, made their selection and vanished behind the curtains.

After midnight, the three men returned unsteadily to the barracks, recalling the night with slurred voices and laughter. Those who had gone to bed earlier were not happy. It wasn't long before men half-asleep began trading slurs.

"Shut up, you bastards!"

"Fucking hell, shut up!"

"You keep your fucking voices down!"

Each man dropped on his bed with a paillasse, stuffed with fresh straw that was inclined to stick through the bag – not all that comfortable until used a number of times. These three were too exhausted to be bothered by a scratchy bunk.

*

At breakfast, silence reigned until John announced loudly, "What a grim lot you are on this lovely summer's morning!"

"I forgot that you were a morning irritation, John, also considering that you were one of that lot that made such a noise after midnight," George replied in a less than cheerful voice.

"George, you are never happy even at lunchtime as I seem to remember!"

Ian arrived and helped himself to a plate of meat and damper. A little while later, Bill followed. Everyone knew that silence was only possible if John was absent, so they settled in to light conversation. John had something on his mind and soon gave voice to it.

"This is not a good subject at any time of the day, but have any of you come into contact with something you cannot see?" John said.

"John, it is a little early for you to be drinking!" George said.

"George, I'm serious. There's something in the bush and your horse refuses to move, rears up and turns away?"

There was silence as the scenario was considered. After a few minutes, Bill and Ian shook their heads. Not something they could recall. The silence continued until George gave a sigh.

"Some months ago while crossing a gully, my horse reared back in fear and turned around to get away. I had a hard time holding her. We had to cross at another place. Later I asked an old native about it, and he told me a little bit. I reckon the missionaries might have got at him earlier because he talked about Europe. He explained that where armies had crisscrossed those lands, the ancient world had been buried well out of sight. Whereas, where we are, the ancient is still on the surface. According to him, we will all encounter their spirit world."

George lapsed into silence while his words seeped into their minds. Bill and Ian were startled by his conviction. George was usually so quiet.

"So we will be having eerie encounters?" John queried.

"I believe so. We are part of the landscape and I don't think we will suffer by this old spirit world," George replied.

"Except getting eerie feelings at night way out on our own!" John commented.

*

The men left the bench after breakfast and went to do various chores before a long patrol. This was a free morning to write letters or repair equipment. The barracks was a fairly primitive building and coming in from a patrol wasn't really a rest period, except for the horses. Being social animals they loved to run free in the horse paddock with the other mares or have a satisfying roll in the grass down near the creek with the sweet running water

Bill, John and Ian were standing outside the stables when George walked briskly up to them and smiled.

"The Sergeant wants you three fellows in the office right now."

"Do you know why?" Bill asked.

"I'd take a punt and say it might have something to do with last night."

"What about last night?" Ian asked.

"I saw that fucking old busy-body Mr. Wickham leaving the office earlier today. No doubt complaining about us again," George grinned.

"So that's what it's about, a simple night out," John said.

"You ought to have known someone would've gone to the boss after seeing you enter that whorehouse," George replied.

"Who is Charley Wickham?" Ian asked.

"He's a merchant who sells to miners and others in the community. He likes to be in charge of everyone. Has a bossy wife. We all say she makes the bullets and he fires them."

"So that's how it is, " Ian reflected thoughtfully.

"Yes ,and we're stuck with him," Bill added.

George left the three men outside the office and went away laughing. "Have fun boys!"

They filed into the office – a small room with slab walls, a desk in the middle, and a bookcase behind the desk chair. It had a feeling of a place in transit. If the community moved, so would the barracks.

Ian had led the way and stood in front of the desk. Sergeant Green looked up from the large open book in which he had been writing. He blotted the book, put a cap on the ink jar, then leaned back in his chair and looked at the three men.

"Now Mr. Percy, I would like an explanation of your activities of last night. I've had to endure an irritating Mr. Wickham coming here this morning to complain about your behaviour."

"What was his complaint, Sergeant?" Ian asked.

"He saw you three go into that grog shanty which has a dubious reputation, and he wants it closed down."

"I thought we behaved in a way in keeping with that establishment," Ian countered.

"That's what I thought too when a few things were explained to me. What you might well have done with a herd of elephants in India, you can't do here."

"But there aren't any elephants here!" Ian looked surprised.

"Yes, but we do have Mr. Percy, which after last night, amounts to the same degree of discord," the old Sergeant said, almost smiling.

Swiftly, John and Bill turned their sudden laughter into a cough after encountering a stern expression from the Sergeant.

"We're sorry to have caused you any problems with Mr. Wickham. We were just having a boys' night out," Ian had the grace to say.

"No matter, I can handle Mr. Wickham, but in future find a less public place to have a night out. You do need to remember we are meant to be respectable members of any community we are in."

"Sergeant, what about relaxation? Most of the activities we enjoyed last night?"

"Mr. Percy, you may find it hard to believe but I was young once. At the moment it feels like a long time ago, but I know what you are saying. You will have to enjoy such activities in a less public place. There will always be people who complain."

"Point taken, Sergeant," Ian replied after a moment or two.

Sergeant Green looked at each man in turn, then gave another sigh.

"Behind the public rooms are some private rooms. One is quite large and the owners are prepared to let you use it in future." He added quietly, "This talk has never taken place. Don't let the Inspector know about it."

"No, Sergeant," they chorused with considerable relief.

Their superior looked down at the Diary of Duty and Occurrences book.

"Mr. Percy, when are you leaving?"

"After an early breakfast tomorrow morning."

He looked at John, "I'm sending you with them for part of the way, I expect you to deal with that problem I spoke about earlier. I think between the three of you there is no reason why you can't bring it to a good conclusion. When it is completed, you can return here. I've got another job for you."

"Thank you, Sergeant," John replied.

The men filed out of the office and John looked back to see the old Sergeant smiling as he removed the cap from the ink pot. John wondered if he was thinking of a memory from before, when he was young and unmarried. They walked down the western side of the barracks towards the horse paddock. It was a warm morning giving every indication of being a hot day. There were trees dotted throughout the paddock leading down to the creek. Ian was relieved to see that the farrier had rounded up the eight horses and put them into the yard beside the stables.

"I thought we'd have to do that job. It isn't the weather to do a run in the paddock," Bill commented.

"John would've enjoyed doing that," Ian joked.

"You thought wrong!" John said cheerfully.

They walked to the horse yard and stood near the farrier who was watching the horses. The farrier turned to Ian and asked, "Which horse is yours?"

"That one with a white star on its forehead," Ian pointed.

Bill indicated a lovely light brown mare standing near the fence, and John pointed to a dark brown horse near the gate. They were led individually with a halter rope to the area outside the stables for a check of their horseshoes and a general inspection as to their overall condition.

"I'll put them back in the paddock and they'll be brought back to the stables early tomorrow morning," the farrier said, once the inspection was completed.

The men thanked him and went away to the barracks to prepare for the next day, before enjoying the company of their colleagues and a few beers.

Chapter Four

Next morning saw the men riding three abreast in silence. They'd left very early and the cool of the morning had now been replaced by the growing warmth of the day. Every so often they would ride in single file around logs or through steep gullies, watched by a multitude of wildlife of which they were totally unaware. Curious kangaroos stood up tall to look at them pass by. Sometimes there was a screech from white cockatoos high up in the trees.

John had been quiet for far longer than either Bill or Ian had expected. Bill turned in his saddle and the pair exchanged smiles while riding in single file around a clump of logs piled together. John was oblivious to their interest in his silence. At last he broke it by expressing his thoughts.

"Isn't it good to be in the open, away from the stale air of the barracks."

"As long as it doesn't rain," Bill countered.

John looked disgusted. "Bill, are you usually grumpy in the mornings?"

"I love the silence of the mornings and hearing the magpies sing," Bill protested. He was certainly not grumpy.

"The mornings are a good time to reflect. The country – it's full of bird life, colours I've never seen before. We are privileged to be here, don't you think?" Ian smiled at John.

"I can see everything as we pass by, but it's just normal countryside. Not as comfortable as places near the coast," John answered.

"Look at the brilliant colours of the undergrowth all around us and the trees. Look at the shape of these gum trees. They must be very old to have such a width. I think they're magnificent and we have the privilege to see this country on our patrols," Ian showed his passion.

"Didn't you see the stunning sunrise early this morning and the colours on the eastern horizon?" Bill chipped in.

"No I didn't. The water was cold in the washroom and I could hardly wait to get dressed. Anyway how could you see it?"

"Through the cracks in our slab walls at the sleeping end of the barracks," Bill winked.

Something clicked in John's mind and he looked at his two friends.

"You two have been ganging up on me. I don't believe you even saw the sunrise. There are no cracks in the slabs."

Bill and Ian laughed and a pair of kookaburras in the trees above joined in, which failed to improve John's mood.

John looked at them both. "You are both serious about the land?"

"It's a stunning landscape. We love the vistas across miles of rolling hills and plains," Ian explained.

They rode quietly for a time before Ian asked John, "What's the job you've been asked to solve?"

"It's a bit complicated – a neighbour sold a draught horse. The buyer decided it wasn't worth the price and refused to pay, so the neighbour raided the other man's storeroom and took his harness and a number of other items," John explained.

"Where do the men live?" Bill asked.

"On the edge of the hills, down towards the plains west of here – about a day's ride, though we could get close by the end of today. There are three settlers in the area and one is a suspect."

"What do we know about these settlers?" Ian asked.

"Sergeant Green seemed to think Gary and Bessie Holt would be helpful. Their land is just across the river."

"Right, we'll visit them first, if possible today, if we arrive late in the afternoon," Bill said.

They rode through rolling hills sloping down to a couple of long valleys before riding up a steep incline. From the top they were rewarded with a magnificent view, hills rolling down to a river in the distance. There were small rises on the other side of this watercourse and flat country for miles away in the distance.

"We'll camp on the other side of the river. I expect we will reach it later this afternoon," Ian suggested.

"Did you bring some fishing line?" Bill was hopeful.

"Yes, it's in my saddle bag. Also a small container of worms which I dug up early this morning. I fully expected that question from you."

"After we make camp, John and I will and try catch a fish, if you're happy to do that."

"Yes, I love fishing and given the size of the river, there's bound to be lots in it," he replied.

They rode down through small valleys which took several hours of crossing uneven ground, gradually descending lower and lower until, at last, they arrived at the water. It was a splendid sight to these weary men. It had been a long day in the saddle.

"Can you swim?" Bill asked John.

"No, I've never needed to learn."

"We'd better find a safe place for John to cross as that water looks deep," Ian warned.

They rode along the bank until some animal tracks lead down to some rapids where the water ran over stones. The track climbed up the other side, just low enough for the horses, who managed to cross easily after having a drink. Once on the other side, Ian chose a place for a camp that they were all happy with.

They were only too pleased to alight from their horses and, no doubt, the horses were glad to be free of their loads. Soon the trio caught four reasonably-sized fish and were very pleased with themselves.

"Bill, maybe you should give John a swimming lesson, as it's still warm?" Ian suggested.

John looked shocked. "No, going into the water is unhealthy."

"John, there'll be times when you'll have to cross a swollen creek or a river and if you can't swim you might drown. We don't want to go to your funeral. So strip off and get into the water now."

"When you put it like that, alright. Do I have to get undressed?" John asked.

"Of course, but you'll soon dry."

Soon, a very reluctant John was learning the basics of staying afloat in the waterhole surrounded by ancient trees. His friends didn't let him get out of his depth.

Later, around the fire after the evening meal of fish and other rations, Ian suggested that over the summer when they met again, it would be good to continue swimming lessons, to which John had no objections. It wouldn't have mattered if he had, as Ian had already decided.

John's last thought before his sleepy eyes closed was thanks for these friends who cared about his welfare. A childhood friend had drowned in a flooded creek so he was afraid of going alone into water. The others had stopped talking a while ago and the only sound now was nightlife in the dark trees.

*

Morning seemed to arrive in a snap of the fingers, like a curtain pulled apart. With the sun rising in the east, the men left their swags to prepare a meal. They were always silent in making and drinking the first mug of tea – warming cold hands in front of the fire. It was a quiet time of gathering thoughts. The last man to leave the fire had the job of putting it out and covering the wet coals with soil, leaving no sign behind.

After leaving the camp and riding westward for a couple of miles in the early morning, a slab hut became visible on a small rise. It was surrounded by a wooden fence. At the side of the dwelling was a yard with farm animals and chooks. A large vegetable garden lay on the other side of the hut.

Whoever lived here clearly meant to take a firm hold of the land. Ian was amazed to see a couple of very small English trees planted nearby. As they rode their horses to the front of the hut, a woman opened the front door and walked out to a neat porch. There was a hitching rail nearby and the men attached their horses to it and walked to the front gate.

Ian introduced himself and his police mates. "Are you Mrs. Holt?"

"Yes, I am."

"Is Mr. Holt anywhere near?"

"He saw you coming a while. He's on his way back from that paddock over yonder," she pointed her finger north.

Within a short space of time, Mr. Holt arrived and introductions were made.

"We don't get many visitors, so you are welcome, though you appear to be here officially?" Holt said cautiously.

Ian responded with pleasant words about their fine ride out. Mr. Holt talked about his choice of country, close to water and the rich black soil, ending with, "It will be excellent for growing seed crops."

Warming up, now he had an audience, Holt added, "In wet weather, it isn't good. Heavy and sticky, and easy to get bogged. I've laid stones on the path and the yards."

The garden fence was so low, they could have stepped over it. Instead their host opened the gate, inviting them in.

"Come and sit down on our log seats under this pepper tree. It's a good shade on these hot days," he announced proudly.

Once seated, the policemen noticed that Gary Holt was a well-built sturdy young man, very likely in his twenties. By his movements, he gave the impression he could give a good account of himself. This was important in an isolated area with no neighbours to vouch for one. Ian felt at ease with Gary Holt. There was something about him which gave him confidence, though Ian could not say exactly what came into his mind.

"My wife is about to make a billy of tea," Holt glanced at his missus. Mrs. Holt was only a young woman with dark hair and her main feature was a pair of sparkling dark eyes.

Bill and John grunted their thanks. The pair never declined the offer of tea.

It took a time for everyone to relax and talk easily. The police trio soon decided that these were good people. The missus spoke well and with respect which meant they treated her with equal care. The young woman clearly enjoyed the attention. This visit lasted almost an hour before Holt spoke up.

"May I suggest we address each other by our Christian names? Mine is Gary and my wife is Bessie."

They agreed – they were all in their twenties and now comfortable with each other. But it was time to get to the point of the visit.

"Our Sergeant Green suggested you may be able to help us with the problem of your two neighbours?" John asked.

Bessie laughed, "Norm Green's wife is my aunt!"

There was silence as this information was digested.

"We wondered why he suggested you both. Now it makes sense. Sergeant Green had a grin on his face as we were leaving his office!" Ian laughed.

The words tumbled out of Gary's mouth.

"Of course, we will assist you in any way. We want it fixed." He failed to mention they were their only neighbours. You relied on your neighbours.

"Do you think there's a simple way of fixing it?" John asked.

"My suggestion is to give the impression of bringing it to the Land Commission," Gary offered. "We all have leases, so it would be simple to suggest that the Commissioner might consider revoking their leases and giving them to someone else. This would solve your problem."

"Can you *do* that?" Ian asked.

Gary grinned, "I don't know, but neither would men who are not well-educated."

"What caused the problem in the first place?" John enquired.

"Bruce Peek bought a draught horse from Barry West but found he did not have enough money to pay for it. He wouldn't give it back. Said it was not worth the money – so West raided his storeroom and took all the harnesses. Bruce couldn't do any ploughing. That's the problem!" Gary explained.

John thought about his words. "Let's bring these two men together and tell them to return each other's property or we will make a recommendation to the Land Commissioner. Is that a good deal?"

"I'm sure it will work!" Gary smiled encouragingly.

"Gary, have you ever been in a legal practice?" Ian countered.

He laughed, "No I've never been involved with the Law, but I've learnt to treat legal minds with a lot of caution."

"No one would believe you," Ian winked.

Gary stared, "You're a policeman. Don't you think of getting the best result with the least fuss?"

"Our work is different. We are doing it all the time."

"Ian, when you live on the frontier, survival depends upon on making the right decisions. Men like me have to be able to find a solution which works. Not go on causing more problems." Gary tried not to smile.

Ian was impressed. "I've never thought about how a man deals with these kinds of problems out here."

"Sometimes, we have to ask the law to come and deal with it."

Bill and John, who had listened without interruption, now nodded in agreement.

"Will you be returning this way after seeing my two neighbours?" Gary asked.

"Yes, we'll need to use the same track to cross the river," Ian replied.

"We would like to know the outcome, if you don't mind."

"We'll let you know the result on our way back," John promised.

The police rode away in the direction of the other settlements. The country was quite flat and very different from what they were accustomed to seeing on a daily basis. The trees weren't so tall and the undergrowth was lower. Nor were there any waterholes visible.

It was mid-afternoon when they returned to the Holt property and John was able to recount, "Problem solved. One mention of the land leases and they instantly shook hands!"

"If ever you come this way again, be sure to visit us," Gary said with a smile.

John grinned as he lent forward on his horse to shake Gary's hand.

"You can be sure we'll come visit you," he said.

Before they could ride away, Bessie came out of the hut and handed a package up to Bill. "This is something for your meal tonight. We know how difficult camping can be. We spent a couple of weeks sleeping under our dray and wondering if our food would last."

Bill thanked Bessie for her thoughtfulness, adding, "We'll send John out to catch fish!"

They gave a final farewell to this nice couple as Bill put the package into his saddle bag and rode away. It was near the end of the day before they crossed the river and made camp on the other side. They spoke about the next day. John wanted to know, "How far are you and Bill able to return with me before you turn south?"

"Probably about halfway, John."

The pair were well aware that John liked being in their company and didn't want to leave it. But he had orders.

In the meantime, Ian sent John into the river with Bill for another swimming lesson. Bessie's gift of food was very welcome, once they discovered slices of damper and meat, some cooked but a good many raw. They now had food for a couple of days.

*

The next day, the three men began the long climb back into the hills. At the top of the first rise, each looked back at a view which stretched for miles distant. The end of the plain wasn't visible, not like in the hills where only the next hill could be seen. This trip was much slower than Ian or Bill had presumed, and the horses were showing signs of weariness.

By mid-afternoon Ian and Bill looked at each other. They had to give the horses a rest – it would mean making camp earlier than usual. The halfway mark was still a distance from their present position. The hills seemed steeper than Ian remembered. He too was tired. He thought he heard a voice. "Bill, did you say something?"

Bill smiled, "You were away somewhere in your mind as you do on these long rides. I've become used to riding alone when you go away like this. What I said was, we could make camp on this creek and John might catch us a fish. We may as well make him useful while we have him!"

"What are you saying, Bill?"

"Never mind, John. We're just looking after you!"

He looked at his two colleagues and wondered what they were up to. They had a habit of talking as if he wasn't present. Nonetheless, he loved being in their company.

John was aware the horses were tired. "The Government could at least provide better quality horses. We haven't done too many miles today and already we are making camp."

Not that John really minded. He was content. At that moment he realised that his colleagues had let him deal with the disagreement on the plain. He was so accustomed to his mates taking charge that he hadn't noticed that shift. It was valuable experience.

"Come on, you need to catch a couple of fish for dinner. You're as bad as Ian wandering off and not paying attention!" Bill called out.

"Alright, I'm coming. Where are we going to now?"

They found a good waterhole and soon John had caught two good-sized fish, one a rainbow trout, all very good to eat. There would be enough left over for the next night. Soon they were gutted and cooking on a flat pan, which Ian had brought along with the fishing lines.

Without a packhorse, there was very little room to carry anything other than necessities. But on patrols which stretched over weeks like these, they was the chance of creative cooking if they wanted any variety. They had also packed a tiny medical parcel in case of emergencies.

John thought about Gary Holt. "I hope we see the Holts again sometime."

All agreed that even with the enormous size of their district, they would find an excuse to go that way again one day.

"If the order comes through, don't forget to take me." John looked at his friends.

"As long as you catch the fish!" Bill laughed.

"That's a deal, but you have to cook it," John countered.

Ian smiled at this banter. He scraped his last piece of fish off his pannikin. John had done a sterling piece of police work. After cleaning up, they retired quickly to their swags. Soon, the only sounds were the horses moving about, along with the occasional hoot of an owl. Their swags were arranged so no one could enter the camp without one of them waking. They were back in the more populated district – which meant many itinerant workers and vagrants wandering about. Theft was common. Possession was nine tenths of the law in these parts.

*

When Ian awoke, he was surprised to see the sun already peeping through the trees. He'd slept very well. Had they stayed up that late? His mates were still asleep. Ian decided not to wake them. Maybe they had stayed up until the wee hours? He moved quietly to the water, did a few jobs, lit the fire and put the quart-pots on to boil. He was relieved that the ants had not found the left-over fish.

He fried these up in the pan for when the boys woke. Ian enjoyed the silence of the morning, punctuated only by birdsong. He checked the horses, satisfied himself that they were ready for the day. He looked down on the still sleeping forms. It was time and he nudged Bill with his boot. Bill rolled over and swore loudly. Ian laughed and gave his mate a resounding shove with his other boot.

This time the response was firmer. "Ian, piss off, it's too fucking early!"

"Bill, the sun's up and you need to get up. Breakfast will be ready soon."

Lots of unprintable words followed, which only caused Ian to laugh.

Bill left his swag and went down to the creek to splash his face to full consciousness. John felt Ian's boot and mumbled half-asleep, "Come back tomorrow."

This sleepy lot were not climbing up the steep hills on their horses until mid-morning. By mid-afternoon they had reached the fork where John was to leave them.

"You will reach Hill Top by twilight. No doubt you'll get a good response for the way you handled the problem. We're sorry to see you go," Ian said quietly.

"Now who's going to catch the fish?" Bill added sadly.

They raised a hand in salute and John rode east. Bill and Ian rode south towards higher country. It had been a good day with a late start. Though they had enjoyed John's company, the pair were happy to be on their own again.

It was a lovely summer's evening when at last they found a place to camp. At this time of the year, the afternoons were long and warm. Bill had kept some of Bessie's food, so they had meat to cook. Ian had kept aside a couple of pieces of fish. They'd have leftovers for the next day. The pair sat quietly by their fire well into the night. Finally they talked about John.

"John was right about the quality of the horses. These ones are okay, they just plod along at a reasonable pace, I like them. But I don't know how we'd get on if we needed to chase cattle or runaways for hours on end," Bill said.

"They'd get knocked up before an hour was up. For what we do, they are okay."

"Do you think the Government will ever give us good quality horses?"

Ian's smile turned into a laugh. "No, they'll always be watching out for unnecessary expenses on their books."

"I fear you are right, Ian."

"If we are careful, we can choose the best horses, like the ones we are riding now. When we return to the barracks, make sure the farrier knows we want them back."

"So that's why you took such an interest and spent time at the stables?"

"Yes, making sure we had good mounts for this patrol."

"Were they likely to be taken by others?"

"I heard a couple of fellows talking when they thought I was asleep about swapping their horses for our steeds."

Bill laughed at the cunning of his friend. He was pleased they had teamed up for whatever their future may hold. The fire had died down and they rolled out swags at their usual distance.

As he lay down, Ian murmured, "We are so privileged to be here without anyone hounding us."

Bill smiled and fell asleep.

Chapter Five

The next morning saw the two men riding up the valley to a steep hill which loomed over another valley. Not wishing to descend again, they rode in silence along the top of the ridge for a considerable distance, all the time going southward. In the distance they could see a range of blue mountains.

"Sergeant Green said we would have to pass through some very rough country before riding down into the long valley beyond," Ian reminded his friend.

"What does that mean? Is it dangerous or just rough riding? Do we need to carry more food?" Bill asked after thinking for a moment or two.

"I don't know. I agree this part does not feel right."

"Did he say anything else useful?"

"He wasn't too sure, but he did recall there was a track beside the river which we could follow where possible. I have the impression he wants to know what is in those hills, and we are to make a report."

"Isn't there a police presence at a goldmining creek down there?" Bill reflected thoughtfully.

"I think you're right, but I don't think it's producing much gold."

"But we may be able to stock up on more supplies?"

The pair rode along the ridge until at last it gave way to a long grassy slope, leading down to flat country which covered a large area of unproductive land. It was swampy in places and generally had poor soil. The gentle undulating country was easy on the horses if they skirted the wetlands. They had been riding for about an hour when blue smoke became visible in the east. As they rode closer, it was clearly rising from near a creek.

"I think we've found our mining camp," Bill nodded in the direction of the smoke.

"I'm sure you're spot on. If you look just beyond the creek, further south, there are the rangers," Ian answered him cheerfully.

"So the camp is on the edge of where we have to go?"

"Yes, it looks like it."

They rode up to the camp and as they approached it, a young policeman stood up from beside his fire and walked forward to the hitching rail. Ian and Bill alighted from their horses and tied them to the rail, then turned to greet him, introducing themselves.

"I'm Bob Pringle, pleased to see you," the other man said. "There's no more gold to be found here in quantities to warrant a police presence, so I'm packing up."

"Where are you going from here?" Bill asked.

"I don't know. I was told to wait and a message would reach me."

Bob was young, still learning and unsure of himself. He was a shade under six feet in height with dark hair and a beard of sorts. He'd been a stockman before joining up for this job.

Ian remembered something. "Who is your Sergeant?"

Bill looked suddenly hard at his friend as if he knew what the answer would be.

"Norm Green, do you know him?"

"Yes, very well!"

A silence ensued as this news was digested. Only time would yield answers. Bill changed the subject, turning to Bob, "Do you have any spare meat?"

"No, but I know an interesting man – one of the miners. He came from Peru to seek gold. He told me the Spanish stole all the gold from his country and he came here to find more of it."

"What could interest us in a man from Peru?" Bill was all at sea.

Bob smiled, as if he was speaking to a child. "He calls it *charqui* which is difficult to pronounce correctly so I won't try. While he was here, he used the flesh of a kangaroo and sliced it very finely. He then dried it in the sun and wind. I've tried it and it's good eaten slowly."

Bill was still irritated with Bob, speaking down to him. He was inclined to ignore the tip, but he persisted with his question about feathered game.

"I don't have any at the present though there are ducks on the creek a mile or so away from the mining camp." Bob tried to be helpful.

Ian picked up on the dried meat story. "I've heard about this method – I think it has other names. I expect people use it on long treks where food isn't plentiful. I like the idea of it. It could be good for us."

"I have quite a few strips and I like it," Bob assured them. "Would you like to try some?"

Ian looked at Bill. "Right we'll give it a go."

Bob handed each a man a small strip of meat, both put it carefully in their mouths and began to chew. Not a word was spoken for about half an hour, before Bill admitted, "It's not too bad, though I'd prefer to eat duck."

While chewing, Ian had been thinking about the journey ahead.

"Bob, do you know anything about the country down in those ranges?"

"No, not much. It begins a couple of miles from here in a gentle slope down to the river and a mile or so further on, it starts to get more difficult. Most people avoid going into it."

"We have to go through it to the other side to do a job," Ian explained. "Can you tell us anything at all?"

"The hills are very steep, there's hardly any good grass, but plenty of water!"

This bit of humour produced smiles, before Ian continued to pepper Bob with questions.

"Do you have anyone here who has been through that way recently?"

"Will you be camping here tonight?" Bob countered.

"Yes, we'd enjoy a bit of company and perhaps you'd answer my question?" Ian replied.

Now he had the desired company, Bob grinned and gave a positive reply. Gold had become hard to find and the miners were leaving. Most had left the camp, apart from a few older men who were not in a hurry until they knew where the next camp would be situated.

"I've asked one of these old men to come talk to you," Bob said.

As Bob was speaking, an old man slightly bent over in dirty clothes walked slowly down to the fire where the police were sitting.

He paused. "What do you want to know?"

Ian introduced himself and Bill, and talked about the need to travel through the ranges.

"Have you ever been in them?" he asked.

The old man smiled and drew breath. "Yes, a lot of years ago. I was sworn in as a Special Constable with a group to hunt down escaped convicts. These men had been terrorising travellers and settlers nearby. They were holed up in these hills and we had to go in and get them. So, yes, I know these hills."

Bill looked very surprised, and replied with considerable respect, "I heard about that job. It was more than twenty years ago, and you caught them too."

"What was it like in the ranges?" Ian asked again.

There was a log near where the police were sitting, and the old man sat down. He was quiet for a little while as if he was gathering his thoughts together.

"Very hard country, few animals because there are very few places where grass can successfully grow. The undergrowth is thick. Lots of plants trying to grow and not doing well."

The old man went silent for a few minutes. No one said anything.

"You will find no food in those hills. Take what you need and follow the water. Be very careful and take no risks. If all goes well, you'd get out in two days, but it could easily be three. It's difficult terrain which may have changed dramatically in the years since I was in those hills. There are big rocks near the river, and near them is a cave where some of us camped one night. Big enough to take the horses into."

There was another silence before he continued, "It was an eerie place. We had no choice but to shelter. We were caught in a sudden summer storm. Somehow those hills attract nasty storms, and the cave seemed welcome respite."

"We appreciate your advice. What could have changed since then?" Ian said politely.

"There are always changes with floodwaters, and in those storms, water pours down from the high hills in torrents. I can only tell you to carry all your requirements, plus a little extra."

"Anything else?" Bill asked, as if he was mentally taking notes.

"Take a raincoat and cap."

Bill nodded. They had these in their swags.

The old man took a big breath. "I didn't know police like yourselves enjoyed adventuring. It'll be a ride that you'll remember for the rest of your lives. Like me, something to be treasured in the mind."

Bob had been listening to the old man with an interest which surprised him. He didn't usually pay much attention to other people's stories. He had always considered them long-winded, but this old man had been a Special Constable on a famous hunt. Perhaps he would pay more attention to the stories of elders.

"Are we likely to meet anyone in these hills?" he now asked.

"There will always be men hiding from the police, so it's possible. If you treat people in the right way, there is never any problem I find."

The old cobber added with a note of caution, "If you do meet anyone, never ask for a surname, and be friendly. This is not a place to throw your weight around. Remember you don't have reinforcements handy."

"We understand. We're not interested in any locals. Our work is a long way beyond. This is just the quickest way there," Ian replied.

Ian had sensed that the word would go out in the night, or early in the morning, that police would be riding through the hills near the water. Any escaped convicts would likely keep out of their way. The old timer's advice was welcome.

The old man stood up slowly and wished them a safe ride the next day. He returned to his camp thinking about his own time in the hills. Behind him, the billy was boiling on the fire and Bob dropped a handful of tea into the water. The aroma invaded their senses. There was always a time to appreciate a good mug of tea while sitting quietly and thinking.

This pleasant occupation was interrupted by the sound of an approaching horseman, who rode up to the camp. He did not get down from his mount, but asked, "Anyone here called Constable Bob Pringle?"

"I'm Bob Pringle."

"I have a note for you."

The horseman handed over the note and, turning his horse, sped away without another word. In the meantime, the envelope was opened. Bob read it slowly.

"I'm to go with you into the ranges," he said, looking up from the note.

"Can we see?" Bill and Ian both asked.

Bob looked into the fire and wondered why he had to go with these men. How would he fit into their company?

"I've often thought what it would be like to go a good distance into the ranges. I've gone a little way while doing some hunting. It has a closed feeling, even at midday in full sunshine. There are dark places in those hills," he warned.

Bob handed the note to Ian, who looked at it and wondered out loud, "What does Norm Green know which he hasn't seen fit to tell us, Bill?"

"Probably the kind of trip that would be better with two horsemen."

"As the old man left, I heard him chuckling to himself, so I assume we are not being told the entire truth about the ranges and what to expect?" Ian murmured quietly.

"What are your supplies like? From what I can see, there is not much of anything in your camp?" Bill queried Bob.

"This camp was moved to another location, so the other policeman who was here took most of the original equipment to the new spot. He loaded up the packhorse. I insisted on keeping most of the flour, salt, sugar, and tea. You see,

I didn't know how long I'd be here, waiting for that note. I kept the spare horse in case."

"Ian and I are low on everything. I like the notion of chewing on meat as I ride along. All the same, I'd like some fresh kill," Bill responded cheerfully. "Bob, where do we find ducks?"

It was apparent that even though Bob had been at the camp a number of weeks he lacked confidence. It was good that he had kept supplies, but the men did wonder how he had been treated by the other policeman.

The day was almost at an end with the sun slipping down towards the western horizon in a shower of brilliant colours, in all the shades of red and pink, tinged with gold. It was the kind of sky which made the world a lovely place to be, thought Ian.

Bill was thinking about ducks and where to find them. Now Bob was to be part of the picture, extra food was essential.

That night, Bill and Ian lay out their swags near one another. Bob was only too happy to keep to his own tent away from his visitors. He had gathered wood for the fire, prepared the meal and seemed quite content to sit quietly at the end of the evening. He created a good impression.

Once in their swags, Ian and Bill were able to talk quietly without being overheard.

"What do you want to do tomorrow?" Ian asked.

"Check our supplies and note what Bob can add to it. Also check our equipment, straps, and what we can take on the spare horse. Bob has a small camp oven which could be very useful if we get caught in bad weather."

Ian had another thought, "We can't overload the horse, Bill. What else do you want?"

"I think we might do some cooking for the first night in the ranges."

"That's a very good idea."

"What are you going to do?" Bill laughed quietly.

"I want to talk to the old man again because I think he knows a lot more about what we might encounter."

"Yup, he was very careful with his words."

"Bill, I noticed you watching him and wondered what you were thinking."

"What was in those ranges twenty years ago will not be there today."

With these words, the men gradually fell asleep. Neither had dreams about the ranges.

*

Next morning, Bob took Bill duck-hunting a few miles down the creek from their camp. It was a successful enterprise and they returned in a cheerful frame of mind. The first part of the afternoon was given up to plucking the birds and cooking three of them. Bob cooked a couple of dampers, which came out of the oven lovely and crisp with a wonderful aroma. They had disappeared in minutes.

Later in the day, Bill traded some of the things they didn't need with the other miners and in this way cleaned up their camp. When Bill had the chance, he asked Ian what the old man had told him.

"What we both expected to hear, Bill."

"I knew it, the native inhabitants."

"Yes, but not recently. He thought centuries ago," Ian continued.

"But what's the catch?"

"There are sacred sites which are still powerful. We need to treat them with caution."

Bill was quiet for a few minutes while he digested the words before asking, "Where?"

"He couldn't remember, but it stopped him from going any deeper into those hills."

"We're grown men. We have to go forward," Bill said. "How do you think Bob will cope with this trip?"

"I don't know, he's very young. What do you know of his background?"

"Not well-educated, only to sixth class. Poor family and was sent to help his father, who was a shepherd, at six years old. He became a stockman, so he knows horses, which is a big plus in this job," Bill replied.

"Well, at the end of this trip he will be a lot more experienced."

"By the way, what was in the note he passed to you?"

"I didn't think you saw that sleight of hand, Bill."

"What was it?"

"From our Sergeant who was giving us a choice of keeping Bob into the next job or passing him to another policeman on our ride south after we pass through the ranges."

This was enough for the men to think about before dropping off to sleep at about the same time as the fire died and started to go cold.

Chapter Six

Before dawn the three men left their swags and prepared to ride out after sunrise. Ian lead a packhorse, with Bill in front and Bob just behind. The idea was to make it easier for the horses once they reached the river. On leaving the creek, the ground was uneven. They needed to climb a small rise but the packhorse, in ordinary times, was a police nag which had never carried a load. Difficult in the first hour, the mare but gradually settled down as the day progressed.

At last, the river was reached and they walked in single file. The first mile or so Ian found ways around logs and stones. The constant piles of flood debris was another matter – there was no way of telling what lay underneath the detritus. So great care had to be taken in picking a path. The debris was spread over all the river flats. At times steep hills rose straight up from the river's edge, making it tough to find a path.

The first day was daunting because of the height of the ranges either side of the river. As they rode deeper into the hills, the trees became taller and the sun rarely shone through to the river. In poor light, they rode in shadows. The river wound itself around the base of towering hills covered in stunted growth. Ian noticed the lack of bird life – it felt a dead landscape.

Travelling single file did not encourage conversation. The time dragged. At one stage, Ian asked, "Do you want to have a break and boil a billy?"

Bob backed up this plan instantly, which made Ian smile. He needed a rest too. After all, they had been in the saddle since sunrise. In no time Bill had a fire burning and a billy in place ready for a pinch of tea leaves. Nothing was as good as a mug of tea with a slice of damper. Bob had brought a small pottery jar of honey from the old camp – a welcome addition to damper.

"Did you notice anything out of the ordinary this morning?" Bill asked.

"No animals I could see," Bob replied carefully.

"It is not so much as seeing … it is more about what did you hear?"

"I didn't hear nothing," Bob replied.

"What about the stones which rolled down the hill a while back?" Bill persisted.

"What stones?"

"About half an hour ago. What do you think, Ian?" Bill said gently.

"Nothing for us to worry about, though we really need to keep our ears open, and our eyes peeled for strange movements. Bob, we don't like surprises in places like this!"

After a minute or two, Bob agreed. "I'll make an effort. I didn't hear those stones."

"Bob, you were daydreaming in your own world!" Bill laughed.

They doused the fire with a billy of water and were on their horses, leaving this pleasant patch of green grass. Leaving this pleasant patch of green grass and sunshine, they rode into the shadows. At times, the hills seemed to grow out of the water as it lapped the stones at their base. When this happened the horses had to cross the river, finding a path on the other side. Then there were stretches so steep the men had to dismount and lead their horses, all the time the hills towered ominously.

Open ground appeared and, for a minute or so, Bill thought they were the first people to stop here, until he saw the black coals not quite covered by the creeping grass. Surely this was a safe place to stop for the night.

The horses were hobbled, and for a change showed no desire to wander away. A fire was lit and Bob cooked the last two ducks on the hot coals, while the others checked their equipment for the next day's ride. Bill gave the packhorse a good rub down and the mare seemed to like it, which made the effort worthwhile. After the meal, the swags were rolled out, close together this time. Bill and Ian whispered to one another.

"Ian, if we were on the plains, I'd say that we'll get a storm tomorrow. The air is too warm."

"Yes, it does feel like it, this heavy feeling will make the morning a challenge."

Bill reminded Ian about the cave the old man had mentioned using in a storm.

"I remember. I wonder why he laughed?"

"Do you think there was a reason?" Bill queried.

"I didn't like the way he laughed, and I don't like these dark shadows."

"Remind Bob tomorrow to keep his rain gear handy."

"We'll need to be very much awake to keep Bob from daydreaming."

"We shall. Sleep well."

"You too, Bill."

The only sound was the trickling of water over low stones in the river and the rustling of the leaves in the trees around the camp. As the black hills soared ever upwards to reach a sky of brilliant silver stars, Ian slowly drifted off to sleep.

*

Before sunrise, Ian stirred and, sitting up, saw that Bill had lit the fire, and had a billy on. Tea was not far away.

"What a sight to wake to," he said.

"It was a case of respect for the old that I let you sleep, Ian!"

Ian smiled and tucked those words away in his mind for another day. He completed his ablutions in the river and, after throwing on a shirt, went to wake Bob, who asked, "Why do we always rise before the sun?"

"In a place like these ranges, it's dangerous to sleep in daylight. I also want to get out of these hills as fast as I can," Bill stirred the tea in the billy.

Bob went to splash himself with cold water, before Bill had any more bright ideas. During the night, the weather had warmed up. While they had slept, a large bank of cumulus clouds had developed. These were now billowing high above the ranges – an unpleasant surprise. In Bill's mind, there was an urgency to find the cave. He wanted to get going as soon as possible without causing a panic.

Breakfast followed and soon they were on their horses.

"I don't like the look of that sky. What do you think about going on ahead with Bob, and I will bring the rear with the packhorse?" Ian suggested to Bill.

This idea suited Bill. "I'd be surprised if we don't get a storm near midday. I'd like to find the cave the old man talked about."

"Yes, that's a clever idea to seek shelter if we can locate it in time. I'm also worried about the horses – the track is so narrow. We can't afford to hurry them, nor can we afford to go slow this morning."

"Ian, I'd like Bob to scout ahead of me. It won't do him any harm to have some responsibility. We'll go and I'll send Bob back to you when we find the cave."

"Good. Keep safe, Bill."

"Don't you worry about me, I'll be out in front of you!"

When Ian turned the corner around the base of a large hill, Bob had vanished, though Bill was still in sight a long way ahead. This had been the plan, that Bill would always keep him in sight, in the case of a problem with the packhorse.

Ian wondered if horses picked up on the emotions of their riders. He thought it highly likely – his mare and the packhorse were quite content for the first few hours. They picked their way through gullies, over stones, and around logs, some big and others of an irritating size, where care was constantly needed. Ian began to feel uneasy. His horse gave a shiver and Ian worried that time was running out. This feeling was intensified by the close atmosphere. So his relief was enormous when he saw Bob returning.

"We've found the cave. It's on the other side of the river just above the water. It's huge. It has an area in front with a lot of green grass."

"How long do we have to go then?" Ian asked.

"Probably about an hour or so. Bill said I was to take the packhorse and lead the way."

"You're welcome to her!"

Handing Bob the long reins, Ian was silently delighted to be released from this police nag. He never wanted a packhorse unless someone else led it. Soon he spotted Bill who had come part of the way back.

"You must hurry, don't look up. Just come as quick as you can. We have very little time to get the horses settled before the storm," he yelled.

"The ground is so rough, it's unsafe to hurry but we're coming as fast as we can."

"Bring the packhorse to me and I'll get it unsaddled and hobbled. Bob, do the same to your horse as quick as you can," Bill called out.

Ian followed suit with his horse and equipment. Just before he entered the cave, he glanced up at the sky. In the space between the hills, magnificent dark clouds hovered above him, dominating the sky, heralding the storm. The light gave way to an even deeper darkness.

There was a sudden oppressive silence as, in the distance, a rumble of thunder rolled across the sky. The bank of surging grey clouds seemed to break as the wind surged into the hills. Sticks, branches and leaves were whipped up and flew ahead. Rocks tumbled down the hills, causing minor landslides on their way to the ground.

The cave very likely saved their lives. The horses were safe – there was no risk of landslides on the cave side of the river. Next came heavy spots of rain – opening the way for the storm clouds to release torrents. A great crack of thunder heralded the surge of water pouring into the valley. A lightning flash changed night into day for an instant before darkness descended once more. The wild winds howled, rushing at a mad pace across the hills, spilling down into the dark valley floor.

Water was now pouring down the gullies out of control, washing away anything not already taken by the wind. The deluge waterlogged the flat ground, morphing the water to a muddy brown.

Bill checked on the horses. They didn't seem to be concerned. He smiled to himself – horses lived their entire lives in the open weather.

Ian was relieved they were well supplied with food. The cave was going to be their camp for a while to come. The horses could not continue in safety until the gullies were less inundated from the surrounding hilltops.

After the deluge, the ongoing run-off created a waterfall at the front of the cave. A brown overflow continued to darken the churning river.

"Did you remember to fill our containers with clean water before the storm?

I didn't think of it until now," Ian asked Bill.

"I didn't think of it either," Bill replied with a groan.

"I filled the billy and the quart pots plus a basin too, the one I use to make the dampers," Bob chipped into the conversation.

Both were relieved that Bob had thought ahead. They didn't like the thought of muddy water in the billy. Ian made a comment to this effect and Bob laughed.

"You can always sift the muddy water out with a cloth. After a couple of goes, it's not so bad to drink," Bob suggested.

"Whose cloth?" asked Bill with a straight look at Bob.

Bob replied equally. He was not going to be intimidated.

"Yours, of course, if you want tea."

Bill smiled. He had deserved that reply, but he wasn't about to give in that easily.

"If it comes to that, surely there's clean water dripping off the stone?"

"Don't you carry anything spare in your swag, Bill?" asked Ian.

"I might, but I'd rather look for a drip, if you don't mind," Bill turned to the fire he was busy lighting.

"Are we moving again today?" Bob asked.

"I don't see how we can with the gullies full of water. The river is still rising. These conditions aren't safe," Ian replied, looking across the fire at Bob.

As if suddenly waking up, Bill asked, "Bob, can you swim?"

"Not well in calm water, so I would have no hope in this river."

"So if you were swept from your horse, we might not see you again, is that it?"

"I wouldn't be able to swim in this."

Bill looked at Ian. "Right, we stay then. This was a local storm I'd say, and the gullies will stop running during the night. In the morning, we'll assess the conditions and make a decision."

Chapter Seven

The cave was quite large with lots of wood left by earlier floods. With some rearrangements of the debris, there was room to lay out swags. Bill began to put this plan into action, moving pieces of wood this way and that, until he was satisfied with the result. They made sure their swags were close as the continuing run-off made it difficult to hear.

Though it was summer, the cave was cold and the floor a layer of soil and sand left behind by flood waters. They stripped off their wet shirts and huddled around the blazing fire to warm up. Bob seemed well aware of the necessity of keeping the fire stoked.

Once the rain had stopped and they could glimpse patches of blue sky, the cave seemed more cheerful. The horses were quite safe, munching the grass nearby and didn't seem bothered any more than usual by the hobbles.

Bill wondered what else was near. Even in the firelight, the back of the cave was in total darkness.

"I don't like not knowing what's behind me. There could be a wild dog," Bill complained.

"We didn't hear any sounds, nor are there any footprints, so there can't be a dog," Ian reasoned, joining in the game to see how it would pan out.

"Still… There's a strange smell coming from the back. I'm going to find out what's making it," said Bill, clearly not satisfied.

He picked up a burning stick and retreated towards the back of the cave. Ian and Bob heard him cry out in shock, "Fuckin' hell!"

He dropped the burning stick and fell on to all fours on the cave floor, as he felt soft wings fly past his face towards the cave mouth. Ian and Bob were enjoying this drama being acted out in front of them. They gave in to peals of laughter, much to Bill's embarrassment. With as much dignity as he could muster, he declared, "There's a bat colony at the back of this cave."

With these words, he escaped to see the horses and be in better company. He returned after their laughter had subsided.

Bill was under no illusion about any chance of moving out the next day. The ground was just too wet. It wouldn't be safe for the horses. He decided to talk to Ian once they were in their swags. The afternoon passed with no other surprises and Bob cooked a good meal. With clean water he made a soup with some leftovers he had brought on the packhorse. The young bloke had a gift of being able to conjure a delicious meal out of basics.

"We'll try and keep the fire going all night. If any of us wakes up, please add some wood," Bill suggested, worried there would be no dry wood to rekindle it in the morning.

There were nods of approval.

Very soon darkness descended, and they were all pleased to roll out their swags and, for a while, watch the flickering light of the flames turn from red to yellow and back again. Ian missed the silver stars of the night sky.

The two friends lay in their swags, unexpectedly comfortable.

"Ian, what do you think we ought to do now we won't be able to continue down the river?" Bill asked quietly.

"I've thought about it," said Ian. "If anything, we could explore the area on foot."

"I have an idea, Ian."

"What is it?"

"After I sent Bob back to you, I went for a walk around the side of the hill. On the next hill down from here, I spotted an old track going up. It was definitely man-made and I'd like to explore it."

"How far did you go?"

"Only far enough to see it had been used to get somewhere."

"Go ahead and see where leads. Also, I think we ought to check out the route downriver – we could walk it sometime tomorrow."

"Right, Ian. I want to get out of this place as fast as we can. It can't be too far away – we've travelled a good distance in the last couple of days."

"Me too, Bill. I don't like the shadows. I want to see the sun."

"What are we going to do about Bob? Keep him? He's a good cook."

"So are you, Bill."

"Alright, so let's wait until we're out of these ranges – give him the chance to tell us what he wants?"

"I'd go along with that, and as you're closest to the fire, you can put another log on it!"

"Which means you will have to do the night watch of it!"

*

Next morning the fire was burning fiercely with Ian sitting beside it, waiting for the billy to boil to make the first brew of the day. Bill had rolled over and, on opening his eyes, looked at the steam rising from the billy, the scent of tea wafting across the cave. As comfortable as he was in his swag, habit drove Bill to roll out and walk across to the fire. He sat down beside Ian, who poured him a mug. They sipped the fragrant brew in silence, only then going down to check on the horses. As it wasn't a workday, there was no hurry to do anything, with Bob being the last one to wake up. During breakfast, plans were discussed.

"The horses are doing well and are close together, I don't like having them hobbled all the time, so let's put bridles on them now and then, and walk them about," Bill instructed.

Bob reported that their food supply was still good.

Ian suggested, "Bob, after lunch, can you and Bill take a walk down the riverside to see what the conditions are like, please?" As if it was afterthought, he added, "One of us must stay behind to guard our equipment and look after the horses. I'll do that job today."

"We're going to examine an old pathway leading up from the river. I saw it yesterday while waiting for you to return with Ian," Bill stared across the fire.

Bob looked pleased with this idea and promptly agreed, in case Bill changed his mind.

After all the jobs were completed and more wood was found, Bill and Bob began to walk down their side of the river towards the hill in question, crossing gullies which still had water gushing down to the river. Soon the path was visible and, on closer inspection, it was definitely man-made, wide enough for two people to walk beside each other.

"I wonder where it leads?"

"Let's go up and see," Bob stepped ahead, eager.

Up the track they walked as it wound its way around the hill, going higher and higher until it reached a flat area of ground with some trees. Beside one was the ruins of a wooden slab hut.

"Bob, these old men often created traps in front of their huts, so be careful. Pick up that stick and test the ground," Bill warned Bob.

Sure enough, the stick found a deep hole. On careful examination, it turned out to be almost two feet in length, a foot wide, and two feet deep, enough to break a leg. Bob looked a little pale. Growth had covered it up and he didn't want to think about what would have happened if Bill hadn't warned him.

Bill pushed open the old door and saw the roof had fallen in. On a firm shelf, there were a lot of items beyond being identified. Bill moved some of the bark roof to one side, which instantly revealed two skeletons whose clothes were rotting away. Shock was quickly replaced by curiosity. Close examination showed that both had been shot at close range – two clean bullet holes in the head.

Bill and Bob looked very carefully for any identification, but couldn't find anything.

"I'll make a report to Sergeant Green, he might know something." Bill said.

"Are we going to bury them?"

"No. Someone may come one day and find things to identify them."

The view from the hut across the tops of the hills was magnificent. There was evidence of an old garden, so Bob foraged around until he discovered vegetables which had come up every year. He picked what could be used and was clearly delighted.

The pair returned to the cave to digest the significance of their discovery. Bill was quiet about the skeletons. Bob's interest was the vegetable garden and what he could do with his find.

In the late afternoon, they returned after a walk down the river and decided it would be safe to travel in the morning. The ground was wet but not impassable, and with care, the horses could walk down the river. They were relieved that this was to be their last night in the cave. Ian had remained quiet about the swarm of bats which had returned at dawn this morning. Now, after sunset, they ducked their heads at the first sound of the bats flying out. No one looked at Bill!

"There go your friends!" Ian smiled.

Bill mouthed some unprintable words, which provoked laughter and the group settled down for the night. Bob went off to his swag for the last night sleeping on debris, leaving the other two to talk in front of the fire.

"What was the story behind the hut?" Ian asked.

"I don't know, but they did have a grim end."

"What did you tell Bob?"

"I didn't tell him that one body was a sheila, she had a locket around her neck and some rings on her fingers."

"Anything else?" Ian was worried

"A container of letters which may be able to identity that poor woman."

"How come Bob didn't see all this?"

"The vegetable garden consumed his interest – just as well."

"When we were younger, we had no interest in dead bodies, so we can't make a complaint. I'd rather have his cooking ability."

They wished each other good night and soon the cave was quiet. Though neither would ever say so, it was a comfortable sleeping arrangement. The only sound was the water surging below in the river. In a place right at the back, in the darkness, something else was asleep.

*

For Ian, morning seemed to come in an instant. There was Bill waiting for the billy to boil. The best part was an open sky. Ian's urge to get started was overpowering. Soon the saddles were on the horses, the camp cleared, and they were riding down beside the river. The horses managed the wet ground without any problems. It was soon apparent that the storm had been limited as a couple of miles from the cave they were crossing dry gullies and the soil was bone dry.

It was about mid-afternoon when without any warning, the horses stopped, ears pricked up, their heads stretched up and blowing air out of their nostrils. They refused to move forward, properly spooked by something. The real surprise was that they had not bolted.

"Is one of those places that George talked about at the barracks?" Bill asked Ian.

"Very possible. We have to get moving."

The men alighted and held the reins firmly as the horses were skittish and unhappy.

"How about Bob and I try taking the horses close to the river, while you scout around?" Bill suggested.

"Alright, I'll go for a walk. Are you sure you can manage three horses?"

"Of course."

The horses were cooperative as they were lead down near the water. Around the base of the hill, there was a picturesque flat area surrounded by foliage. Bill decided to make camp. He and Bob hobbled the horses, removed the saddles and set up the camp.

"One of us should stay. The other needs to look for Ian. What do you want to do?" Bill asked.

Bob realised that he was an important part of the team. Their trust motivated him to pull his weight in meal preparation.

"I'll stay and prepare the vegetables for dinner," Bob replied, knowing that Bill wanted to find Ian.

"If you're sure you'll be okay, the horses are hobbled and won't cause any problems."

"Go on Bill, I'm not two years old, y'know!"

Bill had the grace to laugh. Waving, he headed back to seek out his friend. It was a pleasant walk in brilliant sunshine. At the base of the tall hill, he spotted a cave entrance and walked closer. He really wasn't keen on caves. "Are you in there, Ian?"

"Yes, come in."

"Really?"

"Yes, you must. There's been another murder."

Bill spied some old bones pushed to one side. Near the entrance was a decayed body, clothed in the remains of some long-shredded garment. There was the same bullet hole in the forehead.

"I found an old saddle bag with a necklace of coloured stones in it. As a quick estimate I'd say they're probably valuable. The big question is why was it left here? I've been thinking about why that locket was left too? There's a story here," Ian scratched his nose.

"Is there any way of identifying him?" Bill asked, staring at the body.

"Not that I can see, I've checked his pockets. Those which are still intact, nothing. By the looks of it, he came in here to escape."

"So, there's nothing else we can do here, Ian?"

"No. I've now to write a report – when we can find some ink and a pen. I'll take the old saddle bag and put it with your evidence to go to Sergeant Green. I'd love to know why he sent us this way."

"Do you think he knows something?"

"Yes, when you think of this route, and collecting Bob Pringle, we could not have made these discoveries without him, now could we?"

"No, I think you're quite right. The cunning old devil!"

Chapter Eight

The men made their way back. Even before they reached camp, they smelt cooking. They smiled at one another, salivating at the thought of Bob's feast.

The next day was again a bright sky. Each man prayed this would be their last day in this grim place. It had felt like a dark world, living in shadows with only odd glimpses of sunlight. With their horses saddled and the camp cleared, even the gum trees looked fresh. The hills looked not so high as before. Around another bend in the river, they were at last able to see open countryside. It was a moment of sheer delight. Within a mile, they'd be in the wide-open land.

They rode in almost full sunshine – the only shadows the old gums on the riverbanks.

"My clothes have gone from white to brown," Ian complained.

"So, what are you thinking?"

Bill knew exactly what Ian was thinking. "Where?"

"It's a lovely hot day, Bill, and a dip in the water seems a good way to…"

Now playing this game, Bill asked, "Where?"

"There's a waterhole up ahead and we could make a camp on the other side of those trees."

Bob wasn't keen on going into the water, and said so.

"Sooner or later, we are bound to come across a settlement. You don't want to look like something the dingo has dragged around for a week, do you?" Ian responded.

Bill laughed before Bob had a chance to say a word.

"None of us want to look like something dragged out of a hole. You ought to know that Ian always likes to be clean and tidy."

"You told me girls liked clean men!" Ian smiled at Bill.

"So I did."

"Very well, let's choose a suitable camp site. Who is going to find a couple of fat wild ducks?"

Bob came up behind Bill with the packhorse. He eyed the water with distaste, knowing he had little choice.

"Bob, our clothes are wet – could cause flu. We need to wash," Bill insisted.

"I don't see why?"

"Believe us, you do need to."

Bob wasn't about to give in. "It doesn't sound healthy to me."

"Bob, when you're preparing food isn't it good to be clean?"

"I always wash before preparing food," Bob snapped, adding, "I've just never gone naked into the water – it doesn't seem decent."

"We're a long way from anyone else, and we're all men. There's nothing for you to be concerned about," Bill smiled at him.

"Oh, all right. Don't go on about it, Bill."

Not for the first time, Bill wondered if Bob Pringle was suited to a long patrol. He tried to do what was required, but his heart wasn't in the police work. Perhaps there might be an answer in the coming settlement – Sunny Flat – about a day's ride away.

Ian had discussed their reports, confident that they could send the evidence back to Sergeant Green from the barracks. Bill wondered if they had a good cook. If not, they might employ Bob. All kinds of ideas ran through his mind, before Ian interrupted.

"What did you say?"

"What about the ducks, Bill?"

He took his gun and headed for the river seeking a few likely candidates for three hungry men. Bill was a good hunter but he didn't like to make anything suffer longer than absolutely necessary. In no time, he bagged four ducks.

Back at camp, Ian had washed his clothes and was swimming quite happily. Unable to swim, Bob kept to the shallows. Bill smiled.

It was just as well that Bill couldn't see into Bob's mind. Bob was shocked to see the colour of Ian's skin. How he had been able to join the police? Perhaps they didn't know. How could Bill be such good friends with a coloured man?

Bob had been taught about the colony's caste system. Now he sat in the water thinking of all the kind things Ian had done for him. People of colour were not meant to behave with such kindness. In the future, he would disregard the barrier of colour.

*

Bob had come to a decision and decided to tell Ian and Bill as they sat around the fire.

"I've enjoyed being with you on this one trip, and I'll never forget it, but I'm not cut out for patrols. What I like is cooking," he said.

"Bob, we knew. We realised that your heart wasn't in it. That doesn't mean to say that you don't have a role to play. If cooking really good meals is your gift, do it."

"My dad taught me to cook out of whatever we could find, and never waste any food," Bob explained.

"You are wasted on a patrol, you're a great cook. You would be much appreciated by men coming back from hard patrols to a satisfying meal. You do realise very few of our meals are tasty," Ian winked.

"I've eaten some terrible meals in the barracks," Bob agreed. "Do you mind that I want to leave?"

"We'll always take an interest, wherever you are in the colony. We'll want a good meal at cost!" Ian added, "There is something else you might like to know. Sergeant Green gave us the choice of continuing the trip with you or allowing you to go your own way. He understood you too."

They sat around fire talking until it was time to roll out the swags.

"A good solution?" Bill said quietly to Ian.

"Yes, if the barracks want him?"

"How big would the barracks be to warrant a cook?"

"At least six men or more."

There was silence as the men considered Bob's chances.

"What's on your mind?" Ian asked.

"I'm not sure yet, just an idea."

"Come on Bill, what is it?"

"There're lots of eating places in settlements, aren't there?"

"Yes, and some are to be avoided if you want a long life!"

Bill continued, "We need to find a young unmarried woman who is a cook in one of these food tents. Take Bob for a meal and see what happens."

"Have you been drinking something I don't know about? That's a mad idea. It could also get us into a lot of trouble," Ian said, laughing.

"But it could work."

"Bill, it's a cunning plan and would solve a problem for Bob."

"Well, it's worth a try."

With this decision made, it was time to sleep.

Chapter Nine

They woke just before the sun rose above the eastern horizon on a clear morning. The weather continued to feel fresh and clean, and they were soon in their saddles. Bob even thanked Bill for insisting on a good wash. Making a steady pace, the horses covered a reasonable distance before midday. Ian wasn't sure where Sunny Flat was and had to ask a couple of travellers at the river crossing in the mid-afternoon.

"Not far. Just a couple of miles down the track – you can't miss it," grunted a man who would have liked to have sent them elsewhere.

Sure enough in the latter part of the day, they rode to the top of a hill and looked down on Sunny Flat. Like most frontier communities, it consisted of tents and a few slab buildings. One of the slab constructions was the police barracks. Its office at one end was exposed to the stench from the cesspits when the wind was blowing in the wrong direction.

Fires were burning for the night, and a haze was slowly moving over the settlement. The horses were in a hurry to locate the other mares in town, so they reached the barracks at a gallop. First job was to unsaddle the horses and let them out into the paddock through a gate beside the stables. The senior officer had seen them arrive and gave the men time to deal with their horses before walking across to speak to them.

"I'm Sergeant Greg Knox. I've been expecting you," he said, introducing himself. He smiled and added, "A messenger has arrived from Norm Green. I understand you know him well."

"We work for him in different patrols," Ian agreed.

"Who is the messenger, Sergeant?" Bill asked carefully.

It had been a dull day, and these young men were a relief from his desk duties.

"I hear you know him well. Constable John Hale is here somewhere!" he replied.

There was silence.

"Sergeant, how did he get here before we did?" Ian asked.

"He came down the straight road, while you came through the ranges. I do hope you cleared up some matters in that area."

"We have evidence of two murders. We will need to write our reports tomorrow, if we may use your office?" Bill blurted.

"No problem. In the meantime, the barracks are almost empty. The visiting area is down at the end, you'll find three beds. Make yourselves at home and I'll see you in the morning."

The Sergeant left them to carry their saddle bags and equipment to the barracks. Bob retrieved pots and pans from the pile on the packhorse, now lying on the ground in the stables. The evening meal was a long way beneath the standard they had enjoyed with Bob, who was not happy with it at all.

Bob was content to remain in the barracks while the others went in search of their friend. They found him in a grog shanty with a lot of men in smelly clothes. Ian wanted him to leave.

"Not until I finish the mug of whatever it is?"

"It doesn't look safe to drink, John," Bill said.

John had no choice. He was removed by his friends and they found a quiet place to talk. For a couple of minutes, they had to listen to him moaning about their high-handed behaviour.

At last, John looked at his friends, "What do you want to know?"

"What you are doing tomorrow?"

"What do have you in mind?"

Bill explained Bob's extraordinary cooking skills. He wasn't cut out to be a policeman. What he needed was an unmarried girl who was also good in the kitchen.

"We want you to canvass the community, if you have nothing better to do," Bill asked.

"I could get killed doing that!"

"Not if you're careful."

"Let me think about it." Then he added, "You're going to owe me for this one day!"

"If it brings it to a satisfactory conclusion, we'll be happy to assist you," Ian laughed.

Thinking it would be very difficult for John to get into a similar situation, they thought it safe to commit.

*

The next day, John explained that he had to return to Sergeant Green with their report and evidence in a few days. Bob asked if he could prepare a meal for the night.

The Sergeant was impressed.

"You have a job here," he told Bob.

"Thank you."

"Don't thank me. The police are not easy at the best of times, but with you doing this job, I won't have so many off sick."

He walked away in a cheerful mood for the rest of the day, to the relief of his staff.

John was looking forward to examining Sunny Flat. In uniform, he could go anywhere without raising comment. He soon discovered that the community had emerged to support a large land-holding a few miles out, which employed a large number of shepherds and other farm hands. A sizable number of people were moving through the settlement heading south. John walked down a muddy track with tents either side. In a few places there were more substantial wooden slab buildings, but these were not prominent. Everything was for sale, some things evidence the community was still at the shanty-stage of development.

Not paying attention as he wandered towards the end of the street, he heard his name being called.

"That's John Hale, I'd know him anywhere."

John looked around to see a face, which he knew very well. A man on a dray being pulled by two horses. John crossed the street to greet the man with his hand held out.

"Well, what a surprise. Mr. Hunt, what are you doing here?"

"Just like a policeman to ask that question, John," he replied with a big smile.

John smiled, "A very natural question, Mr. Hunt."

"I'm making a living, John."

"I don't understand. When I knew you, you had a good living."

"Some things change."

"I'm sorry to hear you're no longer a teacher."

"When I was told you'd joined the police, I thought it would suit you very well. I seem to remember you could never keep still in class for more than a few minutes."

Both men smiled at memories of a small schoolhouse overlooking the Nepean.

"What made you give up teaching kids?"

"My family has grown up, and you know my sons. We decided to create a family business together. What are you up to wandering about in a daydream?"

"You are never going to believe this story and you've heard a good few from me!" John smiled.

"Try me."

John decided to change his story.

"I have two colleagues who have just arrived from a difficult patrol in the ranges north of here. The third member is a young policeman – an excellent cook, but not very worldly. I'm looking for a cooking tent with a young unmarried woman – might become a match in time."

Mr. Hunt looked at John in mild surprise.

"John, anyone else – I'd give them a sore jaw, but coming from you, it's priceless. What Betsy will think I can't imagine? What sort of a man is he?" He regained his composure.

"Just under six feet, trim, dark, beard, in his early twenties. He really is only interested in cooking."

"Anything you'd like to add?"

"His friends thought he needed a push in a new direction. The barracks are not a good place for him."

Hunt had listened carefully and knowing John as well as he did, this gave him an edge.

"Do you think he would leave the police?"

"Yes, like a shot, if an opportunity presented itself. Why, what have you in mind?"

"We need a good cook to run a food tent. Presently my wife and daughter Betsy, whom you might remember, are running it. Betsy could do with a teacher. My two eldest, Dick and Tom, help me in the carrier business, my youngest Jason runs a shop beside our food tent."

"Is Betsy married yet?" John raised his eyebrows.

"Not yet, she is only keen on cooking – no interest in boys."

"This could be a solution for you too, Mr. Hunt," John grinned.

"What about you bring your friends to lunch tomorrow? We don't generally open then, so it will be a good time to make an… assessment. It should be interesting!"

"Do I introduce you?"

"No, I will advise my wife not to recognise you."

"I'd love to see her face," John laughed. "Betsy will remember me too."

"She doesn't know you," the older man said, surprised.

"Mr. Hunt, I hate to disappoint you, but Betsy and I are old friends."

"Are you? I didn't know."

"Betsy loved going fishing and her elder brothers refused to take her, so she came with me. Always brought the biggest worms."

"Is that all?"

"And her mother's small cakes!" John grinned.

"So that's why I could never find any cakes to eat!" Mr. Hunt roared with laughter, wiping the tears from his eyes.

"Mrs. Hunt was a very good cook, and they were the best cakes ever."

Hunt wondered how close John had been to his daughter.

"Why don't you come to us for lunch today?" he suggested.

John was delighted, given the Hunt children had been his childhood playmates.

In the meantime, Mr. Hunt called his eldest boys and told them Hale was coming for lunch. He also told them of the "request". This caused laughter and a few stories about John's activities years earlier. He'd been a favourite friend.

Jason asked a friend to mind his shop for an hour or so. When John arrived at lunchtime, the three boys were visibly thrilled to welcome an old friend from their school days. Soon they were swapping memories. The Hunt parents were thankful the boys had grown up without damage given these escapades. Mrs. Hunt greeted John with a big hug, "Whenever you came to visit, my small cakes would vanish!"

"Mrs. Hunt, your small cakes were legendary, so of course they vanished on a regular basis!"

They all laughed. This was John as they had known him as a small boy. Betsy just stood aside and listened. Though she had been young, she had clear memories of his kindness.

"You all gave me grey hair. I missed you greatly when you went away to police. When you were nearby, I always knew what my sons were doing," Mrs. Hunt admitted.

The boys all laughed. Jason recalled, "We used you as a shield. Mum never worked our plans out until you left us. Then we had to re-think our activities."

"I have wonderful memories of the Hunt home," John smiled.

Mr. Hunt spoke about the plan for the next day.

"Best if John brings them here before introductions. We need to do an assessment on our own. Betsy, you and John need to go and talk in the kitchen."

John and Betsy went to the slab hut behind the tent, which served as the kitchen.

John opened up. "Betsy, you know I wouldn't bring anyone who wasn't a decent man."

"I know that, John. Is he really a very good cook?"

"He is the best police cook I have ever experienced. My friends tell me on patrol he produced extraordinary meals out of almost nothing."

"What have you been doing since I last saw you?" Betsy looked down.

"Learning the trade of staying in the saddle for hours at a time. Learnt how to cook food I can eat! How to sleep on a firm surface, how to question people," he replied.

"Have you thought about me at all? We were such good friends when we were younger?" she asked quietly.

Betsy had a lovely slim figure with shiny black hair and a pair of brown eyes which seemed to speak of a long time ago when they were children on the riverbank.

He was quiet for a few moments.

"Betsy, It would be impossible to forget any member of your family. You are still my sister. We share memories which are special. They belong to us for keeps. If your folks employ Pringle, I'll be telling him that you are my beloved sister, and heaven help him if I hear you ever suffer at his hands."

Betsy gave John a great big hug. "I knew the moment you walked in that nothing had changed. You will always be my fourth brother. No doubt we will see you in other places for years to come."

"Betsy, I hope so."

They returned to the main tent to be greeted with questions.

"Now if you are happy with a new cook?" he said.

"It's amazing how many stories Betsy and I haven't known of in our own family. I think John ought to visit more often," Mr. Hunt remarked.

To which Dick replied cheerfully, "Dad, we are all innocent, it was John leading us astray!"

"Don't 'Dad' me. You forget I've taught lots of boys and listened to every story under the sun!"

Mr. Hunt then reminded the company that there was work to be done.

"I'll see you tomorrow at lunch," John said.

John walked back to the barracks. How would he tell his friends about Betsy, without revealing his lunch? The first man he saw near the stables was Bill.

"How did you get on today?" he asked.

"I had a good walk all around. It's an interesting place."

"No. I mean who did you talk to about employing a cook?"

"Bill, I did find a family who are interested."

"Well, speak?"

"There is to be a lunch tomorrow at a tent at the end of the street."

Bill was like a dog with a bone. John tried to be careful. Bill was very good at reading between the lines.

"There is a lovely girl – perhaps a little young. You will have to wait and see."

John managed to escape any further integration by Bill, who was distracted by Ian calling out to him.

"We'll talk later. We've almost dealt with all the reports and bagged the evidence for you," Bill promised.

He hurried away and John decided to make himself scarce, knowing he'd never survive another interrogation. As a pair, Ian and Bill were relentless in finding the truth. John managed to keep out of their way until the next day. He met them outside the tent very pleased with himself.

The previous night, in the quiet, Bill and Ian had talked as usual.

"I think John is holding something back from us," Bill whispered.

"What?"

"I don't know, but I'm curious to know why he's kept out of the barracks this evening. He's up to something, I'm sure of it! He's out of character."

"Well, we'll find out at lunch tomorrow."

John greeted Ian, Bob and Bill at the door of the tent and ushered them in. There were a couple of others at two other benches. Conversation was light as they ate a good meal.

"I've been told you are looking for a cook?" Ian at last asked the girl.

"Yes, do you know of anyone?"

"This man here," Ian replied, touching Bob on his shoulder, "is a very good cook."

Bill noticed the girl look swiftly at the older man, who got up and walked across to their bench.

"I'm Mr. Hunt, and this is my daughter. We have decided to give you a trial. John spoke well of you."

"Thank you Mr. Hunt, I'll do my best to return the confidence," Bob replied.

"You have good friends. It's fortunate I recognised John Hale as he wandered down the street. I've known John just about all his life as he and my boys were forever getting into mischief. Things haven't changed much!" Hunt smiled.

"Mr. Hunt, if you've known him that long, you will know it's a losing battle!" Bill grinned.

"Mr. Todd, seeing you put it up to John to ask the question, what do you really think?"

"Mr. Hunt, whatever you do, don't become a policeman!"

The laughter left Ian to make peace.

"Mr. Hunt, on behalf of my delinquent friends, thank you for giving Bob a much-needed job. The way we went about it was unusual, so…"

"We are delighted to catch up with John again, so all is forgiven."

It was another hour before Bob had a chance to talk with the Hunts about his new position.

Chapter Ten

Walking back to the barracks, Bill and Ian had a lot to say to their friend. John just smiled and endured a very long lecture.

"Where are we going tonight?" John asked when at last Bill ran out of breath.

"Did you hear anything we said?" Ian asked cheerfully.

"No, what did you say? Was it about tonight?"

"Where would you like to go?" Bill asked.

"There's a small shanty which has a light beer and is cheap and safe to drink – popular with the traders."

Bill looked at Ian, "What do you want to do? "

"We'll almost certainly meet Dick and Tom there. We can ask some questions about their business on the tracks."

"How did you know, Ian?" John smiled.

"I'm sure you'd want to spend your last night here with your childhood friends. Am I right?"

"Of course – old friends and new ones!"

The tent had benches made of logs. These had just enough room to move about with full mugs of beer. By the time the men arrived, the tent was full of loud chatter about the day's activities. Tom waved and they crossed to join him and Dick, who each had jugs of beer. Before long, any tension left from lunch had vanished.

"How safe is this area travelling with your drays?" Bill asked.

"Nowhere is all that safe, it depends on what the gossip says you're carrying," Tom admitted.

"How do you protect yourself?" Ian queried, his elbows angled across the bench.

"In travelling long distances, this a major problem. I can't divulge how we do it – security concerns," Dick grinned.

"I don't think that was Ian's question, Dick, he meant how we cope with bushrangers?" Tom corrected.

"I tried to avoid that," Dick laughed. "Acting as if there is nothing of value is a way out – felons want valuables."

This gave rise to a long and interesting discussion. Tom and Dick had had little to do with the police, so were cautious at first, but soon relaxed.

"Are you going to resign?" Tom asked Bob.

"It may not be for a few weeks."

"Dad is thinking of moving to a bigger settlement. If he does it will be better for. No one will know you've been a policeman," Dick countered.

"A good idea, even if Bob doesn't leave until you move. What do you think?" Bill spoke quietly.

The brothers exchanged glances, before Tom replied, "Bob can do a couple of meals so we can assess things. Then we can work out the way ahead."

Bob seemed happy with this plan. The conversation moved on.

"Will your father ever go back to teaching?" John asked.

"Dad is planning on opening a larger establishment in a bigger settlement – a meal room, possibly an inn, with a school attached . He loved teaching," Dick looked at his brother.

John thought, "Why is he a carrier now?"

"He could see a future in it for all of us. We think he's right. While it will be demanding work, already it is proving a very good decision," Tom said.

Bill looked around the tent.

"Many of tonight seem to be travellers?"

"The carriers come here after making deliveries. We pick up news and hear about which roads are dangerous at the present time," Tom said laughing.

"If we ever wanted to get word to you, how safe is it to use the carriers?" Ian, who was paying attention to Tom's words, now asked carefully.

"What have you in mind, Ian?"

"Sometimes we need to alert people about problems in a certain area."

"Some are good men and some would kill you for pennies," Dick cut in.

Tom turned to Dick and had a quiet conversation. "We can give you a list after we've had a talk to them. But what can you tell us about highwaymen in certain places on the frontier?"

"I take your point – we'll need to think about it. I do think we can benefit one another."

The night was getting late and the crowd in the tent was thinning out.

"Dick and I go are going to another tent if you want to come. It's of a better quality than most if you catch my drift," Tom said.

Bob said he'd go with them.

"What about it, Ian?" Bill asked.

"I've paperwork to complete for John to take north in the morning."

John looked as if he'd like to go, but thought of the long ride next day made him hesitate.

"You and Bill enjoy exploring the lay of the land!" John said.

Ian stood up and shook hands with Tom and Dick.

"Pleased to have met you both. I'm sure we'll meet again," he said, before turning to Bob, "I do hope we haven't interfered too much. This connection will be very good for you. We'll be interested to know how you get on."

"I'll always have a soft spot for that patrol through the ranges and beyond. I do thank you," Bob said cheerfully.

With these words the men went their separate ways, some further into the night while the other two began to walk back to the barracks.

"John, you're most fortunate having that family as close friends, they're lovely people," Ian said.

"I hope we come across them coming or going the way we do," he replied.

In the barracks the next morning, John was up early and had his horse saddled and prepared for the trip north. The reports and evidence were packed away. He was very relieved he would have company of two other police for the first couple of days – only the last day would he be on his own.

Bill and Ian were up early in the day. Glad to escape their very lumpy straw beds. Both were looking forward to the next assignment further south. This was the very trying part of police work. They might never hear more about the murders in the ranges. Obviously, somebody knew, otherwise they wouldn't have been sent down that river. There were always questions and rarely answers.

At last, Ian and Bill were granted permission to leave.

"How far is our next job?" Bill asked.

"I wasn't told exactly, except it's quite a long way. How are you this morning, I didn't hear you come into the barracks, so it must have been late?"

"Just keep your voice down!"

"So that's it, did you go drinking with the others?"

"They could put it away, like they didn't have to get up in the morning."

"I hate to disappoint you, Bill, but I saw Tom and Dick out on two drays going north long before John managed to leave."

"I don't want to know!"

"What happened last night?'

"Do you really want to know?'

"Yes, on the off-chance I join them in some future activity of a similar nature!"

"I think you'd be too old for these games, Ian!"

"Come on Bill, talk! You know you want to."

"No, I don't!"

No matter how much Ian tried to get Bill to talk, he shut his mouth and it remained closed all day. It was unusual for Bill to behave in this way – so something must have happened. As curious as Ian was, he knew the subject was closed.

Ian never mentioned the subject again. This was not to say that he wouldn't ask Tom or Dick if he came across them when Bill wasn't anywhere near. Men liked to know all kinds of things about themselves, what worked and what didn't, this was the nature of being male. The frontier was really a frontier for everyday life, always learning.

Chapter Eleven

They rode in silence for about ten miles, before Bill asked, "Do you know anything about the job we are going to do?"

"Not really, no one seems to know what the problem is. A great silence has overshadowed the community."

There was a stillness as Bill digested this slim piece of knowledge.

"That's not much to go on, is it? No doubt we'll find something."

"When are we going to make camp, I really don't feel well today, that beer wasn't as safe as I thought it was after several mugs of it."

"We'll make camp at the first place that you choose."

Bill was quite happy to stop at the next good waterhole. He wanted a good wash to cleanse the beer out of his system. Shortly they found a suitable camp site. With saddles on the ground and the horses hobbled, Ian began to make a fire, while Bill stripped to his skin and dived into the water. The river was clear enough to show everything below the surface. Ian watched Bill for a few minutes to see that he was okay. The beer in these camps could be quite lethal. The toxic brew was brought out after most men could not tell the difference. Ian was annoyed the boys had not kept an eye on him, but knew full well that he was being totally unreasonable. Bill was a grown man.

Bill fell asleep almost as soon as he had eaten. Ian was happy to do odd jobs in preparation for the next day. He even caught a fish which would be a tasty breakfast for them both.

*

Next morning, Bill was the first to leave his swag and get a fire going to make tea. He was feeling a lot better. The swim last night had done him the world of good. He wondered why Ian was still asleep. It was so unlike him not to be up and doing things. Moving a cloth over a pan, he discovered the fish was ready to cook. So that's why he was still asleep after sunrise. He gently nudged Ian with his boot.

"Time to get up, the day is almost gone!"

"Why are you up so early?"

Ian stretched his arms, rolled out of his swag, and went down to the river for a wash. Standing up, he watched Bill begin to cook the fish. It was a lovely morning and he looked up at a flock of galahs fleeing a large gum tree nearby. They were beautiful birds. The scent of cooked fish meant his empty stomach growled.

"How long before it will be ready?"

"Just a few minutes longer."

"How are you this morning, Bill?"

"Much better."

"Was it bad beer?"

"The worst."

"I don't know how you stayed in your saddle."

"Neither do I!"

"The fish is ready."

"Thanks, Ian. I really need a good meal today."

"We both need one".

They left the camp about an hour later. Even the horses seemed pleased. The land was flat compared with the ranges – small hills with few large trees. It was odd country. It had a feel which he didn't like. The grass was low and poor quality – not in the least suitable for the horses to graze on. In places there were boggy areas, where water had not soaked away in a month or more.

"Sour country – not in the least attractive, I wouldn't want to live anywhere near here," Bill remarked, looking around from his saddle.

"Who were the two policemen going north with John?" Ian asked as they began to ride up a long, sloping hill.

"Someone said they were from the other side of the Blue Mountains."

"What are they doing in our patch?"

"It's a bit hard to put the job together. Apparently they had been tracking a thief and caught him in the grog shanty drunk," Bill replied.

He was enjoying making Ian ask questions. Bill would pay for it later. As he waited for the next question, he smiled.

"What had the thief done to cause them to track him so far inland?"

"He stole a gold presentation watch from an important individual in the city, plus a wallet containing five pounds. He was put in front of a local Magistrate."

"Did they find the watch or money?"

The banter was keeping Bill's mind engaged as they traversed some extremely dull country.

"They found the watch on him and a couple of pounds. He went down for a few years on the road gang."

"Bill, you've stretched that story out about as far as you can."

"It could have lasted a lot longer!"

"After this effort, I will owe you one."

They both laughed. Their target was perhaps not too far away if the blue smoke rising beyond the hill was any indication. At the top of the hill, a creek was visible before a wide flat area leading to a rise above the water and a hut.

"It's odd. Some of these small creeks are called rivers. I wonder if the early explorers saw them in full flood and mistook them for rivers," Ian stared at the creek.

"I don't know, but I do get your point. Only when we have to cross a flooded creek, it feels like a river!"

"Bill, can you see anyone near that hut?"

"There's a shepherd with a small flock of sheep down near the water on the other side."

They rode confidently across the creek where it was running lowest over gravel stones and up the other side, coming close to the shepherd. His sheep bounded rapidly to the hill beyond, only curtailed by the man's dog. The shepherd stood quite still and waited for the police to approach.

It was easy to tell if such men had done time – the way they behaved, the expression on their faces. A silent question: "What now?" or "Can't you leave us alone?"

The man was poorly dressed and thin.

"We're seeking a settlement called Rockdale where there have been problems?" Bill asked in a measured tone.

"You mean where tents be burnt an' slab 'ut's go up in flame too?"

"Yes, that would be it. How far away?"

"Over them 'ills for a way."

"What happened to the people when their homes burn?" Ian asked carefully, trying not to frighten the man into silence.

"They be sent away by settlers."

"What if they don't want to leave?" Bill asked, shocked.

"They go, not safe to stay," the man said firmly.

"So they have no choice?"

"Nasty to see poor families flee."

Bill continued to ask questions but received no new information.

"Who is the person in charge?" Ian tried one more question.

Now the man appeared afraid. "I can't say. Me get supplies, not safe to say."

He looked with an expression which Bill understood.

"Sorry," the man said very quietly.

Bill spoke equally quietly. He understood the man's position. His information was safe. They turned their horses away from the flustered sheep and rode in the direction of Rockdale.

"This is not a good business – burning tents and huts to force people out. It's more than a crime. How are we going to handle it?" Ian asked.

"We have to find who runs the place."

"Who has the power, do you think?"

"We both know it rests with women!"

"Alright, are we looking for a front man? If so, what does he do? Who has the most power in a growing community?"

"I'd say for a settlement in its infancy, whoever supplies victuals would be have the upper hand."

"Not a big landowner?"

"Not in the settlement itself. Communities have hierarchies. In the wider district, the power is in the hands of the largest landholder, given his connections."

Soon Rockdale came into sight situated on a rise above a small creek in the lee of a large hill. Not perhaps the best location. A track ran through the middle of a number of tents and a rather large slab general store dominated the track. Further down there were a few burnt tents and two ruined slab huts. Bill alighted and walked over to the remains of one hut. Bending down, he touched the black coals.

"They are still warm. This fire was only last night."

"This is a nasty thing. We'll go to that store."

Bill led his horse, while Ian remained seated as they approached the steps leading up to the store. On the top step stood a man and a woman looking almost defiant.

Bill began the conversation, "Where are the people who lived in the hut which burnt down?"

The man, at a nudge from his wife, answered, "They've gone."

"Where?" Bill countered sternly.

"We don't care."

"We don't want them here," the woman, who had sharp features, replied.

"Why they were unsuitable?" Bill looked at the woman.

"This is a community of people born free. We don't want others."

"We'll be making a recommendation for a policeman." Ian had been silent until now, "If any further dwellings are burnt down, arrests will follow."

Bill mounted his horse and they began to walk out. On the outskirts, an old man sat on a log. Bill led the way across the track to speak to him and Ian followed.

"You've had a fire here?" Bill asked.

"They weren't careful," the old man scowled.

"Altogether?" Bill asked.

"It were a good bonfire, it was!"

"Where are the people now?"

"Gone, them be people we don't want."

"Who doesn't want?"

"Them who own the store, them say who can be 'ere," the old man laughed.

"Not very fair, is it?"

"It be life."

They turned their horses and rode slowly up to the top of the hill. At the top, overlooking the settlement, Bill suddenly sat very still. Down below he could see a man moving carefully towards the back of the store. He had a firestick in his hand and was setting alight various sections.

"We really ought to stop him," Ian said.

"It's the best justice, better than any we could organise," Bill admitted, without remorse.

"You're right."

"I'd like to know where the people are who lost their homes."

"Let's get as far as possible away before we make camp," Ian said quietly.

"We can ride for another couple of hours. Which direction?"

"North-west away from the smell."

Bill was only too happy to get as far away as possible. This event was not unusual. Many migrants brought their prejudices with them. The mix of free and convict stock in an emerging frontier society meant every type of human spread slowly across the country.

Chapter Twelve

Ian and Bill rode in silence until they sighted a group on the side of a track under a cluster of trees. There was an older woman and about four children playing with each other. There were a couple of handcarts nearby. The police rode across to speak to the woman. She stood up protectively as they approached, unashamed by the shabby clothes giving away their poverty.

"Where did you come from to be out on the track today?" Bill asked, looking down from his horse.

"We move from Rockdale," she pointed her finger back down the track.

"The people who set fire to your tent?"

The woman was silent.

"Why were you not allowed to stay?" Ian probed.

"We be there a long time. My man be shepherd and have work, then new people come an' we not wanted. Told to go. We stay an' it get bad an' badder, then fire at night. We save little and move."

"Where is your man now?" Ian asked gently.

"He coming soon."

Was the man they had seen with the firestick her husband? He wasn't about to say anything. Sometimes justice was best served outside the courts. This was one of those times.

"Will you give a message to your man from me please?" Bill asked.

Bill saw that she knew what her man had been doing. She waited, half afraid.

"Tell him not to make a habit of it."

Suddenly she smiled. Her hard features broke into a reluctant smile.

"Me tell him an' he not do agin".

"There's a community called Welcome up ahead", Ian nodded. "You ought to be able live there."

"There be a place for us, we work hard".

"I'm sure you'll never give up," Ian smiled.

"Me never give up."

The children had surrounded their mother, listening to the strangers with interest, surprised to see no one was shouting. One of those little boys would one day wear a similar uniform.

Bill and Ian rode away, the small group watching as they disappeared into the trees.

"What's it like, do you think, to be so poor?" Ian asked as they reached the crest of a hill.

"I've seen a good deal of it. Many rise above it with hard work. I bet that one will see her children able to read and write."

"Do you really think so?"

"This land is new. We don't have a dominant class."

"You're saying there are more opportunities?"

"It depends. There will always be powers trying to control. That can't be avoided."

"I'm glad I'm here now."

"Where are we going to camp?"

"The next good waterhole without anyone in sight. I've had enough of people today."

They rode along beside the creek looking for a suitable site, which wasn't easy given the debris and other rubbish on the banks. At last Bill found a spot high above the water.

"We might find dinner in there?" He looked down into the muddy creek.

"So that's what you were looking for?"

"We could do with a nice fish. Let's have a swim."

"When did you first hear strong swear words?" Bill watched the flames change colour in the fire.

"On the ship going out to India when I was sixteen years old. It was normal amongst the sailors."

"I heard them in the brick kiln. Now, we get abused with vile language all the time. It's so ordinary I hardly register the words. It isn't that I don't hear them."

"Sure in the barracks and grog shanties where there're no decent women. I never heard my Dad use strong swear words."

"Dad use to say there were work words – used in the kitchen shed and words used a long way from Mum!"

"Bill, I wouldn't like any woman to hear the language I use on the job."

"I was just thinking the same thing."

"Strong words are common – basic to descriptions of anything!"

Bill laughed and gave the fire a poke. Sparks rose into the night sky.

"Yes, you're right. Very common words in a certain class of people."

"I wonder if it will ever be an offence to swear at a policeman?"

"Ian, what did you have in your tea?" Bill shook his head. "The courts would be full. They would never get any work done!"

Both men decided not in their lifetime. There was silence. The fire was just red hot coals. Bill was the first to roll out his swag.

"What are we doing tomorrow, Bill?"

"We need to visit that Welcome place to see if they'll accept that poor family."

The pair stared at the stars and rising moon.

*

Sunrise seemed to happen at once, despite the many hours they had slept.

In the trees, the galahs never seemed to stop talking to each other – loudly as if they had hearing problems.

They headed north-west along the top of a ridge which gave a good view in all directions. Soon smoke from the distant Welcome settlement was visible. All settlements had to be near water, though too near and they suffered from flooding; too far away and carting water was a problem. It was nothing for a family to struggle with buckets of water five miles a day from creek to hut.

Welcome was beside a creek, well above the flood lines, shown by the debris on its banks. Some of the well-spaced tents and slab huts had gardens. Things already felt welcoming.

"Beware of the beer, Bill," Ian spied the grog shanty.

They rode up to a large slab hut well-situated above the water mark. Alighting, they tied their horses to a hitching rail, close enough so they could drink from the adjacent trough. It was a store, well stocked with tools, cheap candles, pots and pans, camp ovens of various sizes and, in one section, fresh meat. The squeak of their boots on uneven floorboards brought an older man from the back of the shop.

Surprised, he grunted, "What do you want?"

"We're interested in the family evicted from a settlement, Rockdale, south of here."

"We're pleased to accommodate them, until they can pay for a new tent and goods," the shopkeeper smiled. "There is a rumour that the Rockdale store burnt down. It couldn't have befallen a nicer woman." He walked behind his bench. "Are you passing through today?"

"Just checking on people," Ian stared at the stock piled up on the shelves.

"Do you use Hunt & Sons?" Bill asked casually.

"Yes, how did you know?'

"They're to our knowledge honest."

"Don't be concerned about that family. We'll make them welcome," the storekeeper nodded.

"Do you have any problems, while we're here?" Bill asked.

"Nothing we can't handle ourselves."

"In that case, we'll leave you," Ian moved towards the front door.

Leaving their horses at the rail, the two men walked down to the grog shanty. Inside they were greeted by the stench of stale beer, tobacco and unwashed bodies, the usual. The room went silent until one man blurted, "Who have you fuckin' bastards come to arrest. No one has done noth'n."

"Just what we were talking about last night!" Ian turned to Bill.

The drunk persisted, "What do ya's fuckin mean 'bout last night?"

"Language!" Bill laughed.

They gave one last look, turned, and walked into the clean air. They were soon in their saddles and out of the community.

Chapter Thirteen

"It's a long time since I used to do that after work. It never made me feel any better. I'd have friends giving me lectures, then I woke to myself and went dry," Bill said.

"I did the same thing after leaving school. Got into trouble… sent to India. Those days were a waste. But I'm here," Ian admitted.

"Where are we off to now? Those hills a little to the west look interesting, what do think?" Bill changed the subject.

"What's interesting about them?"

"I'm not sure if they're the right hills. A colleague talked about them at the barracks – a bare middle hill and the two either side covered in growth."

"Let's ride up and have a look," Ian shrugged.

They rode along the valley floor and began to climb up the first hill. Yet both now felt uneasy. Near a clump of trees, a black emerged, calling out, "No go near him… spirit man… go back."

The man vanished again amongst the black shadows of trees. The pair paused for a couple of minutes.

"What do you want to do?" Ian hesitated.

"I'm curious to see what's up on top."

They rode carefully, keeping away from any clumps of thick growth. It was a lot steeper than it had looked. Both men were aware of the flickering shadows. They were being observed. Near the top of the hill was a flat area with a pool of water under a couple of trees. The horses stood absolutely still, pricked up their ears and looked at the water. They refused to go anywhere near it. Ian and Bill turned them away and managed to continue to the top of the rise.

At one side under a tree sat a very old black man. The old man showed an interest in these strange white men. His fire had gone out.

"We may as well boil our quart-pots here. Do you have a spare mug?" Bill grunted.

"Yes, we can spare a bit of that fish too."

Under the gaze of the old man, they soon had his fire going. From a spring of water nearby, they filled two full quart-pots, pushing them amongst the coals. Ian threw the fish pieces on the flat pan. No one said a word. The old man was content to watch. Ian produced a third mug.

"Do you understand English?" Bill spoke up.

The old man grinned, showing missing teeth and lively eyes.

"Me 'unna stan' bit."

"Why were we warned not to come up here?"

"Me ole man, time come to meet spirit."

"You are waiting to meet your spirit world?"

He nodded his head.

Even if he was waiting to die, he devoured the fish and tea.

"Is there anything we can do for you?" Bill asked.

The old man turned his head on one side, just looking at them. "You not usual men who be police. You kind to ole man who near spirit time. You two live many, many seasons, till you ole like me, I know me Kadaitcha."

He smiled, but his eyes flashed a warning. Bill and Ian had shown no fear.

They made haste to leave before sundown. The horses were also keen to be gone. By the time the sun was low on the horizon, the hills had disappeared behind a long valley. The valley, well protected from windstorms which might come up during the night, was an ideal camp. It wasn't as hot as usual, and the fish were easy to catch. The fire was soon alight and the quart-pots on it.

"We were in danger, if that old man had felt even remotely threatened," Ian pondered.

"Were we? He was just an old black man."

"No, I felt something radiating out of him. I had experiences like this in India. There were men with the same presence. They were never treated lightly. I think he knew that."

"How?" Bill asked.

"I received a wink and a smile. Before you lit the fire."

"I didn't light it."

Ian laughed. "The old man told you to. He watched you do it."

Bill was quite shocked for a few minutes.

"So that old man was both hungry and thirsty and we provided," he sighed at last.

"No, you lit the fire!"

"Ian, I've just had an old man making me do his will. That's spooky."

"It's just what some people do – ancients like him are part of their societies, it's just we don't understand it."

"Ian, don't put your swag too far from mine tonight."

"You don't want anything unusual to happen tonight?"

"None of your misplaced humour either!"

"Okay, just don't think about it. Begin to plan for tomorrow."

For Bill, the ability to inhabit another's mind had never occurred to him. Nor did he understand he could be made to do something of which he had no control. This spirit world was an unknown.

Still thinking about this extraordinary experience, the pair rode northeast towards the barracks. It was not possible to make this return journey in a day. But neither man was in a hurry and it was pleasant in the sunshine.

*

In the mid-afternoon, blue smoke from a campfire became visible in a low valley as they reached the crest of a hill. They rode closer.

"That's Jack May, also a mounted policeman who told me about that place."

Bill swore quietly. "We crossed swords over a matter. We aren't camping here, but we can use his fire to cook up lunch."

"Why send you to that hill?" Ian frowned as they rode closer.

"No doubt to do me mischief of some kind."

At the sound of the approaching horses, Jack stood up and glared.

"What the fuckin' hell are you lot doing here?"

"We thought it would be a good place to cook a fish. Now we've discovered a colleague, so isn't that nice?" Ian replied cheerfully.

"Why don't you just ride on?" the man scowled.

"We've got lots to talk about. Then we'll ride on."

"I have nothing to say to you."

Ian alighted from his horse and unhitched his flat pan from beside his saddle. Bill handed him the fish and Ian put it on the pan, then sat down opposite Jack.

"Talk Jack. Why did you send Bill to those three hills?"

Jack May was overweight and didn't look in good health. His black hair was unkempt. It probably hadn't been combed for a week. His beard was poorly trimmed – he looked a mess. Jack wished they'd go away – except their fish smelt good and he hadn't kept any food down for a day or so.

"As you're using my fire, I want a good slice of that fish."

He glared at Ian, adding, "I didn't invite you."

There was a silence as both Ian and Bill digested the hostility. Nevertheless they needed information so decided to endure it.

Bill touched Ian on the shoulder. Ian turned to Jack.

"You are welcome to the fish."

Jack didn't look the least bit gratified and glared some more.

"You needn't be so polite about it. I'd much rather be on my own after I've eaten your bloody fish."

"We'll go after you've told us about that…" Ian replied firmly.

"So you went there?" Jack interrupted.

"How far did you go?"

"To the top."

Jack sat up straight. "I don't believe you, those effing blacks wouldn't have let you."

"The views were magnificent," Ian smiled.

"They'd gone when you got there?"

"No, Jack, we were warned by an elder, but we had no intention of harm."

Jack stared at them with loathing.

"I was the only survivor. I'm not well, I can't keep food down. I never want to see that effing hill again."

Bill handed Jack a large piece of the cooked fish and the remainder they shared between themselves. Ian took the pan and cleaned it. They boiled their quart-pots and enjoyed mugs of tea. Jack refused a mug.

"A mug of tea is good for you," Bill muttered.

"Can't you mind your own fuckin' business?" he glared at them.

This was not a man to be trusted.

"The only survivor, what happened?" Ian asked gently.

"We were asked to do some culling of them blacks, they'd been spearing stock. Two sworn-in Constables, two trackers and me," Jack looked up from the fire.

"They were probably hungry," Bill interrupted.

Jack glared. "Do you want to hear it or not?"

Jack continued.

"We surrounded their camp at a water hole and did a fair job. One old man looked as if he'd been around for centuries, begged for his life. He told us about a gully on a hill with gold in it. He described the three hills."

"Did you let him go?" Bill asked quietly.

"One of us shot him in the back and we laughed."

Jack didn't notice their horrified expressions.

"When we gathered them up for burning, we couldn't find him. He wasn't where he'd fallen. Our two trackers were the first to get sick. They carried on about eagle claws on the first night. They died, they couldn't keep their food down. We found the hills and the gully. I had a mate with me – he said we ought to leave. I dunno his problem. Anyway, this black came out of some trees and told us to leave. He vanished before we could shoot. Effing queer it was."

Ian opened his mouth to ask something, but Jack went on.

"We weren't in control, though we had the guns. Our horses reared up and tossed us off. My mate's horse came down on him – broke both his legs badly. He died that night. The two Constables died like the trackers, crying out that something was inside them. Now I'm getting out of this place, as soon as my belly settles, and I can ride comfortably." He soured, "I thought I'd get even with you for that matter, you're a right bastard."

Ian had quietly moved to his horse and untied the reins, with Bill joining him.

"Jack, we wouldn't want to be in your boots. Make peace, while you still have time," Ian shook his head.

"What do you mean, while I've got time?"

"What did your mother teach you?"

"Piss off, both of you."

The sun had set some time ago. They rode down the valley in the brilliant moonlight, almost like day except the shadows were pitch black.

"Jack's not going anywhere. We'll have to report his position. I'm sure the old man has punished all who took part. It's justice and I can accept it," Ian sighed.

Bill looked at his friend. "Using the mind to get justice?"

The moonlight scattered grey shadows across the ground.

"Bill, we use guns to enforce. Are guns justice?"

"When are we making camp? I think there's a waterhole up ahead, unless my eyes are deceiving me," Bill changed the subject.

"We'll stop here."

Chapter Fourteen

In the morning, Ian lazily watched Bill do the odd jobs and make tea. He thought about the culling. Everyone knew it took place. Ian was relieved the old man had used his own powers of retribution.

Bill asked, "What are you thinking so early in the morning?"

"That Jack is having a lonely death in the bush."

"And as he dies, the wailing of children calling for their mothers will haunt him."

"What will we say to that elder if we see him again?"

"I don't think it will matter all that much, it's all about learning," Bill added thoughtfully.

They began to ride towards Hill Top and their barracks.

"It's our land," Bill mused.

"Make no mistake Bill, their beliefs, their stories, belong to the old man and others like him. Even our horses recognise the unseen."

"It's too early in the morning," Bill groaned.

"Can't you feel the beauty of the land? We respect our environment, so don't worry about the unseen."

As the two men rode, they talked about these ancient people and their land. Slowly the conversation veered to Hill Top. Would it become a permanent community? Some rose and vanished as people moved on. The frontier was never stable. It depended upon rain and income. Bill wondered if they would see John Hale.

As they approached the community, it appeared different. Tents had given way to more slab huts. Their town was safe for now, unless a major drought changed things.

Their fillies were welcomed by the other police horses, causing a spring in their step. Soon the horses – being social animals – were galloping off to greet their friends.

The farrier checked their equipment for any needed repairs, before Ian and Bill lugged their saddle bags and swags, dumping them beside their barrack beds.

Sergeant Green had seen them arrive and waited impatiently. He knew he'd be questioned about the murders. In no time, Bill and Ian had recounted their foray.

"What can you tell me about how Jack's party died?" Green asked.

"They spoke of eagle claws and not being able to keep food down," Ian replied.

Sergeant Green was silent.

"I've heard of this – pointing the bone. I was told the actual killing was done by old men, willing the victim to die," he said.

It was very quiet in the office before Bill spoke.

"I thought we were the superiors."

Sergeant Green laughed.

"Be careful and show respect," he added.

Ian asked about the murders in the ranges. The Sergeant opened up. "A year ago a man was executed in Sydney for a brutal murder. He admitted to three others, out in the ranges where you were. He mentioned a hut on a high hill. He had a girlfriend whom he loved, but a violent temper meant he treated her badly. So she left him for another man. They fled the city, found sanctuary in that hut. Many seek shelter there and one of his friends informed on the couple. So he went and killed them in a jealous rage. He raped her before cutting her throat. He had a mate who took part – pinched her necklace. On the way out, they camped in a cave. He saw the necklace in his mate's saddlebag while he slept and shot him the same way."

They were quiet for a few minutes.

"Did she have any relatives?" Ian asked.

"Yes, a sister, we have sent the jewelry to her, plus a carefully worded report."

"We did wonder why the jewelry had been left behind," he added.

"A sad ending. Someone should have warned them to avoid a place used by crooks," Bill sighed.

"I don't think it's simple. Jealousy knows no boundaries. Nowhere is safe in that kind of rage," Ian commented.

Sergeant Green agreed and talked about some of his experiences.

"I have another job for you. A young detective Fred Hall from the city will be joining you. This will be a new experience for him," the Sergeant smiled. "Also for you!"

Ian wasn't too sure he liked the grin on his Sergeant's face. "Why are you smiling in just that way?"

The Sergeant laughed and wiped the tears from his eyes. "Mr. Percy, you and Mr. Todd have had an easy time on your own, now you will be part of a planned operation run by another Sergeant. He has a lot of experience but no familiarity with the country districts. You will meet him tomorrow. In the meantime, make sure your equipment is in order for a long patrol. The farrier will provide a packhorse. I will see you here tomorrow quite sober, Mr. Percy and Mr. Todd."

*

Sergeant Rich was tall with grey hair and beard. He had the demeanour which demanded instant obedience. He had arrived with four Constables to hunt down three criminals. He made it plain that he wasn't in favour of using local resources. He could not vouch for their abilities.

"I have chosen Constable Ben Holt to join you on the forward patrol," the Sergeant looked at Bill and Ian.

Sergeant Green chipped in. "Has Holt had country experience?"

"He has never been across the mountains."

"Then with respect, he will be quite unsuitable for this work."

"Sergeant, you are out of order, explain or keep silent."

The old bush Sergeant smiled grimly.

"He'd stand out like a pig on a post. You need a man who can be seen as a local."

The city Sergeant rumbled, "Well, you've made your point. But they can all ride and are intelligent, so this shouldn't be difficult."

"In the city, how would you like it if I told you how to do your job?" Sergeant Green asked.

"I'd give you short shift."

"This is what we are going to do."

There was no sound, so Green continued. "I will send Mr. Percy and Mr. Todd ahead, and your Mr. Holt will go too. They will scout the district – check if they are laying low as 'shepherds'. Mr. Hall will lead the main party forward."

The city Sergeant scratched his head, but stayed mute. These men weren't half as smartly attired as his charges. Yet his posse of city men were now sprawled around the office as if they owned it.

The only seating benches hewn from rough logs – not easy to lounge on. Bill wondered how the visitors would cope with the drafty slab barracks. Ian was thinking the same.

Sergeant Green coughed. "Let's meet tomorrow at seven thirty to finalise plans. And now a briefing about the crime?"

Sargeant Rich spoke. "Three men held up a gold-buyer returning from a miners camp. They made off with quite a few gold nuggets. He had been staying at an inn and they stole jewelry from the womenfolk and … took their liberties. We have evidence they ran a gaming tent with overproof drinks and fleeced anyone. Depraved vultures. The settlers burnt down their tent. Only then did we hear of their activities."

The Constables filed out. Ian and Bill now made an effort to be friendly.

"Avoid the grog shanty beside the tree – it isn't a good place," Bill advised.

One of the men looked as if he'd never missed a meal. He replied curtly, "We are quite able to look after ourselves."

"Be it on your own head," Bill waved them off.

*

At seven thirty next morning, there was no sign of the city Constables. Sergeant Green frowned. "What happened last night?"

"Told us they could look after themselves," Ian shrugged.

Their Sergeant sighed, "In the city we don't have grog shanties – all closed down years ago."

Sergeant Green interrupted, "My Constable will be responsible for your men, he will have them onto their saddles and out of Hill Top within the hour."

The city Sergeant resigned himself to handing over the lead, "What else?"

"A signature from you giving authority to Fred Hall to be in charge. I don't want any trouble out in the field."

Sergeant Green barked instructions from the office doorway. Soon all could hear the farrier whistle as he rounded up mounts. Saddles and bridles were brought out, men arrived with their saddlebags. Minutes later, Fred was leading four ashen-faced Constables out into the bush.

Rich looked at the older man. "You remind me of my first Sergeant. He knew everything. I'm beginning to feel sorry for my men. I didn't see a packhorse."

"The land will supply their food."

Sergeant Rich was suddenly pleased to be staying in Hill Top.

Sergeant Green called out to Ian, "Mr. Percy, I'll be sending John Hale. He'll return with Ben Holt, otherwise he could get lost in the bush."

"Right, Sergeant."

Sergeant Green added with a smile, "Please keep him out of trouble."

"Who?"

"Both of them!"

Ian caught up with the others on the outskirts of town. Ben was like most policemen, tall with wide shoulders, slim waist. Strong looking, he had black hair, a neatly-trimmed beard and a cheerful disposition, which made him good company. He was surprised that they didn't have a packhorse.

"Are you any good at fishing, Ben?" Bill replied.

"I've never done any fishing."

"Well, we're about to find out!"

"I don't understand?"

"We'll find a good place to camp and see if we can find a waterhole or Ian might shoot a couple of ducks. They're a treat cooked in clay."

Ben smiled not sure if he was being played. Twelve hours later, he discovered Bill hadn't been joking. He was given a fishing line and told to get to it. With his line in the water, he felt a fish tugging. But, startled by two gunshots, he jumped and the fish was gone. Ben groaned. He cast again. He was going to get a bloody fish, no matter how long it took.

Bill smiled as he caught a second catfish at the top end of the waterhole. Those shots suggested a roo. Along with the fish, they'd have a good meal tonight. He was pleased to see Ben returning with a fair-sized fish in hand.

Ben was relieved Ian had suggested an early camp. It had been a long day in an unfamiliar land. The waterhole had large old gum trees either side – a magnificent setting, though he was surprised the camp was so far from the tree branches.

"For your own safety," Bill grunted. "And watch out for snakes. If you see one, freeze – they'll likely slide away".

Ben realised the bush was as dangerous as his city streets.

"Where did you grow up, Ben?" Ian asked.

"My parents had a fruit and vegetable barrow in the city – they did quite well – were able to buy a shop. They were able to send me to school."

"After school, what did you do?"

"On the wharf unloading ships – hard toil. They had me on medical detail because I could read. Fellows were always getting hurt, accidents were common."

Bill raised his head, "I've no doubt you could give a good account of yourself in a fight?"

"There were fights every day. Men wanting to dominate other men, " Ben laughed.

"You'd be handy in a fight," Ian commented.

Ben asked about their work.

"We do a lot of scouting, checking up on the settlements, making reports on potential problems," Ian explained. "How far have we ridden today?"

"Police mounts are lower quality – they manage about three miles an hour. So twelve hours, thirty-two miles. Thoroughbreds will do about five miles an hour," Ian admitted.

"So how long will it take to reach the place?"

"Enjoy the ride. Don't think about the end. We'll be joined by John Hale in a day or so."

"John will take Ben back , so he won't get lost in the bush."

Bill spoke carefully, "Ben, if you become lost, we might not find you in time. If ever you become separated, find yourself running water."

After dinner, Bill and Ian talked quietly about their companion.

"If we get into strife, he'll be handy," Bill said.

"Yeah, he has medical knowledge and is good company," Ian agreed.

Chapter Fifteen

The next morning amid pink clouds and the rising rich light, the galahs rose from their night's roost on the gums along the creek and took to the sky, screeching.

Red kangaroos stood up tall to watch them ride past. Two emus took one look at the horses and bounded away before stopping and turning around to watch.

About the mid-afternoon, Bill noticed a stranger coming down the valley.

"Let's stay in full sight of him, in case it's John?" Bill suggested.

Ahead was a plain with little rises. A very long way away were blue hills on the horizon. It was a vast open land. Slowly, Bill recognised him. "It's John."

As he rode closer, Ian felt something was wrong.

John spoke up. "I've come from a stock theft a couple of days north of here."

At the second camp, it was soon obvious that John was spent. He went straight to his swag after eating a meal.

"Something isn't right with him. We'll have to keep an eye on him. He hasn't been eating properly either," Bill commented quietly.

"We'll have a longer stop at midday." Ian was concerned.

Well before midday the next day, John fell from his horse. Ian saw the colour drain from his face. They undressed him, uncovering his injuries.

Ben had a look. "He's in no state to be moved."

Ian carried some medical things, but nothing was appropriate for John's injuries. Bill went to look for a herb called Arnica to treat the severe bruising.

John remained comatose all day. Not until the evening did he wake, digesting a small piece of fish before collapsing again.

Most of the next day, John slept fitfully. Each time he woke, they tried to get him to eat. He was refusing food.

*

Meanwhile in the other team, Fred's city Constables were sick as dogs the first day out. They called Fred every name they could. He ignored them – called them a bunch of sissies. They kept nothing down that first day and night, except mugs of tea.

Next morning they still looked a sorry lot.

"Charley, go put a line in the river," Fred barked.

"Go catch yer own fuckin' fish," came the reply.

There was no breakfast. Slowly the men realised they didn't have supplies.

Charley watched Fred enjoy the fish he had caught the night before. Quietly, Fred doused the fire, buried the dead coals, saddled his horse and rode out of camp.

Half an hour on, he heard the young Constables coming up behind. He increased his pace. Fred didn't stop for twelve hours. Finally he found a good camp site.

By the time the others arrived, the flames of a campfire were licking the twilight. Fred vanished, returning thirty minutes later with a dead kangaroo.

Sid pulled him up, "Why did you shoot it – we don't have any dogs?"

Alex enlightened his city friends, "There are no dogs, but we need a meal."

Charley swore, "I'm not eating that fuckin' thing."

"Don't be a fool, Charley. We're not in the city now with a stall around the corner," his mate reminded him.

Fred skinned and gutted the roo. A swarm of birds fought over the entrails, and Fred expertly dissected the various cuts and spread them on the grass.

"Fish isn't a good diet all the time. For a group this size, a good-sized roo is better. The leftovers can be carried your saddlebag." Fred turned to his city charges. "Are ye carrying salt ? Good for preserving in the bush."

While they cooked their own meat, Fred stripped off and dived into the waterhole. Alex soon joined him, kicking his long sinewy legs expertly to keep afloat, as he arched his arms, floating on his back. Neither of the others could swim.

After the meal, even Charley grudgingly admitted that the roo filled an empty spot.

Sid wanted to know which police were picked to stay in the settlements.

"Need to be able to sit all day in a saddle," Fred explained.

Given none of the city Constables were married, Fred suggested they might seek a regional to transfer. Silence fell over the men.

*

The next day, Fred led his city men across a couple of gullies, each with exposed clay glistening in the sunshine. These were so deep, they were forced to lead their mounts along the base of the gully for some distance before finding a route up the other side.

At the camp that night, Fred's city Constables were far more cooperative. They now understood their dependence. Fred had picked a spot close to a clump of Casuarina Pine Trees beside a flowing creek. As the evening progressed, a wind sprang up and an eerie whistle sounded though the pines. Not until early morning did it subside. The men could not saddle up fast enough.

Fred was now uneasy at the lack of contact from Bill's party. He began to make a plan for a camp where his men could look after themselves for a couple of days. Riding beside Alex, Fred confided in him, "You'll be in charge. I have to ride ahead to find the others".

Fred chose a site, shot another good-sized kangaroo, and slung it off his horse onto the dirt for Sid and Kevin to prepare. Faced with being on their own a couple of days, Alex, Sid and Charley wished they'd paid more attention.

Fred barked instructions, "You've water, meat, and fish in the river. Don't go out of sight of this camp. Alex, you're in charge."

"Fuckin' hell," Charley swore.

"Cut it out, Charley," Sid cut in.

*

Indeed Fred did turn up alone the next day to Ian's surprise.

"I almost missed you except for the blue smoke," Fred blurted on arrival.

"How far behind us are your companions?" Ian asked.

"I left camp early this morning, so half a day's ride."

"How are my colleagues?" Ben was full of curiosity.

Fred grinned, then laughed out loud. "Let's just say they can hardly wait to get home!"

"Will you camp the night?" Ian asked quietly.

"Sure."

Given John's condition, it was better to stay in camp, keep him warm and as comfortable as possible. Fred leaned back against his saddle on the dry grass and filled in his new mates.

Fred and Ben turned in, which left Bill and Ian to discuss John.

"When can we move him, do you think?" Ian asked.

"We'll have to wait and see how he is tomorrow."

"I think Fred enjoyed being nursemaid to the city boys. I couldn't have managed as well as he's done. A group of men is never easy."

"I agree, he's done a good job to get them here."

Chapter Sixteen

In the morning before sunrise, stirring the embers of the fire, Ian turned to Fred. "Bring your men up to this camp. We won't be moving until John's well enough."

"Are you sure?"

"They can camp in the hollow near the river, close enough to be in contact with each other."

"If we're quiet, no one will be aware that a large party are camped here," Bill added.

Fred considered this. "It's risky. If they get wind of us, they'll be out of that hut and away."

"No one can go out on to the plain too far. There's no water, they can only go up the river," Bill reminded him.

Ian continued. "We'll prepare a fire in the hollow for tonight, and food. This way you'll be able to slip in quietly and no one will be any the wiser."

Fred rode back to his camp arriving at midday. He briskly commanded all to pack up and get ready to move out.

"We have a six-hour ride ahead. Bring any food and keep the pace."

He warned the men en route about John.

Alex moaned about the trouble Charley was giving him, "I don't know why Charley is a policeman?"

Just after sunset, they arrived at the camp to find Ben beside the fire, keeping it burning and grilling the meat. They dug holes for their swags and saddles, more savvy now to a comfortable sleep. They yearned for the relative luxury of their city beds.

In the top camp, John, now awake, was coaxed to down a good meal.

*

Next morning, John felt a lot better, unaware of how close he had come to death on that first night. His mates were not going to allow a relapse. Ian and Bill went down to the other camp to make plans to catch the crooks.

"I left out a couple of fishing lines if John gets bored. It won't do him any harm to begin moving his limbs and feel he's helping," Bill murmured.

In the hollow, they found the city men beside the fire with quart-pots bubbling with tea leaves. Bill and Ian took a mug each.

"We can use that patch of sand to plan our operation," Ian nodded toward the bank.

"It's effing sand!" Kevin protested.

"Haven't you ever used a mud-map?" Bill countered.

Alex and Sid rolled a log over to the sand and sat on it. The others sat on the ground watching Bill as he took a stick to sketch the hut and its door, adding the cover of trees and bushes nearby. He'd been in the vicinity yesterday and made notes. Bill began to explain what he had seen.

As expected, Charley was skeptical, "You've got fuckin' good eyes, mate."

Ian handed a small brass tube to Charley.

"Look through it," Bill said.

Ben put it to his eye, removed it rapidly and shot them a glance, "What is it?"

"An Indian telescope – they've been around since the sixteen hundreds."

It was passed around the men. Bill continued, "We don't know where you got the idea that your crooks were shepherds. Yesterday they were lying around the hut on the grass."

Ian looked at the men, "I presume you fellows have the equipment for moving prisoners on foot?"

"We do. They'll give us no trouble," Sid answered.

Bill continued outlining the plan.

"Sid and Kevin, you'll move to the top side of the hut, get behind those bushes, and keep out of sight."

"Do we shoot if they come in our direction?"

"A bullet or two won't go astray, if you have no choice." Bill thought for a moment and added, "Shoot without question, of course."

Charley was grim. "We mightn't need to take the whole bloody lot back."

Neither Bill nor Ian commented. Their job was to bring in these men, make the arrests. Ben also remained quiet.

"We'll see how it goes once we announce our presence, but you may be right, Charley," Alex agreed.

"Charley, Alex and Fred, you approach from the river, get as close as you can to the door," Bill continued.

Charley wanted to know where Ben was going to be. Bill was clear. "Ben will be in the hollow with the horses. If they make a run for it, Ben will head them off, though he'll have no protection from bullets."

There was silence. Bill asked, "Any questions?"

"Once we begin, it's our deal, right?" Charley stated firmly. "We know what we're about, we've been dealing with crooks every day, we know how to treat them."

Bill felt a chill run down his spine. These guys were inhumane.

"And after we capture them?" Charley asked Ben.

Ian answered. "Charley, Ben has medical experience in his previous job. He'll come back with us to take care of John on the way to our barracks."

Charley added, "You fellows happy with Ben staying to help?"

There were nods of consent.

"I'll be escorting all of you back, but you're responsible for the prisoners," Fred commented.

"So once we get our prisoners, we journey back?" Sid queried.

"Providing you don't have to bury anyone," Fred corrected.

"Can't they do it?" Kevin pointed at Bill and Ian.

"Charley, this is your job … you bury them," Fred replied.

Sid and Alex told Charley exactly what they thought about him taking over.

At last, honour was satisfied and they moved to catch the crooks.

Chapter Seventeen

In the cabin, no one thought to keep a look out for police. They had seen no one in weeks. Last night, they had finished a flagon of firewater and were still drunk. One man staggered outside to relieve himself. He found himself staring at a copper. He stood in total shock, before shouting, "Bloody hell! Get up, you bastards, and defend the fuckin' place!"

By the time the crooks had stumbled outside, the hut was surrounded. The police dived as shots were fired. There was little cover available for those in the hut. Plenty of shots penetrated the wooden slabs.

A bullet grazed Charley's shoulder, as he let out a curse and fired a couple of shots into the hut. He grinned as a cry rang out.

"Go, get Ben to attend to it!" Fred yelled.

Fred and Alex crawled behind old logs, reaching a spot close to the hut door. Sid and Kevin retreated to a safe place near the side of the dwelling.

The Constables were still firing and the return shots were getting weaker.

"Come out! You're surrounded!" Ian shouted.

"Come and get us, you bastards!"

A barrage of shots peppered the hut. At last, a weak voice called out, "We're coming out!"

Two men emerged, supporting a wounded man, bleeding profusely, leaning heavily on a stick. Alex stood up, approaching the advancing men.

"Alex! Get down, it's a gun!" Sid yelled.

As the man raised the gun to fire, Alex dropped flat on the ground. Sid fired in fury. His target instantly dropped – a bullet to the chest. A second man grabbed for the gun. Kevin shot him. The last man quickly threw his hands above his head. The police moved forward, arresting him, checked for more weapons and searched the hut.

Sid, Kevin and Alex took turns digging the two graves. The jewelry was found, but only four of the gold nuggets were in the saddlebag.

By the time the cleaning up was complete, it was too late to leave camp. Bill wrapped up Charley's wound. "This will hold until you get to Hill Top."

Fred went over to talk to Ian.

"Are you okay to leave early tomorrow?"

"Yes, though it'll take a couple of days."

"The city men want to get away." Ian was tired.

Fred laughed.

"Charley is a tough man from a poor part of the city, where the weak didn't survive very long. I've found him to be a sturdy type, who I'd want to have beside me in bad times. In this case, he'll see the crooks get to the Magistrates court," he said.

"We'll see you sometime, so have a good trip back with your charges." Bill thanked Fred for his help.

Fred shook hands all round and had a few words with John, before returning to the hollow. The city police left before sunrise.

*

The bush police settled around their fire. John knew he wasn't well, but the desire to help was overwhelming. It had been an effort to prepare the line and sit quietly, almost willing a fish to take the bait. Of course, Ian had been vocal about it, but that was expected and endured with a smile. Ben adjusted the native weeds so they better covered his wounds.

"We leave tomorrow, Ian?" Bill asked.

"What do you think, Ben?"

"The sooner we get him back to Hill Top the better. A slower pace on the first day."

"You'll ride beside John," Ian instructed Ben. "He's a strong lad, otherwise he wouldn't have reached our camp."

"Yeah, he's as strong as us, but he's also concussed."

*

They were in their saddles and riding towards the distant hills early next morning.

With Ben's cooperation, they made very good time – twelve hours in the saddle before stopping to camp. As soon as he had eaten his meal and hot tea, John slept. The others sat around the fire talking. Ian and Bill liked Ben's company, which prompted a question from Bill.

"How would like to get a transfer to work on this side of the mountains?"

"I have thought about it," Ben grinned. "I've really enjoyed working with you. I'll think some more."

Ian continued, "If you do decide on it, write and we'll try to get you into our region."

"I will, Ian. Who knows what the future holds," Ben winked mischievously.

It took several days to reach Hill Top, by which time John was almost fully recovered. They arrived the same day that the other party had left with their prisoners.

"Sergeant Rich has left instructions for you to return the jewels and gold nuggets to their owners," Sergeant Green informed Ben.

Over near the barracks, Bill caught sight of Fred putting his mount in the horse yard and called out to him. Fred turned and looked over. After putting his bridle in the stables, he came across to where they were sitting.

"How did your city men get on?" Ian asked him.

"I suppose you had to ask." Fred smiled as if he had secret.

"Come on, Fred, spit it out. We can see you're dying to tell us!" Bill urged.

"Bill, you'd be excellent in ferreting out secrets."

"Fred, come on, what happened?"

"We thought it best to put them in civilian clothes, before letting them loose."

"So what happened?" Ian was interested.

"Charley met the Wickhams but had no idea of their place in the community. It was outside that tent of ill-repute. Charley thought Wickham was a client. Had one of the girls on his arm . It was his wife!"

There was a stunned silence, then wicked smiles. Bill filled Ben in. Fred continued, quite satisfied with his story.

Ian regained his composure. "What happened?"

Fred continued, "Our fellows went behind a tent to escape being seen. Charley told him his choice was poor given the bad light. Told him to put her back and he ought to be sober next time he chose."

He paused until their laughter stopped before continuing.

"Sid, Kevin and Alex knew something wasn't right – acted as if they were miners. Charley caught their drift and told Wickham he ought to be more careful how he spent his gold."

Another peal of laughter. Fred was enjoying the telling.

"They paraded around the tents that night spouting off about old street women being a trap for decent men out for a good time, to the delight of everyone who heard."

"How did they get back to the barracks without being seen?" Bill asked when he could draw breath.

"Snuck behind the tents and back through the horse paddock. Needless to say, the city police were not allowed out of the barracks. They left today well before sunrise, while everyone was still asleep."

But there is always someone awake. One man saw shadows of men on horseback riding out. He wondered what was going on.

"What's new in Hill Top?" Bill asked Fred.

"A new lot of young girls doing good business at the end tent. I'm told they're a lot better than the place you went to last time."

"How do you know about that?"

"Very few secrets in this place, Bill."

The three men went out drinking, well into the early hours of the morning. The morning after, each slept until midday, only getting out of bed because there were reports due. Then, after delivering their reports, another night of revelry – this time in the "tents". But they were back before midnight, given they had an early morning meeting with Sergeant Green.

Sergeant Green raised his head from scribbling in his work diary as the three men entered.

"Mr. Percy, am I likely to have a busybody coming to complain about any of you after two nights here?"

"Unlikely, Sergeant."

"So you were well behaved?"

He was delighted to see their surprise. Surely, they understood he had been young once. But they saw his rank and his grey hair, dismissing anything else.

He smiled inwardly, adding, "Mr. Percy and Mr. Todd, it isn't possible for either of you not to cause talk in this small community. Now you have taken Holt under your wing, it will probably send me grey."

They didn't like to say he was already grey. Bill's face lit up.

"Did you wish to say something, Mr. Todd?"

"No, Sergeant."

"I quite thought you were about to speak?"

"Not a word, Sergeant!"

He looked down at his desk for a moment, then up at his men.

"Now you've recovered those valuables, there's no reason to stay in town. The best course is to keep looking for Mr. Jones. Are you happy with this plan, Holt?"

"Yes, Sergeant."

"Good! You'll have an escort. Mr. Percy and Mr. Todd will return both the gold nuggets and the jewelry to their owners."

He shuffled some papers on his desk, finding one which had been out of sight.

"I've spelt the details out in clear language. Mrs. Allan Lake lives out on a plain north-west of here, so allow for several days riding. Albie Jones is thought to be on a goldfield east of where you are going now. You'll just have to find him."

"How long do we have?" Ian asked.

"There is nothing else at the present time, though that's not an excuse to take the job easy. I'd expect you to address any problem which crops up en route."

"We will, Sergeant. How is John Hale?"

"Doing well, I'm told. Ought to be back in the saddle any day."

"When will I be returning to the city, Sergeant?" Ben asked carefully.

"After the property has been returned, if you come across any city police, you may return with them."

"Thank you, Sergeant."

"Are you ready to leave?" Sergeant Green was impatient.

"We arranged all our equipment yesterday. We can leave this morning," Bill nodded.

"Mr. Percy, what is that round leather container hanging down near your saddle bag?"

"Sergeant, a metal frying pan, with some fishing lines and hooks in it."

"I see, not quite regulation, but on long trips a necessity, I'd think?"

"Yes, Sergeant. It's good equipment on a long patrol."

"Even you couldn't do any harm with it!"

There were smiles all around the room. They filed out after the older man wished them a safe patrol.

They went to the barracks to collect a few last items not yet packed. Soon the horses were saddled and they were riding out. Wickham's store was open, though there was no sign of any miners anywhere. No doubt they were keeping away until the disturbance had died down.

The news on the street was that Mrs. Wickham had much to say to her husband on their way home that night. The locals had been most amused for a few days.

*

They rode over the familiar country of hills and valleys and, at the end of the first day, reached a favourite waterhole in a tiny valley. There were always fish to be caught and, being a deep and long hole, a good place for a swim on a hot summer's afternoon.

To Ben, it was so good to be out in the wide-open spaces, away from the cramped Hill Top settlement and smell of cesspits. They all dreamed of finding a wife one day, but the call of the bush was too strong to be tied down just yet.

*

The next day took them to the top of a large hill overlooking a great valley. It appeared to be several miles to the next range. There was a splendid view of grasslands destined for some fortunate landowner one day. Ian never tired of gazing at the countryside, the brilliant colours of the sky at sunset or sunrise. Staring at the cloud formations, he would decipher wondrous shapes and designs. Ian remained fascinated by this ancient country.

The following morning, Ben was awake before the other men and soon had a fire going. Ben often thought this hour was the best. Soon they'd be in their saddles, ships crossing green seas of grass, except horses were much preferable to ships. Ben had lost interest in the sea after the heavy work of loading them.

The other men woke and Ben stopped his daydreaming.

Chapter Eighteen

As they rode across the plain, Ben asked, "What kind of place are we heading to?"

"Have you looked at the jewels you'll be returning?" Bill answered.

"They look to be really valuable stones – might only belong to a well-to-do lady," Ian suggested.

Bill was now curious.

"So this place might be a more substantial dwelling?" he asked.

"Probably – though many with land, cattle and sheep still live rough about here."

Bill queried Ian, "What do you know?"

"I asked Sergeant Green to explain Land Leases. You know – we heard about them on that job with those farmers."

"What did he say?"

"There are few surveyors in the colony. Only the nineteen Counties have been surveyed. Outside these, land can be leased from the Government on a yearly basis. Later, squatters may be able to buy their land. The holding we are headed to out on the plain is a big landholder. But with people all flooding to the goldfields, farm workers are in short supply."

"So who are working these farms?" Ben asked.

"The owners employ superintendents to manage. These guys usually live in bark huts, or slab dwellings – whatever's available."

Ben's education was being given a new depth.

"What about the trouble on the goldfields?" he asked.

"Do you mean when Wentworth brought in that Act making every man pay three pounds for a gold diggers' licence?" Bill asked.

"Yes, why did he do that when money is so tight anyway?"

"To keep men on the land. Landholders needed their sheep to be washed and shorn, the state needed the wool exported. That's apart from all the other farm work."

Ben had not yet finished asking questions.

"I read there was big trouble on the Turon River?" he continued.

"Eventually it all went quiet, saving a lot of bloodshed. Lucky we aren't involved in that kind of work. A nasty job," Bill shook his head.

"A weekly wage is only eight shillings. Where would a man get three pounds?" Ben persisted.

"It was a cruel Act," Bill said thoughtfully.

Ian's mind wandered as he mused.

"Sometimes those in power don't concern themselves with anyone but those who support them. Land ownership has always been sought after. Only once has an Englishmen lost the right to land – when the Normans invaded in 1066. The Saxons bought land when their Kings wanted money."

"Where does the Norman Invasion fit in with our story?" Ben was confused.

"Only that when there are enough surveyors here, it will be opened up. No one can keep land forever out of reach of those who desire it."

Bill stepped in, asking Ian, "Did your family come over with the Normans?"

"No. My great, great grandfather came to England in with William of Orange, when he was offered the English Crown through his wife Mary Stewart. I'm from old Viking stock," Ian laughed.

"Where did your parents come from, Bill?" Ben asked

"Dad told me from middle England. What about you, Ben?"

"Apparently the city of London."

"Well, we've more opportunities than in England. Freedom is more valuable than all the gold," Ian reflected.

They all agreed. As the day drew to a close, another campsite was chosen beside a waterhole on the open plain, the hills now behind them. In the west, the sun was now low on the horizon, as their fire burst into flame. Before it could go off, Bill cooked the remaining fish from the previous night.

The men could see horizon to horizon, a vast open land. Their job was to follow the river, where the trees towered higher than on the hills. Nor were the wild animals so plentiful as on the rich grasslands. There was a beauty here on the flat land – the colours were different, not as rich, but a soft glow in the twilight.

*

In the mid-morning, they noticed a drover approaching with a herd of cattle along the river. The stock were moving slowly, munching grass as they walked. The drover looked to be in his late thirties, with a long beard streaked with grey. Bill stopped, then rode up. They talked about stock and where he was taking the cattle.

Ben observed the whole group – a woman with two children probably about seven or eight years old – on a dray pulled by one horse.

The youngsters started asking Ben questions. Ben replied cheerfully, rewarded with a smile from the woman.

"Do you know the Lake property?" Ian asked the drover.

"Sure do, mate, just up the river a couple of miles. Nice place and good people. They let us camp. Not like some who wouldn't give a fellow the light of the day."

The woman added, "The missus gave honey to our children."

Saying a farewell, the men rode up the river following the drover's directions. Soon a belt of green trees became visible. Ian was amazed to see English trees, so foreign in this landscape.

"They're English, I've seen them in the city, and these ones are Pepper Trees and Cedars," Bill rode closer to inspect the imported specimens.

There was a wooden garden fence and gate painted white. Near the entrance was a hitching rail for horses. The men alighted and tied the reins to the rail, under a Pepper Tree whose wide branches offered the horses some shade. There was a water trough within reach of each horse.

Ben carried his saddlebag as they opened the gate and walked up towards the front steps. Their arrival had not gone unnoticed, and a man stepped down from the wooden verandah to meet them on the path.

"Are you Allan Lake?" Ian asked.

"Yes I am."

Ian introduced himself and his colleagues. "Is Mrs. Lake at home ?"

"That she is."

"May we speak with her, please?"

He called his wife out on to the verandah. The fellow was clearly curious as to why the police had ridden so far. A smart lady of middle years emerged from the doorway – simply attired in a good quality dress. Ben stepped forward, greeting her formally.

"Mrs. Lake, a while back you were robbed of a number of personal items at an Inn. We've located them and arrested the culprit."

Ben handed her a small parcel from his saddlebag, asking her to check the contents. She did so, her eyes sparkling, enormously pleased.

"If ever we can assist the frontier police, please don't hesitate to ask," she gushed.

As they turned to leave the garden, she stopped them, "Won't you stay a while, I've just made a damper with honey?"

Mr. Lake confirmed the invitation and Ben, without hesitation, replied, "Thank you, Mrs. Lake, we'd like that."

Conversation flowed, as Ben learnt to eat fresh damper with dripping wild honey, without soiling his uniform. Bill talked about the plain they were to cross. Mr. Lake could have talked for hours. Ian asked about the garden and the English trees.

"Mr. Percy, I had to have a bit of home in this new land. The summers are hot as you know, we do well on the river, but even so many plants struggle in this climate. The Pepper and Cedar Trees are natives and they are doing well," Mrs. Lake explained.

Ian indicated with a sticky finger the wooden buildings behind the brick house.

"Don't you have trouble with white ants?"

"The timber is Cypress pine and the ants don't like it."

"What an amazing country this is, Mrs. Lake."

"Yes, it's a hard life but hard work never hurt anyone. A good life can be created here. Our children love it too."

They stayed for a couple of hours and were made most welcome, given visitors were rare, because of the distance. The Lakes filled their saddlebags with food for the return journey.

"As you're planning to cross the plain tomorrow, ride downriver until you reach a big bend. About twelve miles," Mr. Lake explained.

"How will we know when we reach it?" Ian asked.

"It's a long bend of a couple of miles. Camp on the bend itself, it's the shortest way across. On the other side is another river."

With good wishes ringing in their ears, they rode back down the river. Such hospitality was rare on the frontier for police.

The men reached the area described at almost twilight, with just enough light to make a camp and create a good fire to cook the meat that Mrs. Lake had given them.

En route, they hadn't seen another human being. Bill hobbled the horses assisted by Ben, while Ian prepared the meal.

The camp was taking shape and as chores were completed, each man came to the fire. Light conversation flowed while watching their grub sizzling on the grill. Ian threw a piece of fish on the pan.

Bill piped up. "Ian, what's with the fish? We're having meat tonight."

"I just thought it would be needed."

Bill sat up straight, looking hard at Ian. "We're on our own."

"Perhaps not?"

"You're being mystical. I tell you we're on our own."

Ben could not make any sense out of Ian. Sometimes he worried about the effects of so much time in the bush on their own.

Bill nagged Ian about wasting food. Ian just smiled at him. There was a full moon. Shadows surrounded the campfire. Dinner had the odd piece of charcoal attached. Ian put a small piece of damper and honey aside.

"It will be eaten, Bill," Ian assured him.

Bill was becoming uneasy. He began to stare at shadows around the fire. His discomfort spread to Ben, who also stared.

"What's the matter?"

Suddenly the Old Man moved silently from the shadows. He sat down beside Ben at the fire. Ben stood up in shock.

"Nothing to worry about Ben, just sit down," Ian whispered.

Their indigenous visitor wore an animal skin around his nethers and nothing much else. He belonged to a caste of spirit men, custodians of the tribal knowledge of the spirit world. He scared the shadow people. Both judge and jury, the ultimate power – the Kadaitcha.

The man smelt of stale animal fat. Ben wasn't sure about being so close, but there was no where he could move to. The Old Man read his thoughts and tapped him on the arm, "Me come, me safe!"

Ben looked into the eyes of this extraordinary man. He felt a depth of centuries. Something changed. Instinctively he knew why Ian had set aside a meal.

Ian handed the Old Man the fish, damper, and honey. Given his advanced age, he had only a few teeth. When he had finished, he gazed into the fire. He spoke about a very long walk north to see to tribal problems. Now in his broken English, he told them about a waterhole which they would pass next day out on the plain.

"Ve bad place, don't drink, your horses won't go, avoid." He spoke of an old spirit sleeping in the black water. "No wake 'im."

He repeated himself until Ian mirrored the words back to him. The Old Man put a hand on to Ian's arm. There'd be no water on the plain. They would have to carry enough for their horses and themselves. Bill couldn't comprehend why they were unable to get water from the black pool. The Old Man grinned at him and then fell silent. Bill's face lost colour. Understanding came instantly.

Ian's mind heard the words, though nothing was vocalised. In his land, there were many spirits asleep in remote places. They were not to be woken.

"Better sleep, safe to sleep, leave alone."

As silently as he had come, he stood up, smiled and turned into the shadows – vanishing from sight. It was as if he had never been in the camp.

The men were quiet as they prepared for sleep.

In their swags close by, Bill whispered, "How did you know he was coming?"

"I didn't know, I just thought he might."

"So you cooked the fish because he has so few teeth?"

"Yes, and the damper and wild honey."

"Where was he going from here?"

"He said tribal judgements many moons from here."

"Ian, I think he travels over vast distances over tribal lands. The shadow people have enormous respect for men like him."

"I know, I have that kind of respect too. He is always welcome at our fire. I wonder what Ben made of him?"

"We'll ask in the morning."

Ian turned, "Don't worry, Bill, you're quite safe, he'd be miles away by now."

"It will take some time to forget that shadow coming to life beside our fire."

"Life is full of shadows. Nothing harms us, so sleep well."

Chapter Nineteen

Ben woke early and lay quietly thinking about the day and the visitor. Ian seemed almost part of the land – some deep connection. The land was a living being in tribal spirituality. The Old Man was the speaking part. Ben turned to watch the horses and slowly dozed off.

While the men dreamt, over a distant horizon, a streak of brilliant lightning was followed by a roll of thunder echoing across the landscape. It was chased by a furious wind, lifting up anything not rooted in the soil, dragging half dead plants from the ground, cannoning this hailstorm ahead of it. Then came plump splotches of rain, drops as heavy as bullets on the parched soil.

At last, the rain eased. The plants – their faded leaves clinging to life – soaking up as much moisture as they could bear, grasping for this nectar of life.

After the storm, a shard of sparkling light pierced the plain. The greenery had shed its dusty coat. The precious liquid soaked a grateful land.

Before sun-up, the men drank their mugs of tea in silence, pondering the visitor of the night before. The bush produced strange events. The Old Man.

At last, Ian stood up. "We need to get moving. We have a long trip today."

They travelled east into the rising ball of light. The plain gave the appearance of being flat, but there were low rises and falls, evidenced by the direction of the run-off. Small marsupials burrowed just under the soil – protected from the extreme summer heat.

Ben noticed lizards and snakes. Care was required to avoid their mounts breaking a leg in an unseen wombat hole. The mares had a better eye for these than their riders. There was no spare horse in case of a mishap.

"No sign yet of the forbidden waterhole. It does make me wonder why such a spring can't be used," Bill mused.

Ian spoke, "Haven't you heard of prehistoric animals, much bigger than men?"

"Yes I've read about them, but what does that have to do with…?"

"I was just wondering if there were some here."

"You mean it could be part of the Old Man's ancestral memory?"

"Possibly, and easier to accept than a mythical spirit deep in the waterhole."

As the day progressed, the heat was oppressive. No trees. The horses plodded along at a slower rate.

"Look at the ground. Rain must have fallen," Ben declared.

"I can see two clumps of trees," he added an hour later.

They rode closer and Ian, out in front, suddenly indicated his horse, "Look his ears are up."

Each mare stopped in her tracks. The riders wheeled them around in the other direction towards a clump of stunted trees. Here, Ian dismounted and tied his reins to a low tree. The mares whinnied uncomfortably. The other riders followed his lead.

Moving now on foot, they approached the second clump of trees that had so spooked their mares. The gums marked the edge of a long waterhole. Strangely, there was no bird life, just an uncanny silence. There were no animal tracks on the bare ground around the pool. The water was black and in total shade, the stunted trees preventing the light from reaching the pool's surface.

"I don't like this place. I get the feeling something from a long way down is looking up at me," Ben glanced down at the stagnant pool.

Bill laughed, "Next you'll be telling us something is speaking to you."

"I'm with Ben, " Ian murmured. "There is something weird – nothing, not even flies or mosquitoes. Can you smell the water?"

"Whatever is here is telling us to leave," Ben added.

Each felt a cold shiver down their spines as they turned to walk away. The walk back to their horses was in silence. Then Ian spoke.

"What do you say we ride as far as we can before twilight?"

This was agreed upon without discussion.

Towards the end of the day, blue hills came into sight in the distance.

"Ian, how much longer can we ride?"

"Bill, can we increase our pace?'

Bill turned to Ben, "Are you happy to up the pace, the ground looks okay?"

"I'll follow you. Just remember we need to water our horses at the end."

They picked up their pace for the next hour. The hills were still on the horizon, the sun lower in the western sky.

"We need to find a camp site soon," Ben grumbled.

"Ben, we need to ride on."

Ben had no intention of giving in. "We can manage, but our horses can't. Ian, can you put water in the fish pan for the horses?"

"There're no problems," Ian answered. He paused. "So that's why you want to make camp before dark?"

"It's easier to see to the horses. We can manage better if there is a moon up."

Night riding required a certain skill – not just to ensure they did not lose their bearings. As advised, this was the shortest route across the plain. When the squatter had illustrated the trip on paper, it didn't look far. But their mounts could only walk so far without water. There was likely none until the other side of the plain.

Towards the late afternoon, they crossed the wide gully of a dried watercourse. On the top side, the rise was like a tiny hill, providing evidence of trees a long way ahead.

"Ian, do you think we ought to reach those trees?" Bill suggested.

"Look to be the only ones offering shelter," Ian agreed. "Maybe water too."

The ground was not as level as it looked. Each rider had to focus intently to ensure no horse lost their footing. At a fast canter, the trees were reached in the late afternoon. Ian had been correct. There was a waterhole, almost certainly dry a week ago, now carried about a foot of water – plenty enough for the horses and some left over for the men.

"The land provides," Ben commented.

"Not always, Ben. We're fortunate we are here after a storm," Bill added with a laugh.

"At least we can enjoy more than one mug of tea."

"I wouldn't be too sure. We have to conserve water until we find the river," Ian reminded him.

Ben frowned, "There's a lot to be said for living close to water in those settlements."

Bill let the horses drink. "Ben, people in the settlements – they aren't as safe as you might think. There are long droughts some years. Water will always be precious."

While they were talking, Ben had gathered dead wood from under the trees for the fire. Bill had put the saddles and equipment for each horse nearby, in case they needed to leave before sunrise. Each man had learnt that a before-sunrise exit without knowing where things were meant chaos.

Ben threw the last lot of Mrs. Lake's meat on the grill. It would not have lasted another day.

"What do you think about leaving early?" Ian grunted.

"How early?" Bill asked.

"It'll be another hot day. We have to get off this plain. As soon as it's light enough to see what we are doing in camp."

"Whoever wakes up first makes the fire," Ben suggested.

This was agreed upon and the men settled down to enjoy their meal and the last of damper with honey before an early night.

*

Just after dawn, Ian left his swag, checked on where the horses were, and quietly made up the fire, wedging the three quart-pots in stable spots to prevent a spill.

Bill was the next to wake. He took a bridle to each horse, removed the hobbles, then tied the reins to the trees, before saddling his horse. Ben was the last man out of his swag.

They rode out in the dawn light and headed east, following the directions they had been given. Ian hoped he had interpreted them correctly. He gave a silent prayer.

Ian was enormously relieved in the mid-afternoon to see hills rising up in the distance. Soon tall gum trees became visible beside the river. The end of the plain. It was twilight before they reached the riverbank, though finding a place to cross took a while in the fading light.

In the gathering darkness, there was no choice but to hobble the horses and get a fire going to make tea. They gobbled leftover meat and rations – not appetising, but it filled an empty space.

"What do you think about fishing in the morning, an equipment clean-up, then a rest day?" Ian suggested.

"Good idea. Once we get amongst the gold fields, we'll be busy. No miners' camp will be quiet," Bill added.

"But it'll make the job longer?" Ben queried.

Ian looked at Ben. "Yes – delete a day from what may well be a long patrol. But we need to supplement our food supplies, wash our clothes. Out on patrol, we don't get many chances, as you know."

"I suppose I'm feeling as if the sea is calling me."

"We all get a little restless when we're away for a long time."

*

Each man enjoyed a late breakfast next day. Bill had gone to the river early and caught a fish in the silence of the morning. It was a time to think. He watched a water rat swim the length of the waterhole. As Bill gutted the fish and prepared it for the fire, Ian joined him and they talked quietly.

After checking their equipment, the three men made off downriver searching for flying foxes or birds to shoot. Ben warned them, "Don't think you can send me into the water like a dog."

Bill laughed and patted him on the shoulder.

"Forget it, Bill. I'm not going into the water. If I fall, guess who's coming with me?"

Both men laughed. Ian yelled, "Cut it out you two! You'll frighten the birds and we won't bag anything."

Ian managed to shoot a couple of ducks and found some clay on his way back to the camp to bake them in.

After the first mug of tea next morning, they were on their horses riding up the first of the hills. Bill noted the direction which Ian was leading them.

"Which mining camp are we going to?"

"Where we met Cedric and Nancy Hall on that creek."

Ben was confused. "Which one?"

"A small camp, we inspected in early summer," Bill enlightened him.

"We may have to check several camps before we track down that Albie Jones. We'll talking to miners as we go," Ian spelled out the plan.

Ben didn't look all that happy. "Finding him could take weeks!"

"Sergeant Green will not be happy if it takes too long. So you needn't worry, Ben. I'd be surprised if it takes more than a few days," Bill replied.

"How far do you think that mining camp is?" Bill wondered aloud.

"I'm unsure, except the country here is nothing like where the men are gold-panning." Ian seemed to think for a few minutes. "Perhaps tomorrow."

Ben was impatient. "If we had faster horses, we'd be there by now."

"That goes without saying. We can't push the horses unless it's an emergency. There are no replacement horses out here."

"So we just plod along at three miles an hour," Ben sighed.

"We do okay. They can go all day, carrying our weight and equipment," Ian spoke up for the police mounts.

Ben lapsed into silence. His mind wandered back into the city. What were his colleagues doing?

Riding was slower given the many small gullies to be crossed. Some were so deep, they needed to detour miles out of their way to find a place the horses could cross. There were constant changes in the landscape. Stunted trees gave way gradually to taller ones. The long grassy slopes suggested a wetter climate. What Ian loved most were the magnificent old man gum trees with their ancient, gnarled trunks.

In the steep sides of the gullies, the colours changed, the rich topsoil replaced by clay. As they traversed the virgin pastures, they imagined cattle and sheep grazing.

They camped in a small valley beside a dry creek, except for a few stagnant pools. The water had to be boiled before drinking. Entering the hill country, conversation moved to the Old Man.

"I wonder where he is?" Bill mused.

"His mind can travel beyond his feet," Ian winked. "I'm sure we will see him again, one night he'll walk in and sit at our fire."

Ben didn't look happy. "You have spooky friends. I hope I don't see him again."

Both Ian and Bill laughed.

It was mid-afternoon next day, on top of a tall hill, when Bill declared, "I know where we are. We're near that camp site where you shot the ducks and that miner complained."

Ben asked, "Near a miners' camp?"

"We're a couple of short valleys away. There ought to be a good camp site near here," Ian explained.

Bill turned his horse to walk down the side of the hill. It was a slow ride down and across a few small gullies now quite dry with hard clay and stones on the track. The water was only just flowing over small pebbles at the crossing. Nearby, they found a reasonable-sized waterhole where they made camp.

*

In the morning they continued along the creek until they reached the miners panning for gold.

"What, three of you and no noise?" one of the miners called out.

Bill smiled. "At your request if you remember?"

"I thought I'd seen the last of you."

Bill laughed, "Nice dream!"

They watched the men sifting through piles of gravel searching for that precious metal. In this area, most creeks had gold in the gravel but it was hard work to extract it.

Right at the end of the workings, Bill saw Cedric at work. As they approached, he looked up.

"Look, our friendly police are back," he nudged his wife Nancy.

Cedric stood up to greet the arrivals. Ben was introduced and the twins, Alice and Alfred, came from the tent to greet them.

"Today is a holiday from school," Nancy explained.

"You have a school here?" Ben was skeptical.

"Not like in other camps. We write and do sums in the sand."

Ben looked surprised. "How do you use it?"

"Each of us has a patch of sand in a square with sticks around it and water. If the sand is wet, the words show up. It's really easy. I'm a trained teacher."

"We had slates and chalk when I was at school. We would've loved teaching out under a tree," Ben smiled.

"You'd never do any work!" she said and laughed.

"You're right, the distractions would be strong," Ben admitted.

"They do stop and watch when men start fights – pretty frequent," Nancy admitted.

"What causes the most fights?"

"Gold."

"How close are you to moving on?" Ian changed the subject.

"Fairly close, the yield is getting smaller – hardly worth the effort to pan it."

"When are you thinking?"

"Within the month most of us will be leaving," Cedric admitted. "What are you doing here? On patrol?"

"Looking for a gold buyer – Albie Jones."

"We've not seen him for a long time. Ain't heard his name spoken lately."

"Not a good sign for us. You have any suggestions?"

"The amount we're extracting wouldn't be worth his effort right now. I'd try a bigger camp further east."

While their parents were talking, Alfred and his twin sister were at a lower waterhole with lines trying to attract a fish or two. Alfred's line suddenly went taut.

"Got something on it," he called out.

"Mr. Todd, come and see what Alfred has caught," Alice yelled. "Probably a stick!"

"It's not a log, it's a big fish!" Alfred was obviously nettled.

This caused a squabble much to the amusement of their parents. Alfred slowly pulled on his line with Bill's assistance. He had indeed caught a fish.

"Not very big," said Alice dismissively.

"Is too! What've you got?" asked Alfred.

Bill eyed both children. He realised they expected him to voice an opinion.

"Alfred and Alice, I think it's big enough for you two. Your mum and dad can catch their own," Bill smiled, in case his words were taken the wrong way.

The children were satisfied. Bill was relieved to mount his horse and follow Ian and Ben out of the camp.

Chapter Twenty

Next day they rode to another small dying community. Ian approached a man and woman packing up their tent and possessions into a small two-wheeled handcart.

"Leaving?" he asked.

The man stopped rolled up his tent. "Yes".

"You know of a gold buyer, Albie Jones?" Ian continued.

"Never had enough gold to sell to no one."

He didn't look well. Ian smelt a small-time thief.

"Has the gold run out?" Bill asked a miner further down the track.

"Yeah, we're all moving on."

Within a short period no sign of this tent community would exist. As they rode on, there was a cavalcade of miners and their women carrying swags, pulling handcarts, all on the move to the next gold field.

They soon became aware the miners were attempting to keep them within sight.

"Why such a hurry?" Ian asked a man puffing with the weight of his swag.

Gasping for breath, he took a minute before speaking.

"There are thieves about here – while you're with us we're safe."

Ian watched the straggling crowd, recognising their fear. He felt sorry for them in their lust for gold.

Another miner came up to ask, "What are all you police doing here?"

"The same as you."

The miner talked for a few minutes before moving on, scrutinising each side of the track.

In the evening camp, Bill and Ian shared confidences.

"The others can deal with any night visitors, if they're silly enough to make trouble," Bill sighed.

"We can relax. No need to be on edge."

Bill shifted his saddle and saddlecloth a little to one side.

"What did that miner tell you today?" Bill asked.

"So you noticed that?"

"You were quiet for a long time afterward."

"And if I said it was nothing…" Ian replied.

"I know you better than that."

"Bill, you don't miss much do you."

"We've been together long enough."

Ian was secretly pleased that Bill was so observant. Now he spoke in a low voice.

"The miners noticed there were more of us than usual – gathering for some unknown activity…"

"What did you say?"

"I smiled and changed the subject."

"When you do that, it's very irritating."

"He was reluctant to talk of anything else."

In the trees and low shrubs, the night was alive with sounds. There was the usual chatter of insects and birds, and the clink of the hobbled horses moving towards water or better grass.

"Do you think we ought to investigate this?" Bill asked.

"I think so. We have Ben to consider."

"That reminds me. I'd like to ask him if he is related to Gary and Bessie Holt?"

This caused Ian to sit up and look at his friend in total surprise. "Whatever made you ask that? I can't see how, considering Gary and Bessie being educated, and Ben's parents with a fruit and vegetable barrow."

"Which has developed into a shop."

"All the same, there is a wide social gap."

"The gulf isn't all that big today."

"'Tis in the social world, we're still close to convicts."

"I'd still like to know, Ian."

"Okay, you ask him in the morning. I'll ride ahead. I want to talk to anyone coming from where the police are meant to be."

"If they're from the city, Ben can join them. Is that what you are thinking?" Bill added.

"Yes, he'd like to go home."

*

The well-worn track crossed a hill, and from the crest, Ian recognised Dick and Tom Hunt. They had camped in an open area to deter any marauding thieves. As Ian, Bill and Ben approached, they saw the Hunt brothers with several other men guarding the drays. They alighted and walked forward to greet them, all grinning with pleasure. Tom introduced them.

"Why don't you join us tonight?" Dick suggested.

"We'd be happy to camp here," Bill agreed.

The guards were nervous having the police so near, but made an effort, talking to Ben given he was also from the city.

Ian was delighted to hear news of Bob Pringle and their sister.

"Their tent is now twice the size it was. Everyone goes there for the midday meal," Dick told them.

Neither Ian nor Bill believed anyone could hear their conversations. Circumstances were about to change. Quite suddenly, the shadows shifted, a disturbance of the air. Ian and Bill sat up in surprise. Tom and Dick sat down close beside them.

"What's this about the police presence?" Tom piped up.

"How much did you hear, Tom?" Bill asked.

Dick laughed quietly, "All of it."

"We've picked up talk about the police gathering for the last week. We knew about the thieves in this district – accounts for our added protection," Tom said quietly.

"Maybe the police have located the culprits' hide-out and are preparing?" Ian asked.

"What direction are you travelling?"

"South, with one stop, and then home."

"We want to be out just after dawn – the moon should still be up. We prefer it then – safer," said Dick.

*

At dawn, the Hunt brothers left while the others mumbled a sleepy goodbye. Later, as they sipped their tea, Ben could hardly wait for the silence to end.

"What were you all talking about?" Ben asked.

"Tom and Dick knew some details… and came to tell us." Bill looked at Ian.

"Ben, you heard a good deal of the talk?" Ian turned to ask.

"In bits and pieces about the police ahead of us."

"The buildup of police ahead… Tom and Dick were adding information – we weren't keeping it from you," Ian said.

That morning, daylight took some time to penetrate the low valleys where men were panning for gold. As planned, Ian rode ahead to question fellow travellers.

Bill asked, "Ben, any family connections this side of the mountains?"

Ben looked surprised. "What an odd question."

"Ian and I came across a family who had the same surname. Wondered if you were connected?"

"Who?"

"Gary and Bessie Holt, in their twenties. Squatters out on the black soil plain."

"My great grandfather had two sons. One – my grandfather – rebelled and left the run-down estate. Went his own way, found other ways to make a living, fell foul of the law, gaol, transported. The other brother stayed, built up the estate. Eventually sold it. What happened after that I don't know."

"So they could be family?"

"Depending who their grandfather was."

"Next time, we'll make an effort to go see them. Who was your great grandfather?"

"Charles Holt. His sons were John in my line, and Richard in the other line."

"Be interesting to find out. We can tell them your father owns a fruit and vegetable shop. Sure you don't mind?"

"No. This is a land of opportunities. Where you came from ain't important here."

Over the next hill, the mining camp came into view beside a creek, as usual.

Ian murmured quietly, so as not to be heard by others on the track.

"We'll talk later after Ben returns Albie Jones' gold nuggets."

They rode down the muddy track between tents and humpies of wood and bark, pulling up outside a tent. A line of men were waiting to do business with. Ben and Ian walked in to see four well-armed strong men either side of an older man with a bushy beard. He was sitting at a log table beside a pair of gold scales.

"What's this all about?" he stood up as the police entered the tent.

Ben carried his saddle bag, walked up, and introduced himself and Ian. "Mr. Jones you reported the robbery of some gold nuggets some months ago. We have been able to recover some of your stolen goods."

Ben tipped his saddlebag and gold nuggets rolled out on the table, to the surprise of Jones and assorted onlookers.

Jones grinned. "Mr. Holt, thank you. I didn't expect to see it again."

Ian and Ben then joined Bill outside. All three mounted and rode out along the creek, ascending a long hill. Travelling east at a comfortable pace, they stopped to talk to a couple of travellers. It seemed there had been several hold-ups of miners who had been robbed of their gold, food, swags, and anything of value. The scoundrels had even robbed children of their toys.

Ian stopped a couple of men. "Going far?"

"Away from being held up by crooks."

"When did this happen?"

"Yesterday, we were held up. Stripped of food and money."

"What will you do?"

"Live off the land until we find more gold."

"Try the goldfield back behind us – it was doing well."

Bill and Ben caught up with Ian. They soon came across a family picking up their goods which bandits had thrown from their old hand cart across the track.

"What happened?" Bill asked.

"We were held up and robbed. Our companions saw the robbers coming and ran away," the woman clarified.

One of the little girls was crying. Her mother went on. "Pixie's cat scratched one of them. They killed it in front of her."

"Can you describe these men?" Ian asked.

"They could be watching. We'd get hurt again," the man hesitated.

"Have you still got that bangle you found?" Ian asked Ben quietly.

"In my saddlebag."

Ben searched for it, looked at Ian, and the penny dropped. Finding it he alighted from his horse and went up to the little girl. "I wondered if you'd like it?"

The silver bangle had a blue glass stone mounted in it.

"Don't cry, little one. Your dad will get you another cat and, in the meantime, you'll have this."

The little girl stopped crying, took the bangle in her rather grubby hand, and smiled. Her mother was equally surprised. "Thank you. She will treasure it."

Ben smiled. After a few words, the police urged their horses on down the track, dusty from the hundreds of feet tramping it all day long.

An array of steep hills rose from the low country with many small rises and sloping grassy hillocks. Blue mountains loomed in the distance, but up close these rises seemed isolated, as if a mother had scattered her offspring over a landscape. The wind and rain had moulded them, wearing away soft stone, enclosing short valleys which could not survive the more arid regions.

*

A group of thieves had inhabited one of these small valleys for more than a year. It had taken a considerable time to gather enough Special Constables to tackle the issue. Now they waited quietly, concealed on one side of the lonely mountain.

Further away, the bush police and their city friends gathered to plan. The repeated holdups were bringing attention to places which many gold diggers would much rather the police avoided. Many preferred to deal with such matters on their own.

The problem was when thieves stole the colony's gold, the troopers could not look away.

The track felt cramped, the hills looming over it. Dotted around the valley were slab huts and tents near waterholes. There were drays, hand carts, coaches, and the odd carriage. The further east they rode, more men were on the move.

About mid-afternoon, a man stood up from beside a log near the track as if to greet them. As they came abreast, he asked, "Are you Mr. Percy?"

Ian nodded and the stranger continued, "At the creek, travel north until you meet with more police."

"Who are you?" Bill asked.

"I'm under the direction of Sergeant Rich."

Ben noticed a horse tied to a tree nearby. "You're one of us."

"That's so. We expected we'd see you sometime today."

"Are you coming with us?" Ian asked.

"I have to meet more Special Constables. Then I'll join the other police coming from the city."

"How did you know where to meet us?" Bill asked.

"We heard Ben needed to meet up with the city police at the gold-buyer's tent."

Ian shook his head. "In other words as the crow flies in the bush!"

"Something like that."

Following instructions, they rode on.

Chapter Twenty One

In the distance, a range of blue hills loomed around a small mountain, towering up from a small creek. A flock of galahs were busy eating seeds on the flat but, with the sound of the horses' hooves, rose into the air with a collective "Rark!". On the flat were a couple of tents and a horse yard fashioned from sticks and a rope. A familiar figure walked over to greet them.

"That's Fred Hall," Bill said cheerfully.

"And John Hale too!" Ben added.

Friends greeted each other and news exchanged.

"Who is in charge of the police here?" Ian asked when he could get a word in.

"We're not sure. We were only told to come yesterday."

"Seems this is a well-planned operation," Fred explained.

"It might be well-planned, but the whole district knows," Ian pointed out.

"Do they now?" Fred looked surprised.

"We picked up the news two days ago," John clarified.

"Fred, there are very few secrets in the bush."

A group of riders was coming up through the trees.

"Is that the rest of our group?" Ben nodded.

"You ought to recognise your city colleagues," Fred smiled. "I see Charley!"

"Also Sid, Kevin and Alex with Sergeant Rich. We'll be in for a good time." Bill smiled.

The new arrivals rode up. Charley looked down from his horse, "What 'ave we done to deserve this lot, Mr. Rich?"

"I don't know, Charley, but I was thinking all my sins will be cleared up working with you!" Fred answered.

There was laughter from both groups. Soon quart-pots were on the fire and tea waiting to be dropped into the boiling water.

Ian reminded Ben he would be leaving with the city men when the job was done. As he rolled out his swag, Ben thought of asking his father about what had happened to the other part of the family.

He was daydreaming about a visit to Gary Holt, when Sergeant Rich interrupted. "Right, you lot of ruffians, I'll tell you about this job."

They sat on the logs and grass. The Sergeant sat down facing the men. He asked Kevin to enlighten the bush police.

"The leader of this pack of dogs is a tubby man – bushy beard, eyes as cold as winter. Moves in social circles as a respectable man. Has a finger in every illegal pie. May have police protection. We want him out of our lives."

The men smiled grimly.

"Ben, now you'll be comin' back to real police work," Charley reminded him.

"Charley, you wouldn't last a day out in the bush without a nanny to take care of you!"

"As long as she was pretty," Charley laughed.

"Cut it out, you two." Sergeant Rich was irritated.

"You bush police may not be aware these thieves have a network of supporters. In the city, the leader can't be touched, out here is another matter," Sergeant Rich continued.

Kevin turned to Bill, "This man controls a network. We think crooked police may be protecting him."

"Is this why we are involved?" Bill was thinking out loud.

The Sergeant sighed. "You won't shoot us in the back. Sergeant Green told me about your experience. You know the signs."

"Who else is to join us?" Ian asked.

"Four Special Constables – brothers whose father owns land bordering the valley. These men have worked in this valley all their lives. They too also suffered."

"Do we know how?" Ian asked.

"They've lost cattle. Their huts were raided when they were out mustering stock."

"What's the plan, Sergeant?" Kevin asked.

"Early tomorrow morning the four brothers will arrive. We will pack up camp, ride to a new camp according to their directions." He looked at Ian, "Do you have everything you need?"

"Yes, Bill and I always travel light."

Charley interrupted, "Alright, we don't travel light because we don't have to do it."

"Stop it, Charley, Ian was just explaining our usual conditions," Bill chipped in.

Charley hadn't finished, "You fellows always act as if you were superior to us."

Fred laughed, "Come on Charley. We have more experience in our district."

"See Fred just said it. How would you like to be in our fuckin' streets?" Charley countered.

Bill tried to temper things, "Charley, you are better in your streets, and we are better out here."

There would always be friction about who were the real police, city or bush.

Charley wanted clarification. "So these four brothers have suffered. Do we know why, apart from the stolen stock?"

"No," Fred added, "Cheer up, Charley."

"Anyone like to join me in fishing?" Bill asked.

Ian found spare lines in his pan bag for Sid and Kevin. Charley and Alex had unloaded their packhorses. Charley, designated camp cook, put a camp oven filled with stew on the campfire.

"What do you know about these brothers?" Alex asked Fred.

"Only what Sergeant Green said. They were the best men for the job."

"Can you give me one good reason why we should trust them?" Alex was not about to give up.

"As young boys they played in this valley. They know it like home, until they were hunted out," John answered.

Until he could meet them and make his own decision, Alex was satisfied. It was near sundown when Bill, Sid and Kevin returned to with four large fish. Alex was fascinated when Ian removed a pan from a leather flat case tied to his saddle. Ian was careful not to offend Charley letting him put the pan on the fire.

Ben laid his swag near Fred and John. The others arranged their swags on the other side of the fire. With so much to think about, sleep was not easy.

*

Next morning, Ian turned to Kevin, "Did Bill talk with you last night?"

"We aren't happy."

"No, but we have to be prepared for a betrayal."

"Kevin, we'll give you whatever support you ask."

"Thanks."

Charley called out, "Come and get it."

Breakfast was quart-pots of steaming tea with fish pieces and damper.

John's expression changed. Bill interrupted, "What are you thinking, John?"

"When are the brothers due?"

Sergeant Rich jumped in. "Coming through the trees now. See?"

Four solidly-built men and a packhorse came into sight. They rode up to the edge of the camp. Each group of men looked at each other, silently. The one who looked to be the eldest introduced himself as Andrew. "These are my brothers Shaun, Patrick and Toby."

For a brief moment, Ian thought about the conversation with Bill last night about some city Constables taking bribes.

"Do they have anyone in mind, Bill?"

"A Sergeant Shaw."

"We'll have to be very careful in that valley. Anything else?"

"Wanted you, Fred and John to know."

"The other city men are suspects."

"Ian, I don't like it at all."

"How much does Charley know?"

"It was Charley who discovered bribes being paid. The guy plays his cards close to his chest. Plays games to make people think he's stupid."

Ian laughed quietly, "He's a master at that game! I've never underestimated him."

The rattle of the bridles brought Ian him back to the present. He and his mates would be need to completely trust these farm men. But they had been recommended by Sergeant Green. He trusted Green.

Sergeant Rich was introducing his men. Each offered a firm handshake. Everyone sized up their counterpart. They would need to work as a team.

Toby walked across to Charley. "How are your meat supplies?"

Packing up his camp oven, Charley looked up.

"You're Toby, aren't you?"

"Yes, and you're Charley?"

They summed each other up. "Not good. We're a larger group than I'd prepared for."

Toby assured him, "We've enough meat for tonight and next morning if we're careful."

"We'll need it."

Each was careful not to offend the other's cooking skills. Within the hour, the camp was cleared – the large group riding northwest. Miners and other onlookers watched from the mountain.

Chapter Twenty Two

In a slab hut with several attached rooms, a middle-aged man, Sam Hade, and his wife, Elizabeth, sat at a wooden table drinking tea. There was a knock on the door. "Come in."

An old shepherd came to the doorway. "Them police 'ave gone."

"Thanks."

The old man left. All their younger shepherds had made for the goldfields, but the old man was happy to remain in his well-stocked hut.

Elizabeth was still a fine-looking woman, though years of hard work had added lines to her face. Sam had once been a strong man, but both remained handsome. They worried for their sons and the danger facing them in the valley.

Elizabeth spoke up, "Norm said Mr. Percy and Mr. Todd will look after them, but I still worry Sam."

"Lizzie, you always worry. You know very well our boys are more likely to look after those two policemen, than the other way around!"

She reluctantly agreed with him.

*

Andrew Hade, the eldest of the four brothers, rode up beside Sergeant Rich.

"Mr. Rich, we know this valley very well, we spent countless hours playing in it as children. We've been talking about your problem. We were chosen to assist because of our knowledge. We've worked out the best way to approach the valley."

"What do you have in mind?"

"A camp amongst those trees to cook meat for tonight, because it will not be possible to cook after tonight, boil a quart-pot, yes, but meat, no."

"Why, Mr. Hade?"

"The smell. If the wind's blowing in the wrong direction…"

"I didn't think about that."

"We did these things as children."

Sergeant Rich was becoming quite curious. "When did you stop going into the valley?"

"When the crooks made it dangerous. They caught Shaun and Patrick – almost killed them. Mum and Dad between them removed bullets from their legs and other places."

Sergeant Rich was visibly shocked. "Did no one come to their aid?"

"Mr. Rich, this is the frontier. We have to look after ourselves."

"There is the law."

"The law is a long way away, as is a doctor."

"Mr. Hade, what are you and your brothers planning?"

"If you're agreeable, with victuals for each man, I'll lead a group of eight men at speed to the back of the mountain," Shaun suggested.

"And the packhorses?"

"Will come later with my two other brothers."

"What do you want me to do?"

"Mr. Rich, you are in charge. I can only suggest."

Sergeant Rich smiled. "I'm happy to be guided. Once in the valley, it will be a combined effort if we're to succeed."

Andrew dropped back to talk to his brother Shaun. Up ahead, the Sergeant called a halt and explained the plan. With a waterhole beside them and lots of wood, a fire was soon burning and meat sizzling on hot coals. There was enough food for a light meal now. When everything was packed up again, Sergeant Rich interrupted, "Gather round. I'm appointing Andrew Hade in charge, so listen."

Andrew sat on his horse and spoke slowly and with respect about the importance of reaching the valley quickly, but not in one group. He would lead the first group. No one must suspect the police were headed to the valley. His brother Shaun would take the second group at a slower pace.

Charley asked, "What about the packhorses?"

"Toby knows the way."

"We can't ride fast."

"Alex, John and Patrick will be there in case there's a problem. Charley, you will need to be in the valley by late afternoon."

"Toby has cooked a lot of meat, what's it for?" Charley asked.

"Depending upon the direction of the wind, you'll be able to cook a stew."

"Why's the bloody wind got to have a say in what I cook?"

"Carries the smell a long way into the valley. We don't want anyone to know we're at the top of the waterfall."

Charley muttered, "Fuckin' stupid mountain."

Everyone began riding towards the blue hill on the horizon. The large group increased its pace and spread out.

The gallop to the foot of the mountain didn't take as long as Ian had thought, given there were no gullies and it was flat grasslands.

"Follow me in line," Andrew said quietly.

He led them up a track between tall trees up into the mountain. Without Andrew, they would never have made out the track. It wound higher and higher, steadily upwards to a flat area, with a ridge of trees to the south and the sound of a waterfall.

"This place we know well. Through the trees is a track down into the valley. Don't go near the trees. You may be seen from the valley floor. This part of the mountain is the source of the creek. It's spring is just behind us. Cool water – one of our favourite places. The horses can be hobbled – they'll be quite safe," Andrew said quietly.

Ian, Kevin and Bill gazed through the trees to a valley spread out before them. Keeping well out of sight, they could see the fall of the water. Behind them, the fresh water spring made the large rocks around it glisten darkly.

"Who will stay with the horses?" Kevin asked.

"Toby and Patrick will remain," Andrew replied.

"John, too," Ian added.

The police were enthralled by the camp site. Charley had never seen water bubbling out of the ground before. Toby showed his friend, "Look Charley, watercress in the creek."

"What do you do with it?"

"It's edible, but a pungent flavour. Here, try some."

Toby lent down and picked a small bunch. He tried it and approved. Though Charley was reluctant.

"Bloody hell, I'm not eating that!"

To which Toby countered, "Come on, Charley! Eat the effing stuff!"

Charley looked at Toby and ate it.

"Hey, that wasn't too bad at all," he admitted.

"Good to know what's edible and what isn't, when food supplies are low," Toby said.

Toby handed around the watercress. Some liked it and others were wary.

"It could be good when no other greens are available," Ian agreed.

The men were relieved the wind was blowing from the south. They were looking forward to a hot meal. Pools of water near the waterfall meant the men could wash in safety. They were shocked to see Patrick and Toby's scars, where bullets had been removed. All retired early after a final mug of tea.

"Bill, I'm not happy about the complications which could arise tomorrow. We can trust our lot, but the others could have another agenda," Ian spoke quietly.

"Surely not all of them, Ian?"

"No, but we have to be extra careful."

"I agree. There are lots of questions I'd like to ask."

"Such as?"

"Sergeant Norm Green for one?"

Ian laughed, "How did he know the Hade men?"

"Ian, I like them, particularly given they're on our side!"

"You do have a point – those men are a formidable team. Determined."

"I get the feeling that this valley is important to Andrew?"

"You're right, I wonder who did the valley investigation?"

"This is a police operation, isn't it?"

"I'm not so sure. Where did the direction come from – the city or the frontier?"

"Do you mean the city police are here to protect the crims?"

"It's possible."

"You think the other group may not know our part?"

"That's it, Bill."

Both men were silent.

*

In the morning, Sergeant Rich asked, "What were you two talking about so earnestly last night?"

Bill was reluctant to speak.

"Well?"

"Sergeant, we were wondering where the directions had originated from."

The Sergeant remained silent for a moment. "Alex and Kevin were right about you and Percy."

He walked away to check on his horse.

Breakfast was quiet as usual, with each man thinking of the day ahead. They would be facing hardened criminals, who had nothing to lose, just words against a bullet. All men faced this problem – to fight for justice or let evil grow. Better not to think. Just go do the job.

Sergeant Rich called the men together for a final briefing. Some sat on the large stones, most chose logs.

"Any questions?" he asked.

"How do we you know the valley is the hide-out?" Ian enquired.

Sergeant Rich looked at Andrew, "Will you answer?"

"Our father contacted a policeman."

The Sergeant added, "We nabbed two men involved. With some encouragement, they gave us the camp layout."

"How do we get into the valley?" Kevin asked.

"At the end of the waterfall, a track leads down. Single file – it's a narrow path," Andrew explained.

"Dangerous?" Kevin said.

"Of course," the Sergeant replied briskly.

Sid commented, "So we take it carefully?"

"What happens if one of us falls?" Charley asked.

The Sergeant glared at him, "Provided you're not dead, stay quiet and we'll get you later."

The men looked at one another and grinned.

"If we took that young bastard who gave us all that cheek, we'd make sure as hell he had a fall!" Charley said.

Alex laughed, "He's still walking the streets a long way from here, more's the pity!"

"You will go down with care, it's really quite easy. Stay quiet. Sound carries," Andrew continued. "Any questions?"

"Where is their camp?" Ian asked.

"In an open area surrounded by thick scrub beside the creek. It won't be easy to approach without being heard. You'll need to be careful," Andrew explained.

"What about the other city police?" Fred enquired.

Andrew looked at the Sergeant. "They are meant to stop the crims escaping in the other direction."

The men were silent. The true situation was at last out in the open.

"I feel sorry for our honest colleagues, working beside others taking bribes. But there are good men here. They know the risks," Alex said quietly.

"What do we know about their camp?" Bill asked.

Andrew spoke up.

"The slab hut is in the clearing. There is a horse yard, humpies, and bark huts. Stolen cattle and sheep for fresh meat. We're not sure of the number there – probably seven men."

"A big effort for that many," Sid commented.

The Sergeant smiled and enlightened him, "We caught four in a trap recently, none of them survived."

He turned to Andrew.

There were sober looks between the brothers before Toby said, "These men are dangerous, like rats in a corner. Don't risk it. They will kill you given the chance."

Patrick spoke quietly, "If anyone is hurt, the closest medical help is at our farm."

Andrew looked at his brothers. "Patrick and Toby will remain with the horses."

The Sergeant was silent, then suggested, "I'd like to leave a few police here in case of a break-out."

"John, how about you and Fred stay?" Ian suggested.

"And miss all the fun!"

The Sergeant interrupted, "Excellent idea, you both stay plus Ben. Andrew, you lead the way down the track."

Charley looked at the path. "It looks easy for a boy of ten, but what about us?"

"I don't expect any problems, but then I'm not overweight," Alex piped up with a grin.

"Charley, speak for yourself, we're going down now," Kevin countered.

Sid finally admitted, "Charley speaks for me too, I never liked walking tracks made for animals and this is a prime example."

Shaun laughed. "Don't look down. I just follow my brothers!"

"He knows we won't let anything happen to him, he's too good a shot!" Andrew smiled.

Charley walked to the edge of the waterfall, standing aside for Shaun to begin the descent. The others followed in silence, taking care where they put their feet. Mostly it was about two feet wide, sometimes less. The drop on one side was a sheer cliff. Some of the men stared at the drop in disbelief.

Ian, though, was relaxed. As he turned a corner, he found Andrew had waited for him. The path became a little wider as it passed through some rocks, away from a gentle waterfall.

Andrew smiled and indicated Charley well out in front of the others.

"Charley has a woodheap on his shoulder, but a good man in a scrap, though difficult to handle," Ian said.

"What you see is what you get," Andrew admitted.

"How did Toby manage with the food?" Ian enquired.

"Toby liked Charley's rough sense of humour. He knew what he was doing."

Kevin stiffened as another policeman walked out of the trees towards them.

"Here's trouble," he said under his breath.

Senior Sergeant Shaw, in charge of the city police, had arrived to give directions.

"I've told my men to spread out across the valley floor. It's only small, so no one can get behind us," Sergeant Rich explained.

"No, the thieves are at the hut. Go and deal with them," Sergeant Shaw demanded.

"I don't agree with you – that's leaving a big gap in our defences."

"I have the authority here. You'll follow my orders."

He turned on his heel, crashing back through the trees, followed by an escort of two city policemen.

"Be very careful today. We know what's at stake," he spoke quietly.

Alex was reassuring, "Don't worry about us."

He turned and followed the others into the undergrowth and out of sight.

The Sergeant ordered his men, "We have to follow the new plan, there's no choice."

Andrew, Ian and Bill moved into the bush together. The others spread out two at a time. They had been advised not to go alone. They checked for footprints along the banks of the creek, as it meandered around rocks between tall old gum trees and thick undergrowth.

John had begged to be allowed to come. Fred and Ben, with the two Hade brothers, were enough to watch the camp. Ian had relented. The police progress was painfully slow.

John queried, "Could go down into the middle of the valley?"

Ian was ready for this. "Just don't get shot and look after Shaun."

"I've been waiting to see who would break ranks. I don't think you need to worry," Andrew said to Ian.

"Is Shaun really a good shot?"

"We all are, but Shaun is better and he'll look after John, don't worry."

"I'm not worried, but John can be very determined. He'll look after your brother!"

Their eyes continually scanned the bush and trees as they walked deeper into the undergrowth. The city police had made no effort to hide their tracks.

"How did they come up and avoid running into the bastards?" Charley wondered.

Sid replied quietly, "Good question. I can think of an answer, but it will give you nightmares."

The Sergeant interrupted, "You've no proof."

They progressed further down the valley with a growing question – Where were the thieves?

The silence was almost eerie. The only sounds were birds high in the trees chattering as usual. But they were being monitored from a couple of tall bushy trees. There were a lot more than six thieves. Reports had come through of a large number of police at each end of the valley. Immediately plans were made to flee. Unknown to the Hade men, they had discovered their secret routes undetected, and now made use of the tracks.

Ian and Andrew heard shots. Instantly Bill wanted to investigate, but they had to keep together. He needn't have worried, as Shaun had seen the movement and fired. A cry was heard, then the breaking of branches and a body fell to the ground.

"Good shot," John said cheerfully.

"I'd do anything to get rid of the bastards."

"John, keep an eye up in the trees."

Shaun stopped and said softly, "See. Up there."

"I see the bastard. Worth a shot do you think?"

Shaun stood aside as John shot the man out of his perch. Shaun and John walked into a cleared area as Ian and Andrew appeared from another direction.

"Lost?" Shaun queried.

"No, we just didn't expect to see you," Ian admitted.

Other shots could be heard from all sides – pained cries and the breaking of branches.

"Where's Bill?" John asked.

"Out in front of us."

"Ian forgets I'm an experienced police officer," John said to his new friend.

Shaun laughed, "Same here, my elder brother forgets I'm a man. He'll always think we need protection."

"Elder brothers always think like that," Andrew clapped Shaun on the shoulder. "I'm pleased with your shooting today."

Sergeant Rich and his men moved through the trees, shooting at branches that shifted under the weight of fugitives. It felt like rounding up sheep, except they were leaving corpses behind. Cattle and sheep grazed near the creek, disturbed by the guns, but there was nowhere to run except into the bush.

Charley saw a hut and they crept close, moving around to the front of it, and saw a body at its entrance.

"I wonder which blighter shot 'im?" Charley asked.

No one answered him. They moved on, coming across other huts scattered with lifeless bodies. Who was responsible?

"There's possibly another getting rid of dead wood in the network," Sid suggested.

"You mean one of their own?" Charley barked.

"The other possibility is a policeman."

"If a man shoots at me, I shoot back. If he puts his hands up, I put him in handcuffs. Most we've seen have been shot in the back," Charley observed.

Chapter Twenty Three

In a clearing on the edge of trees on the valley floor, Sergeant Shaw held the leader as Bill trained his rifle on the man.

"I've got him covered, give me your rifle and handcuff him," Shaw advised.

Reluctantly Bill handed his gun to the Sergeant, and approached the felon with handcuffs. He froze, watching his target's hand reach for a long knife in his belt. Looking on, Andrew realised the guy needed discouragement. He aimed, as the felon grabbed his knife.

"Andrew, fire," Ian yelled.

The knife flew through the air, piercing Sergeant Shaw in the chest.

"You bastard, you double-crossed me!" the thief cried out.

Bill stood quite still. Ian and Andrew walked into the clearing.

"Do you think it's now over?"

"There's a cleaning up job to do, it may never be over."

As the men talked, a Special Constable arrived with a dray to cart the bodies to the local burying ground.

"We could bury the Sergeant here?" Bill queried.

"Not in my valley," Andrew shook his head.

More shots rang out. The frontier farmers frequently lost stock and the Special Constables were all from grazing families. These men knew the ruthlessness of these thieves. They were merciless in response.

Both police groups came together near the main hut and a brief rundown given of Shaw's death.

"We have lost a couple of others too, connected to Shaw. We'll see that they're buried locally. Thanks to you, local men, for your help," one of the city men said.

Sergeant Rich took charge. "You go ahead to the city. There are people we have to thank."

The city men headed out of the valley, the others back to the waterfall. At the bottom of the path, Andrew looked up.

"Look over there, that's two bodies, just down from our path, they'd have to have fallen from our camp. What the bloody hell happened up there?" Charley growled.

The men raced forward, fearful of what they would find. The camp was a mess, there was blood on some clothes, but no sign of life. Four horses were missing.

"Look here," Sid beckoned them over.

Andrew hurried across to a message scrawled in the bare earth. "Gone to farm, all alive, need help."

"We'll stay here the night and tomorrow ride to the Hade farm," Sergeant Rich spoke.

"Shaun, you stay and lead them home. I'll take Ian and Bill tonight. We'll travel by the secret track – the route they would have taken," Andrew said.

Shaun was surprised, "You know it?"

"Toby lost a bet and had to tell me!"

"So you know it leads to the shepherds' hut?"

"Yes, that's where we'll go tonight. If they reached it, they'll be safe. But they may have met trouble on the track."

They were soon on their way, riding single file through dense undergrowth.

"Don't lose me. Don't talk and keep your eyes open for trouble," Andrew commanded as they rode into the late afternoon.

It was a subdued camp they left behind. Shaun was not happy at having to remain. John and Shaun were close and Shaun was worried. It was the bloodstained clothes which concerned him. Who did they belong to?

John could read his friend's thoughts. He put a hand out to him in his swag.

"We're all safe in this camp."

Shaun nodded and turned into his swag.

*

Next day, Shaun led them back down to the base of the mountain. It was slow going, but they quite enjoyed the twisting and turning between tall trees and around fat rocks and over gullies. For a few hundred yards, they had to walk up a tall bank.

"I don't remember this track, Shaun?" Charley asked.

He turned to face Charley. "One of our secret tracks, it'll cut miles off."

Charley worried out loud. "What if something happens to you ?"

"You will have face the challenge of finding your way out. Then you will have to face my brothers. How fast can you run?"

The men laughed, warning Charley not to tempt providence in such a dense wilderness.

At last, the track reached open country – grasslands as far as the eye could see. Now they could canter their horses. As they looked back, they saw that the track had hugged the side of a steep rock face. Now they were within a couple of miles of the valley entrance.

Shaun's features were strained, as they rode towards the shepherd's hut.

The old shepherd came out and talked to Shaun a few minutes. Shaun turned to his men. "My dad was here in a dray. Ben and Fred have been wounded. He took them to the farm."

Shaun sat quietly on his horse thinking about where were Andrew, Ian and Bill had got to. There were other tracks out of the mountain. They had to be on one of those. Perhaps they were on their way to the farm now. Shaun turned and rode towards Sergeant Rich.

"Fred and Ben are wounded and have been taken to the farm. Andrew had organised a dray in case anyone needed medical attention."

The Sergeant asked, "Do you know where your brother, Mr. Percy and Mr. Todd are now?"

"No."

"So, they could still be on the mountain somewhere?"

"They are three tough men. Perhaps they are solving another mystery?"

The Sergeant smiled. "We'll go to your farm."

"Yes, there's a good creek and deep waterholes for fishing."

"I'm looking forward to a rest with a line in my hand!"

*

As Patrick, Ben, Fred and Toby sat around the campfire talking, gun shots rang out down in the valley.

"How do you police manage facing gunfire so regularly?" Patrick asked, then clarified, "I wouldn't like to risk your lives, now I know you. Nor would I like to think we would never meet again."

"We try and make our frontier safe. We're on the same side on the problem," Ben offered.

Toby laughed, "He's got you there. We go out of our way to keep the frontier safe. What about that recent kidnapping?"

"What kidnapping?" Fred raised an eyebrow.

Toby was distracted by the horses. Looking down into the valley, he froze, drawing the attention of his friends. With his hand he signalled for silence. Instantly they reached for their guns.

"We have company coming up the path," Toby said softly.

Toby peeked over the edge and continued quietly, "Two approaching, armed."

The men took cover away from the horses. Behind a cluster of rocks, they watched as heads and bodies came into full view. Patrick fired, followed by Fred.

Ben took a chance and ran to get a better position on another angle, but he neglected to notice a man kneeling with his gun raised. As Ben lunged towards was a safe position, he felt the sharp sting and tear of gunshot ripping into his shoulder.

Toby saw Ben fall and kept up a steady fire. The newcomers took a few steps back, unaware of the precipice behind them. Fred felt a bullet burn through his upper leg, but he kept firing, edging the men back until one slipped, fell backwards and gave a cry. The other turned to look at his mate as Patrick shot him.

There was silence. Toby stepped forward three paces and with his foot pushed the injured man over the edge with a grim satisfaction.

Ben and Fred needed medical attention. Toby wrote a message on the earth in a clear area near the campfire, while Patrick found cloth to stop the bleeding. Toby saddled the four horses, attached their swags, and added as much food as he could locate.

"Can you get on your horse from that rock?" Patrick asked Fred.

"I don't know," Fred grimaced.

"We have a long ride, we have to go now."

Toby helped Ben on, assuring him, "We have a secret path out. It's a rough track – just stay in your saddle. Call out if it's getting too difficult."

"We can endure it, can't we Ben?" Fred winked quietly.

"We can stay this ride," Ben agreed with a weak laugh.

Toby wasn't sure but they started down a track which had been invisible until now. It began beside the spring, crossing the top of it and down among the trees. The route twisted across the shady side of the slope, with a steep grade between the trees.

Ben winced.

"Hold on, Ben, we are almost at a flat area and we can rest," Toby encouraged him.

Patrick rode ahead to check the track. He returned and explained, "There is a second track down to the valley from here. We'll stop a bit but stay on your horses. I've found other tracks – fresh ones."

"We're not alone," Toby commented.

"We need to have our guns ready. Can you manage, Ben?"

"No trouble at all."

Fred laughed quietly. "Patrick, Toby, we'll keep up with you."

He was also worried about Ben, staying upright through sheer willpower. Toby knew Ben would rather die on his mount than fall, so he watched hawk-like.

After a rest, the track continued up another hill, before a long descent. Patrick paused constantly, listening for the lack of normal bird chatter. They entered a clearing where a second track joined theirs.

"Toby, hide the horses and get Ben and Fred into that thicket of growth. All guns out and we wait," Patrick ordered.

"Fire on sight. Aim for the chest. We haven't the time to flush 'em out of this bush," Fred suggested.

They waited and listened. Soon approaching footsteps could be heard and then talking. Toby estimated about three men. Guns trained on the path they waited. And waited. As the three men came into view, at a nod from Patrick they fired – four lethal bullets.

"Check their bodies for papers," Fred suggested.

Toby handed coins and a bag of papers to Fred.

"These will interest you," he said.

"Toby, make sure Sergeant Rich gets them."

"I will, Fred."

He put the papers in his saddle bag, leaving the bodies on the track.

They continued down the steep hill, along winding tracks, around steep gullies, careful not to slip on the narrow path. Through the trees, they could see the open plains in full afternoon sunshine.

At last Toby could see the shepherd's hut and a dray harnessed with two horses. It was their father waiting. A dog barked and two men came out of the hut – the old shepherd, Dan, and Sam Hade. Patrick rode up to his father and pointed to Ben.

"He's in a bad way".

His father walked over. "A brave man, Mr. Holt. Now I need you to get down from your horse. I've got a dray ready and I'll take you to our farm."

Ben looked down at Mr. Hade, smiling weakly.

As he dismounted, Ben swung himself askew and began to fall. Sam Hade caught him in time and laid him on the dray. Toby and Dan helped Fred onto the same dray.

"Maybe you'd be my escort in case we come across trouble?" Sam suggested to his sons.

"Of course, Toby and I will lead their horses. Those men saved our lives."

Their father whipped up his horses, waved goodbye to Dan, and drove away across the plain with his sons just behind.

*

Andrew, Ian and Bill had taken the secret path behind them in the late afternoon. Andrew thought he knew the track, described to him by his delinquent brother. But the boy had wanted to keep this route a secret, so his directions were not accurate.

Andrew and his colleagues had headed up the crest of the valley and into a clearing. Now Andrew admitted, "I don't think this is the path."

"We can't keep going after dark, if we're unsure of where we are," Ian warned.

As they sat silent, a faint sound could be heard. A child's cry. Andrew drew his horse up beside Ian.

"There was a girl and a child taken from a squatter's hut recently. No one knows why. We ought to investigate that cry."

The two policemen nodded and followed the sound quietly through the bush. In the twilight, a bough hut appeared. The men alighted, walking carefully towards the hut. Bill moved quietly to the front, spying a girl and a small boy sitting on some branches. Bill made a sign with his hand for silence.

"Where is the guard?" he asked the children quietly.

"Gone for water. Who are you?" the girl gasped.

"Police."

"Please take us home!"

"Which direction did he go in?"

She pointed down towards the valley floor.

"Why were you taken?" Ian asked gently.

"Something to do with my dad." The girl shrugged helplessly.

"We should all get as far away as possible," Bill suggested.

All agreed and scooping up the youngsters, they rode back until they were on the path. Twilight changed to moonlight as the track turned down towards the distant plains.

After crossing a small creek into a clearing, Ian suggested, "Let's make camp here. Bill, you get a fire going and let's eat."

"Won't the fire draw attention?" the girl said frightened.

"We're too far away from the hut. Also, it would take a brave man to attack a police camp," Ian replied gently.

"I'm Betty and this is Angus," she replied in a doubtful voice.

"How old are you, Betty?" Ian asked.

"I'm fifteen. Angus is five going on six."

She smiled tentatively. "Angus refused to leave me alone with him, just before you came."

Betty lifted Angus' shirt and showed them a nasty weal across the boy's back, blood seeping from the wound. In the light of the fire, it looked grim.

Andrew made up his mind. "We ought to take them to the farm. My father was an army doctor."

"What do you think?" Ian looked at Bill.

"The farm's the best place to begin any investigation," Bill agreed.

Betty asked, "Do you have a mother at your farm?"

"Yes, I do and she's a good woman."

"Alright. We'll go with you."

Then the girl asked, "Why are you going to this man's farm, what's he done?"

"Don't know, but we aim to find out!" Bill laughed.

"Our colleagues were shot," Ian explained.

"You mean you fought those bad men and got rid of them?"

"There are always men who take advantage of others. You know the name of the man who kidnapped you and Angus?"

She looked into the fire before speaking in a faint voice, "My dad said not to say a bad man's name, because he will hear it and come take us away. That's what happened."

Ian recognised this thinking from criminal gangs – to keep children silent. They needed a name from a frightened girl.

"Betty, if you whisper his name, he can't hear you," Ian spoke gently.

Ian lent down.

"Thank you, Betty. Now, you and Angus wrap yourselves in your blanket and go to sleep."

"Will you be here when we wake up?"

Ian felt a sadness. What they had experienced?

"Yes, we'll all be here, making breakfast when you wake."

Bill had applied a bush remedy to the boy's back, which had stopped the bleeding. The lad gave him a hug.

"Angus, you're a brave boy. Now it's time to sleep," Bill said.

"Will you take me on your horse tomorrow?" Angus asked sleepily.

Bill looked down into the lad's pleading eyes.

"Yes, you can ride with me tomorrow. Now go to bed, or I might change my mind."

The men now had time to talk about the situation.

"What do you know about her family?" Ian asked Andrew.

"Father's name is Alf Thorne, from a squatting family on the edge of our district. They've kept to themselves. The mother can read and write. Alf was an office clerk. I don't know what changed. Gossip says he found gold and chose the land to settle."

"What was the name of the kidnapper?" Bill asked.

"Dennis Stone."

Ian watched Bill as he sifted through his memory a multitude of names.

Andrew felt a bit ashamed, surprised at the level of compassion his mates had shown the youngsters. After all they were of questionable parentage.

"I remember there was a hold-up on the road on the way to the Blue Mountains. One of the men was recognised as Dennis Stone – he served time. A few years ago now," Bill said at last.

"Possible Alf Thorne was the other man?" Ian queried.

"He'd have to be a lot older than he is now."

"Andrew, any idea of Alf's father's name?"

"No. But we can find out later."

*

Next morning, it was Betty and Angus first up who had a fire burning brightly.

"There were coals still hot," Angus admitted.

Andrew found some meat and soon they were enjoying a meal. Andrew took Betty up on his horse and told her to hang on. Angus was on Bill's horse and had no intention of letting go. Ian rode behind, as Andrew led the way to the farm.

Elizabeth Hade stood outside her home on a slight rise above a creek. She had been looking east, several times already.

"Jenny saw dust on the plain. Dad's coming with two men on horses, leading two mounts," one of her daughters told her at last.

This was not cheerful news to a mother worried about sons forever involved in dangerous activities. She stood at the highest point of the verandah gazing out to the plain. Soon the dray was in full sight. Elizabeth gave a sigh of relief and called her daughters.

"Jenny and Jane come! Dad's home – with two wounded men."

Mr. Hade stopped as close as he could to the slab hut doorway. His wife and girls ran up to hug him, glancing at the wounded men, as if they ran a field hospital.

"We're not in such a bad way, are we Mr. Hade?" Fred grinned at the pretty girls.

"Not yet, Mr. Hall!" Sam replied.

Patrick and Toby greeted their womenfolk and helped Fred out of the dray.

"Toby, take Ben first. I'll wait while Mr. Hade takes that bullet out," Fred clutched the side of the dray and stood up.

"Right, Patrick and Jenny, help Mr. Holt on to the bench."

Ben lost more colour when he noticed knives and saws amongst the equipment lining the walls.

"Don't worry, this is our meat room. Dad uses this bench for anything medical, usually on us. It's stable," Toby laughed.

Elizabeth used a cloth to clean up Ben and remove his shirt. "I'm a trained nurse, so you're in good hands."

Ben tried to smile.

Mr. Hade arrived in a white gown, looking as if he meant business, and Ben looked a little uneasy. Patrick and Toby looked on with their sister Jenny.

"I have to take the bullet out. It will hurt. Toby has a stick which you might close your teeth on it. I'll have to probe around to find the bullet but I'll be as gentle as I can. My wife will put a cloth over your eyes," Mr. Hade spoke gently to him.

Ben was held steady for the next hour. It was a relief when he passed out so Hade could find and remove the bullet. When Ben opened his eyes, he was in a bed, Jane sitting beside him.

"Mr. Holt, do you want something to drink?"

He smiled and drifted back to sleep, feeling so very tired. Meanwhile, Fred was enduring the same treatment, biting hard on another stick.

At last, the bullet was located and removed. Fred, still conscious, was put on a stiff board and carried to bed.

"I don't want you to move that leg, until I see how it's healing," Mr. Hade explained.

In the meantime, Patrick and Toby filled in their family about their escapades. Toby swore their police friends had saved their lives. Patrick added graphic details of hearing the fighting and the approaching criminals. They thoughts turned to Shaun and Andrew.

*

The ride across the plain to the farm only took half an hour. As they rode, Sergeant Rich realised he would have loved to have had this playground as a child.

Soon the wood slab farm buildings came into clear sight. There was just one brick structure. The main homestead was on a rise well above the meandering creek below. Shaun took them up to the side of the house, where his father came out to greet them.

"Welcome! We're grateful for your efforts!" Mr. Hade called out.

"Mr. Hade, I'm sorry it's taken so long. How are our men doing?"

"They are doing well – still sleeping, which will help the healing process. I had to probe a bit to find the bullets."

"I suggested the area down near the creek, below the house, would be a good place for the men?" Shaun said to his father.

"Yes, it's close enough for anything needed. Sergeant, we're sorry we are unable to accommodate you – your two men are in our spare room."

"That's alright, Mr. Hade, I'm happy with my men."

Shaun led the men down to the camping area. Sam Hade followed to make sure they settled in, given they were so far from home. While he talked to the men, Sergeant Rich unsaddled his horse giving him time to think of what to ask Mr. Hade.

"How long before Mr. Holt can ride a horse?" he asked.

"About three weeks, and Mr. Hall will take longer."

"As expected, Mr. Hade. Are you happy to keep the men here until they're able to ride?"

"We will be happy to accommodate them until then," he smiled, adding, "if we attempted to move them, my sons would revolt."

"I have that impression too."

Shaun asked his father, "Where is Andrew?"

"I don't know – not here."

"But he left last night to follow Toby and Patrick."

"I wouldn't worry about your son. He's with two experienced police officers. I have rarely met a more determined man than Andrew. Who knows what they found to do," the Sergeant smiled. "They are as determined as your son – wouldn't let anything happen to him."

With these words, Mr. Hade and Shaun walked back up to the house. Shaun went to see if Ben and Fred were awake in case they wanted anything.

*

The city men talked about the farm, so far from their city streets.

"How long are we going to be here?" Charley asked.

"Probably until Ian and Bill turn up, if they do," Kevin looked up from sorting through his pack.

"Of course they'll come – where else can they go?" Charley rose to the bait.

"Charley, you always fall for it," Kevin grinned.

"By what Mr. Hade said, Ben and Fred'll be here for a few weeks," Alex said.

"How in the fuckin' hell do you know?" Charley scratched his beard.

"Remember that fellow – shot in the leg about a year ago?"

"That policeman, in the next station from ours?"

"That's right – he took a long time before he could get on a horse."

"I do remember, but he was a fucking idiot and no loss to us," Charley added.

"Shot by that bastard who attacked those travellers – we didn't get him till much later," Kevin recalled.

"Got ten years' hard labour," Charley replied.

Shaun came down with some meat. "Where's John?"

"Went up to see Ben. He'll change his dressings," Kevin said.

Alex went fishing, enjoying the peace of the creek and birdsong. Turning, he looked across the open plains to the blue of the mountain in the distance. Rubbing his eyes, he realised they had not deceived him. Andrew and Bill were riding this way – each with a small passenger. Ian rode behind them.

Alex was not the only one who saw them approaching. Everyone stopped and stared. As they rode into the horse yard, the questions started.

Mrs. Hade took Betty, and Toby lifted a reluctant boy from Bill's mount. Angus was tearful until Bill assured him, "I'll see you soon, Angus."

Andrew had some private words to his brother about the bet.

"No harm done, Andy, and you had an adventure!" his younger brother grinned.

Sergeant Rich wanted all the kidnapping details to make a report.

Betty and Angus would stay until the matter had been settled. Bill joined Alex fishing on the banks of the creek.

John slept next to Ben and Fred, so he could attend to their needs during the night.

He also spent time with Toby who explained, "We've money coming in, so decided to replace the wooden slabs with bricks. Dad employed a brickmaker. Andrew worked with him."

"Where's the kiln?"

"Not far. Everything was going well until the bloke left to find gold. Now we all spend time brickmaking."

"Toby, you won't believe this. Bill had time in a brickworks before policing."

"Dad will be interested."

They found Sam Hade talking to Sergeant Rich, who had requested that Andrew accompany Kevin to the police camp, with Dennis Stone's arrest warrant for kidnapping. Sam had agreed, and they had left an hour or so ago.

Sergeant Rich would leave with Charley and Sid. The papers discovered with the deceased thief would prove invaluable in tracking down other parts of the network. Sergeant Rich wanted them in the city as soon as possible.

"Now what have you two been up to!?" Mr. Hade asked John.

It hadn't taken the family long before they all addressed John by his Christian name – he was so like Shaun and Toby. He was good in a sick room, dependable. Toby told his father about Bill.

"Well now, that is welcome news, we need some more help working with the clay."

John was only now realising the men worked their own kiln. It explained the roughness of the boys' hands. His life was on horseback. It was easy to forget that others improved their lives as they could afford to.

John returned to check on Ben and Fred. They wanted to get up – sit in the sun.

Mrs. Hade shook her head. "Not yet, give it another couple of days. You stay in bed, I don't want a relapse."

They had no option but to agree.

She smiled. Before leaving, she ensured the door was wedged open to allow the fresh air.

On Sergeant Rich's last night with Charley and Sid, Sam Hade sent down meat and damper with wild honey.

As Shaun made the delivery, Charley remarked, "Shaun you're always welcome in this darned camp!"

"That's a bit tough Charley, this is his own land!" Ian laughed.

"Best honey I've ever tasted," Charley continued.

"Probably the only honey," Kevin added.

"Old Mick has beehives."

"What? That old skin flint? I bet he never gave it to you out of the kindness of his heart."

"Well no, he reported some stolen goods. We couldn't charge him, so he gave us some honey."

"You took honey from that old devil when you knew he was as guilty as hell?" Kevin was surprised.

"Don't take on so, Kev – we couldn't charge him."

Kevin groaned, "We aren't meant to encourage men into bad habits, Charley."

"The Sergeant took the honey away, so they learnt that this was a bad act."

Ian had to ask, "What about your pot of honey, Charley?"

"I wasn't with the men when the Sergeant discovered the honey pots."

Shaun walked back to the house chuckling to himself.

*

Next morning, word came in that Dennis Stone had been arrested and would be taken to the nearest magistrate to be sentenced – likely another prison term or a road gang.

Sergeant Rich left, leaving Ian and Bill to deal with the children.

The Hade family were happy to support the remaining officers until Fred and Ben were well enough to leave. Ian convinced Bill to help with firing bricks.

Ian now called the shots, "Kevin, you can assist Bill. And Alex, you can help me with the Thorne family."

Kevin was not so keen. "As soon as Ben can ride a horse, we'll be leaving."

Sam Hade was delighted. Bill had already had a look at the kiln and made a few suggestions. The family became accustomed to seeing Bill's shadow – a small boy following him everywhere. Bill coped well with Angus and gave him time, asking questions which the boy answered with the honesty of the very young.

As Sergeant Rich was rolling up his swag and about to leave, a messenger arrived with a request.

"It is believed a cache of stolen goods has been hidden in the valley. When located, you and your men will escort it by dray to the nearest large settlement," it read.

Chapter Twenty Five

Police work always took precedence. Sergeant Rich wondered if this would ever change. He had really wanted to leave the two men to bring Ben home in a couple of weeks. Instead Ben would have to rely on his bush police friends.

It was hard to care for your men in a system which put work first and welfare last. Nonetheless, his men seemed only too pleased to be on a new assignment.

At the camp that summer night, Ian turned to Bill, "I saw you talking to Angus, what did he say?"

Bill lay on his side watching the flames. "I sometimes feel guilty questioning people who have no idea of what they are actually saying to us. Angus is a little boy who loves his family. Dennis Stone attacked him, pushed him out of the shelter, told him to 'Get lost'. He saw that beast rape Betty – not that he understood through her tears."

"The bastard," John said forcefully. "Can he be charged with that?"

"Probably not, but ten years for kidnapping, at least".

"Andrew suspected Betty had been raped," Bill admitted. "That's why he was keen his father saw her."

"What's our next step?" Bill asked Ian.

"We ought to visit the Thornes. Sort out this mess, so the children never suffer again because of these secrets."

They talked into the night.

*

Next day, John left the camp early to tend to Ben and Fred. Ian and Bill walked up to their hut later and met Mr. Hade leaving their room.

"How are they doing today?" Ian asked.

"Strong, young men. They're doing well. Mr. Holt will be able to get up and move with care. Mr. Hall's leg, it's taking longer to heal."

"When will Ben be able to move out?"

He shrugged. "Ask me in a couple of weeks. I'd like to keep both men here until I'm sure. Don't think they'll be a problem to us."

"What about Ben travelling by coach to the city?" Ian asked, making one last effort.

"Entirely out of the question, exposed to such jolting for days. I wouldn't let my boy endure it, so no, Holt is staying here."

"Just thought I'd ask. I'll send word to Sergeant Rich with your recommendation."

"You do that, Mr. Percy. Have the police found the stolen property yet?"

"I don't believe so."

"Toby or Patrick could offer an idea as to its whereabouts?'

"Why am I not surprised?" Ian laughed, then remembering a story asked, "Where were they caught by the thieves?"

Mr. Hade looked surprised. "I don't really know. I was too busy removing the bullets from their legs. Those bullets left scars. I don't think I wanted to know at the time."

Toby was at the horse yard and his father called out. He came over, "Where were you caught those four years ago with the bullet wounds, Toby?"

"In the valley," he answered surprised.

"But where in the valley, Toby?"

"Does it really matter, Dad?"

"It might do. The police are still searching for the stolen goods."

"So that's it?"

"Yes. Do you know where they could be?"

"No, but Patrick and I can go and have a look."

"Will you take Bill with you, please?"

"We'd rather go on our own."

"Bill will be safe company for you, with so many strangers in the valley now," Ian commented.

"Oh! Alright Ian, we'll take him with us."

Mr. Hade looked surprised.

"We're on a first name basis, it's easier in camp, and apart from myself, most of my men are about the same age as your sons," Ian explained.

Bill was located and Ian explained about the coming expedition with Patrick and Toby. He was there to provide protection. Bill was thrilled.

His young protégé Angus though had other thoughts, crestfallen that he was to be left behind. The kid glared at Ian.

Ian tried to soften the blow, "You'll see Bill later today and he'll take you for a ride."

Angus walked towards the yards to see what Shaun was doing instead.

In the sick room, Ben and Fred had perked up.

"We had Jenny and Jane bringing food in, they are lovely girls," Fred winked.

"Jenny mended my shirt, it's as good as new. And she mended Fred's pantaloons." Ben seemed lovestruck.

"Jane read to us from a Captain Marryat book," Fred added.

*

Bill, Toby and Patrick arrived in the valley near the waterfall, following one of their secret tracks.

"Have you found the goods yet?" Bill asked a policeman.

"No, not yet."

"Follow us, these men know the secrets of the valley," Bill advised.

Patrick and Toby tied their horses to a tree and walked up beside the fall of water, shaded by undergrowth. They walked behind the fall, along a thin path into a cave. It was full of barrels, boxes, bottles and other goods.

"Is this what you were looking for?" Bill asked.

"Could be."

A few minutes later, after opening a box and finding a small bag of gold dust, he turned to Bill. "Yes this is it. We'll bring up a dray and take it to Hill Top."

He turned to Patrick and Toby. "Thank you. I've heard you suffered in this place."

"How did you know?" Patrick asked in surprise.

"A man I shot took a while to die. He told me he'd shot at two boys in a cave. When I came in here, I remembered."

"We almost never made it out alive," Toby said.

Bill, Toby and Patrick mounted their horses and started for home. Before leaving, Bill turned to the brothers. "How did you escape?"

"We crawled out from behind those rocks, up to a patch of blue sky," Patrick pointed to one side of the cave.

Bill sensed he had hit on a traumatic memory. It showed in their body language and their short replies. The nightmare probably still visited them in dark moments.

"Tell me about what you experienced?" he asked quietly.

"We've never talked to anyone about that. Still have nightmares – but it's time we talked. Toby, you go first," Patrick nodded.

"We left our horses in a thicket of undergrowth and had gone on foot, which we'd always done. We knew thieves were in the area but assumed they didn't know about the cave," Toby explained.

"We'd been extra careful, watching before entering. Perhaps we didn't wait long enough. We'd only just entered when Toby heard boots on the rocks outside," Patrick took over.

"We couldn't get out the front. The only choice was a patch of blue sky, visible from the back – a thin chimney on an angle, and steep," Toby continued.

Patrick, his voice loaded with emotion, explained, "We were a few years younger – fit and strong and thinner. We climbed as someone fired a gun up the chimney. We were hit in our legs as we fled, worried we wouldn't be able to get out."

Patrick's head dropped as Toby picked up the story.

"In that chimney, we were unsure if there was a way out, or what we would discover at the top."

Toby did not say it, but remembered images of his parents, his siblings, flashing like cards through his vision. "There was a fair chance we would not survive. That climb up, with shot-up legs, took a long time. We drew strength from each other."

"We reached the top of the chute. There was a ledge just wide enough to crawl on to reach some undergrowth. Off the ledge was a sheer drop. Grabbing tree roots, we made it to the other side of the waterfall. We had to walk a fair way to find our horses," Patrick spoke quietly.

"The first person we saw was Andrew. We both hugged him, oblivious to our bloodied bodies," Toby continued.

Patrick remembered Andrew's face. "He went pale, shouted hoarsely to Dad, who was putting his horse in the yard. We were always hurting ourselves, but this was a new level of injury. Soon we were put on that same bench, as Ben and Fred."

Toby added, "When we were better, our wounds healed, we went back to that cave, this time taking extreme care. We put maggots in their meat barrels, poured out their liquor – left that cave in a mess."

"It was a risk we had to take. That man could have killed us in that chimney and no one would have ever known. That's our nightmare," Patrick explained.

*

Back at the farm, as they unsaddled the horses, Bill put his hand on Toby's shoulder.

"I hope by speaking up, the nightmares will not be as bad. Talking about the tough stuff helps Ian and me."

"I'm going for a swim," Bill volunteered.

"I thought you might," Ian winked. "Best keep the girls away from our camp tonight."

"Are you joining me in the water?"

"I need a good wash and so do my clothes," Ian grinned.

Both men stripped, immersing their sore bodies and day's clothes into the cool lagoon. John came and joined them in the shallows after doing his washing.

Andrew stood on the bank watching them.

"Come in Andrew," Bill called out.

"No thanks, you look like a lot of bloody fish."

Andrew was standing close to the edge. Bill nodded to Ian and swam in close to the bank, reaching out for Andrew's feet. There was a cry as Andrew toppled in. Andrew, usually so controlled, swore ferociously, to the delight of his friends in the water.

A barrier had been broken. Andrew had no choice but to strip and join in. They had a couple of races. Though Andrew was an excellent swimmer, Ian was stronger and easily beat him.

With clothes draped over nearby bushes to dry, they sat beside their fire and talked.

"I came to thank you for getting Patrick and Toby to talk about their nightmares in that cave," Andrew admitted. "But Uncle Norm didn't tell us about your love of pulling men into the water!" Andrew said.

"Uncle Norm?" Bill queried.

Andrew explained, "Norman Green, my uncle."

There was total silence, before Andrew laughed at the expression on their faces. Gasping for breath, "It's payback time, boys!"

John could not help smiling. He could hardly wait to tell Fred and Ben.

Ian asked Andrew, "Do you want to stay for some fish for the evening meal?"

Andrew grinned, "I'd better stay until my clothes are dry, otherwise I'll have to explain how I fell into the water, and I'd rather not say."

*

While the men sat around the fire, talking and laughing, cementing their friendship, up at the house, the family sat around a table at their evening meal.

"Why did we have to keep away from the camp this afternoon?" Jenny asked.

Her father jumped in. "Girls, when I was treating the boys, Fred told me that Mr. Percy had been in India and was accustomed to bathing every day. Both are expected to wash regularly."

"Is it normal to wash every day?" Jenny asked.

"It isn't an English custom, because it's so cold, but here it's a healthy way to live."

"Where's Andrew tonight?" Patrick asked.

Toby grinned, "I saw him go down to the camp, Ian and Bill were swimming in the waterhole. Andrew was standing on the edge and fell into the water."

"Men horsing around," Elizabeth winked.

Jenny wanted to know exactly what happened.

"Were they dressed for swimming?"

"No more than we are."

Toby clarified, "They swim naked, the way we do sometimes."

*

In the early morning, Sam Hade went looking for Bill, finding him checking the horses.

"I've been told you worked in a brickyard. I'd like you to teach us some of the things you did back then."

"Sure, and John can come too. It's time he did some real work!" Bill smiled.

"You'll need some old clothes and boots. Andrew's will fit you."

"I'll ask Ian to come too," Bill suggested.

"In that case, I will get some more old clothes."

Once it became known the three policemen were going to the clay pit, the four boys made no complaints, although none of them liked it. Bill was impressed with the set-up. It was primitive but it worked. There was a stock of bricks to be put into the kiln, and the first job was to empty it.

The dray made several trips back to the house, while Patrick and Ian filled the kiln with the new bricks. It was hard work but satisfying to see the progress.

"I can hardly wait for the men to return. It's an awful job," Andrew confessed.

He wasn't the only one. At the end of a gruelling day, even with all the humour, the men left the clay bog looking like walking mud. The waterhole was the ideal escape.

In the afternoon, Ian and Bill went up to speak to Elizabeth about Betty and Angus. They found her making an apple pie in the kitchen with something bubbling in a pot on the open fire. Were the children ready to go home?

Elizabeth was silent for a moment. "Not until it's safe. First you need to talk with Alf Thorne and suggest his wife come here, until this mess has been sorted out."

"Angus?" Bill said.

She smiled. "Quite naughty at times, my boys handle him and like him. Toby and Shaun keep him in order."

"We thought we'd go tomorrow. Ask Andrew to be our guide?" Ian suggested.

"Andrew likes your company. I have no concerns."

"Andrew has no interest in police work, so we're no threat. His sole interest is to own the valley one day. In the meantime, he's learning much from us and, as you say, we enjoy his company," Ian added.

"You've put my mind at rest. You've had a lot of influence on our sons, it's been good for them," Elizabeth patted Ian on the knee.

This conversation had been needed. In the clay pit yesterday, when Jenny and Jane brought their midday meal, Ian had been uneasy. This family was a unit – one day each would go their separate ways, but not yet.

"Ben and Fred?" Bill enquired.

"Will be thoroughly spoilt by our daughters. Don't worry about them!"

"Thank you, Mrs. Hade. We'll talk to Andrew when we find him," Ian replied with a smile.

They found him near the water trough. He turned to see who was coming and instinctively moved away from the water.

"You're quite safe, Andrew, it's too shallow" Bill remarked.

"I've no doubt I'd fit if you wanted to take the trouble."

They walked to a couple of nearby logs.

"What have you in mind? Spit it out!" Andrew asked.

"Just a little ride to the Thorne place tomorrow," Ian reassured him.

"Their place isn't too far away, but that won't be the problem. Alf will be. I'll organise the food and, if it suits, you we'll leave at sunrise," Andrew assured the pair.

"We'll introduce you as a Special Constable, so you have every right to be with us," Ian clarified.

*

They left at sunrise riding south along the creek from one valley to another. The landscape changed from rich grasslands to floodplains. They climbed into the hilly country – low growth, stunted trees, and pale grass – with gullies washing good soil down to the plains leaving stones and gravel behind. Despite the poor soil, the landscape was beautiful, with stark dead trees and windswept vistas, looking over valleys to distant hills.

"Hard to make a living anywhere here," Ian yawned.

"Poor country and it borders the Thorne farm," Andrew answered.

"Making a living here could amount to taking money from a hold-up?" Bill suggested.

"That's the question been rolling around in my mind since you mentioned the hard living conditions," Ian added.

"Money is difficult to come by, although there is game to be caught. A hold-up could be a solution," Andrew replied.

"A big risk, if caught – seven years on a road gang," Bill mused out loud.

"It's food and it's free," Andrew smiled.

"For seven years, I don't think so," Ian shook his head.

"Perhaps you've never been hungry enough to steal," Andrew continued.

"I do know what that's like, but it's about self-respect. I didn't give in, survived in the army, learnt a few hard lessons. It has been a test," Ian admitted.

They talked on. Ian was saddened to see ring-barked trees, where there was no good soil to plant a crop. At the far end of the valley, a slab hut became visible, with yards near another slab shed. As they rode towards the hut, there was no sign of anyone watching their approach out in the open clear ground.

"I feel we are under observation," Bill said quietly.

"Me too," replied Ian.

"In that small shed behind the hut? Is it Alf do you think?" Andrew asked.

They rode up to the hut, securing their horses to the hitching rail under a nearby tree. Ian, Bill and Andrew walked to the hut, met by a middle-aged woman. Wearing a long dirty apron, over a coloured print dress, she had a careworn expression.

"Mrs. Thorne?" Andrew asked.

"Yes. Where are my children?"

"At my parents' farm, in the care of my mother."

"Why have you not brought them?"

"My mother thought best they'd stay until safe to come here. She suggested you may like to come stay for a time, until this matter has been cleared up?"

"What matter is that, Mr. Hade?"

"The matter which caused your children to be kidnapped and Betty raped."

Mrs. Thorne grasping the door post, lost colour, and replied choked, "I wasn't aware. No one told me."

"No one's business except yourselves and us. A private matter."

"Was it Dennis Stone?"

"He's been arrested and will do time for kidnapping," Ian replied gently.

"But the other?" she asked sadly.

"Not likely and better forgotten," Ian murmured.

"That is always the way of it," the woman moaned.

"Where is your husband?" Bill asked.

"Somewhere around."

"Mrs. Thorne, we have to ask Alf some hard questions, before your children can be returned," Ian said carefully.

She indicated the shed at the rear of the hut and turned back inside, closing the door.

Bill and Andrew walked around one side, and Ian went the other. As Ian passed an open gap in the hut wall, he heard a sob.

They found Alf at the back mending a poorly constructed yard with some branches.

Ian recounted exactly what had happened at the hands of Dennis Stone. Alf was stony-faced, then glum. Bill filled in the gaps, talking about his arrest, and what the police knew about the hold-up, including the unidentified man.

"Your children will never be safe until he's caught. We know Dennis Stone visited you," Ian stared.

Alf showed no expression as he considered his diminishing options.

"What do you want?" he asked at last.

"The name and whereabouts of the suspect," Ian demanded.

"Can't do that."

"You'd prefer to see your daughter raped again?" Bill stepped forward.

"She'll get over it."

"You will tell me or face arrest," Ian countered sharply.

"What for?"

"For failing to prevent a crime."

"That's not true."

"Dennis Stone threatened you. You refused him, told him he could do whatever he liked. He took your kids. You made no effort to stop him," Bill replied coldly.

"Alright, but no one can stop Dennis when his blood is up."

"You have to make amends if you want a relationship with your children," Ian chipped in.

Alf sighed, "The man you want is my brother."

"Where?" Ian asked.

"A shepherd on squatter's land."

"Whose land?"

"Jeff Hake."

"What's your brother's name?" Ian asked.

"Jim Thorne."

"What was his share of the hold-up?"

"It's gone now, but he got half – about ten pounds."

"Why did Dennis Stone want him?" Bill asked.

"To punish him for the seven years he had to do."

"So you sacrificed your children to keep your brother safe?" Bill said with disgust.

"He's my brother, the kids will get over it," Alf scowled.

Bill ignored him. "We'll send your wife to the Hade farm for a month. Give you time to make improvements to your hut and land, before…"

"And my brother?"

"It will be up to the magistrate," Ian speculated.

The Constables found Mrs. Thorne at the door of the dwelling.

"Mr. Hade, tell your mother I will come in a day or two. And thank her for her invitation, please."

"I will, Mrs. Thorne."

*

As they rode down the valley, Andrew pulled up his mare. "You didn't ask about Jeff Hake's hut?"

"We've heard about him. He has a reputation for employing men of questionable backgrounds. His place is in rough country, bordering a run where stock go missing," Bill replied.

"Where's the land?"

"It isn't far from you. South amongst the high hills. Travellers avoid them, given the risk of hold-ups in the area," Bill replied.

"We know that area – the Black Hills, best avoided as you say. Mum used to tell us stories about them – ghosts and goblins and evil men," Andrew commented.

"No doubt designed to keep you away," Ian laughed.

"Yes. Shaun and Toby would have loved to have seen the hills, but they never did get there," Andrew said.

"Then you'll be the first," Bill grunted.

Andrew shook his head. "I'm not sure I want to go – given those childhood stories."

"We ought to make camp soon. It's getting late," Ian suggested.

They found a clearing on the creek with gnarled gum trees beside a long waterhole. The water looked inviting. The men fished and swam as the sun's late shadows warmed their bare bodies.

Andrew fried up the fish in a blackened pan in companionable silence. Words were not important. Instead the men tuned to the sounds of the bush. A chorus ringing out from the tops of the trees, the deep grunt of the bullfrog.

Ian put a piece of fish on each man's tin plate and a handful of watercress, which Bill had dug out while out fishing. Seeing the green on his plate, Andrew smiled.

Vegetables were difficult to bring on patrol – mostly bought from squatters or found in overgrown gardens. A well-balanced diet wasn't easy out here.

"How do we handle Jim Thorne?" Bill asked.

"Let's ride towards the farm and see what turns up."

In this night soundscape – a bush lullaby – each man was lulled to sleep. Before the moon rose, the night enfolded each, an extra covering unseen and comforting.

Chapter Twenty Six

They left camp before sunrise and were surprised to encounter another patrol, led by George Nash. With him was James Wade, a new police recruit. James had been a stockman for a couple of years, a tall man and slim – the way those men usually are – with a keen-eyed expression.

George looked at Ian, grinning. "Look who I've found on this bright morning? Not a care in the world!"

"Where did you come from, George, to spoil the day?" Ian called out.

"Our well-connected Sergeant told me if I was to see you to give you a note," George winked.

As he was speaking, George withdrew a note from his saddlebag. Leaning across the gap between the horses, he handed it to Ian. "I hope I've brought you good news."

Ian broke the seal and read, with no change of his expression.

George knew how the game was played. "What did the note say?"

"Work."

The men laughed at George's non-plussed face.

"George, he got you there," Bill said.

"So you're not going to tell me?"

"A personal note of no relevance to work."

"You sure?"

"There is one sentence of interest to we patrollers."

"Yes…?"

"If we need help, you will be glad to give it. I assume that's correct, George? For in fact, we're on our way to make an arrest."

George laughed, "Of course. What's the plan?"

"We'll be riding into the Black Hills. You know them?" Ian asked.

"Heard of them. Supposed to be dangerous. We're not going there, but we'll meet you this side at the base of the hills. There's a campsite which I like."

Ian was silent as he considered the proposal.

"Good idea. Don't know how long it will take to make the arrest. How long can you wait?"

"I'll give you two days."

"Ample time. The hills are only an hour away."

With the arrangements in place, the two patrols split and went their separate ways – George and James to investigate stolen stock, Ian and his friends to the Black Hills.

Bill couldn't resist asking, "Ian, what was in that note?"

"Another job lined up after this. Okay, there was no mention of George helping us – it just seemed a good opportunity to get rid of a prisoner," Ian smiled.

Andrew and Bill bent over in their saddles laughing. They guided their mares at a steady pace up a track – their mounts now expert at avoiding prickly bush and the hazards of low scrub.

"What did your mother say to keep you from exploring these hills?" Ian asked.

"As I told you, ghosts and goblins."

"What else?"

On the crest they stopped, looking back over miles of country, then turned their horses to face a winding onward track.

Andrew continued, "She told us trees are social beings. Their roots hug each other. Above ground they talk to each other. Some are happy trees and some are old with dying limbs. Some use their branches to attack because humans assault them with axes and saws. We are enemies."

Ian smiled, "You sure your brothers have never been here?"

Andrew looked perplexed as Ian continued, "Look at the trees."

Bill and Andrew stared at the avenue of dead trees in a stunned silence, until Andrew broke in laughing, "Those young devils!"

Into most of the dead trunks, someone had carved faces – some aggressive, others with droopy mouths, and others sad. To a lone traveller with an active imagination, the spectacle might well spur them to flee. Andrew alighted, approaching the nearest face on an old trunk.

"It captures that grumpy expression on the faces of old men," he turned in surprise.

"Which one of your brothers might have…?" Ian asked.

Andrew smiled. "They have hidden talents. For this effort, Patrick or Shaun. I reckon this was a group effort."

Bill examined one of the faces and agreed. "Your brothers, eh? Raises plenty of questions."

"I'll try them first," Andrew offered. "Though whether they'll tell me, I don't know. Those boys are careful in what they reveal."

Talking about the faces, they rode on through the stunted trees across the top of the hill.

Bill mused, "The effort to design those faces, then carve them, shows determination. What else were they capable of?"

"We're a close family, but those younger boys did get up to mischief. One time, they came home all bloody and hugged me." Andrew's skin prickled at the memory.

Down ahead, smoke was visible coming from a hut.

Bill persisted, "You say you own that valley. I think the four of you do. Those boys have no doubt played knights and dragons here their formative years. I wouldn't take those hills away from them."

"You're a deep one," Andrew turned in his saddle.

"Andrew, has it taken you that long?" Ian laughed.

The hut they had seen was unoccupied – the smoke must have another source. It drifted along the creek on a gentle breeze. Oddly there was no stock to be seen.

"Any ideas?" Ian asked Andrew.

"We ought to check the valley beyond."

"Come on, Andrew. What are you really thinking?" Bill looking hard at his friend.

"This hut could be a decoy – give the impression of occupation."

"Are you saying it isn't?"

"That's correct. This is poor grazing country. I bet the landholders are in the next valley."

"Squatters are as wily as any street urchin. I'd never have thought of a trick valley," Ian mused.

They rode quietly into the next valley, following the creek, the horses walking on soft grass with little sound. Their approach went unnoticed until they rounded a bend – there a group of men were drinking beside the creek.

One gave a sudden cry, "Mary, mother of …"

A few tried to stagger to their feet, grinning. One fell in the attempt.

"Jim Thorne?" Ian asked sternly.

One man grunted waving his arm loosely in acknowledgement. Bill alighted his mare and, in a few breaths, secured the fellow with rope.

Jim's mates swore a string of profanities. There was no sign of an overseer. He was known and that was sufficient for the time being.

Leaving the drunken group behind, the Constables and their mounts plodded on, now with a prisoner on foot grumbling about his head.

The climb up the hill was slow. Bill had to stop to let Jim get his breath. In the avenue of gnarled trees, the carved faces spooked Jim to the point of panic. Andrew chuckled – his brothers would enjoy the story.

At the crest of the hill, Bill stopped. "I smell smoke." They had found the other party.

They rode down in early twilight, every man thinking about a rest, not least Jim who wasn't sure why he'd been arrested.

George stood up and walked to see the prisoner.

"Well Jim, it's been a long time," he observed.

"Yes, Mr. Nash, a long time."

"I arrested you for that pocket watch. You did time on a road gang?"

"That's right, Mr. Nash. Four years."

"What's more, you are our suspect in a hold-up. Dennis Stone did time and came back to seek revenge."

"I haven't seen him."

"No, he kidnapped your niece and nephew, because Alf wouldn't say where you were."

"Did he harm them kids?"

"Yes." Ian explained in detail. The old man, unkempt and dirty, made only one request.

"Mr. Nash, I'll plead guilty, you'll have no trouble. But let me do my time with Dennis."

"I will see what I can do, Jim."

"Thanks, Mr. Nash."

Jim was given food and chained to a tree at a distance. Ian wondered about meeting up with George. Perhaps Sergeant Green knew more about Jim.

Before returning to the farm the next day, George requested, "Ian, given I'm taking your prisoner, will you check the road out from the large property at the other end of the range?"

Ian raised his eyebrows.

"There've been reports of hold-ups, so you need to show a police presence."

*

With this job in mind, the three men set out before sunrise. By mid-morning a driver, with a woman and two children, turned out of a gate in a brougham, accompanied by a stockman.

Glad to have news, they pulled up. Ian rode closer, recognising the young woman.

"Sally Pearson, fancy meeting you here. Are these children your charges?" he commented.

"Yes, Mr. Percy. I am engaged to a stockman. Life is an adventure, as we talked about on the ship over here."

"Yes indeed, Miss Pearson, I hope you'll be happy."

"I'm sure. Now, if you'll excuse me, we must get going."

She indicated for the driver to proceed. Ian wondered how he had ever thought her a pretty girl. Perhaps because there were so few girls on the ship. He had considered a life with such a girl. There would be others.

*

This was one of the jobs Ian found irksome. It was called police presence and usually a job for men in training. After a short time, Ian had had enough.

"We're returning to the farm," he stated.

Bill agreed. "What was in the note from Sergeant Green?"

Ian rummaged around in his saddlebag until he found the envelope, and handed it to his friend silently. Bill open it, staring in confusion at the words.

Bill raised his eyes to see Ian looking at him. "What do you make of it?"

"That Sergeant is a devious old man. He has no choice to control the number under his command. He talks to everyone and people talk to him. He knew we were on our way to arrest Thorne."

Bill laughed, "Shows he's on his game! He isn't going to retire – that's just an act to keep us thinking he isn't aware of our movements."

Ian appreciated Bill's nous. "I've been thinking the same since reading that note."

They grinned. Andrew spoke up, "Give me a look?"

Bill handed the envelope over. Each moved their horses so they could watch his face as he read it. Andrew unfolded the note, and looked at it in shock.

"It's blank. There's nothing on it!"

*

They rode on, leaving Andrew to think. After all, Norm Green was his uncle. Andrew was pleased he had chosen to stay on the land. As much as he had enjoyed policework, it was time to return to the farm.

"I think it's time to leave the farm," Bill said quietly to Ian.

"I agree. We'll have a talk with Mr. Hade this evening."

They arrived in the early twilight. Andrew went to the horse yard and the men rode down to the camp to discover John had made a fire.

"I saw you coming across the plain," he explained.

That night, Ian let John know, "Bill and I think it's time to move back to our barracks."

"Yeah, we are close to outstaying our welcome, I think."

"Right, Bill and I will go up to speak to Mr. Hade about moving Ben and Fred."

Mr. Hade was sitting on his verandah. After general conversation, Ian broached the subject.

"We do appreciate your care, but it's time to return to our barracks."

Mr. Hade gathered his thoughts.

"I've had a letter from Norm Green with the same request to get you all to Hill Top. My wife is becoming concerned at how familiar our girls are with Ben and Fred."

"Mr. Hade, you have beautiful daughters," Bill felt awkward.

"Sir, it would be better to act quickly. It won't help to draw our departure out longer than a day or so," Ian spoke carefully.

"I can do better. I replied by the same messenger. The plan is that I will take

Ben and Fred in my dray, with two of my sons as escort, to meet one sent by my brother-in-law."

"When do we leave?" Ian asked.

"Tomorrow." Then he added, with a chuckle, "Our girls will be away visiting a neighbour, they'll be leaving early with Patrick and Shaun. Easier that way."

"Your brother-in-law, he's just as devious," Bill said.

Mr. Hade laughed, "You're fine ones to talk, after I've been listening to Andrew."

"Did he tell you about the carved faces on the dead tree trunks?"

"Yes. We have every intention of making a trip to see them. We do hope you will visit us again?"

"You can be sure we will, thank you," Ian shook Hade by the hand.

Early next morning, they received a visit from Patrick and Shaun, who stayed for a mug of tea. There were firm handshakes and they departed as the sun rose over the horizon. They would remain good friends in the years ahead.

*

Ian, Bill and John watched Jane and Jenny leave with their two brothers as the sun touched the top of the trees. Soon after Ben and Fred were helped into the dray. It was sad saying goodbye to Mrs. Hade. Though it had been a wonderful place to stay, their barracks – though not so comfortable – were home. What they missed the most was the camaraderie of their police mates.

The escort was cheerful, slow and determined. Mr. Hade drove for five hours to the meeting place. Duck's Corner camp lay on the edge of a swamp – actually an overflow from the river. Ian found a man and dray waiting plus a fire burning.

"Do you know who's waiting for us?" Mr. Hade asked Ian.

"It's Tom Hunt. He and his brother run a carrying business. We met them some time ago," Ian nodded.

Introductions were made. Mr. Hade probed Tom on the capacity of his business, making sure to follow up the connection. With mugs of tea consumed and final goodbyes said, the drays headed off, one back to the plains, the other to the barracks.

Ian wanted to know how Bob Pringle was getting on cooking.

"He's doing very well, but it's a bit stormy given Betsy and Bob argue, and neither will give in!" Tom answered.

"Last time you mentioned the food tent had been extended?" Bill asked.

Tom thought for a moment. "They both work hard, nothing is wasted. Everyone comes for a meal if they have the money. The police certainly do, so there's never any trouble."

"What's the chance of a marriage?" Ian was curious.

Tom laughed, "Your guess is as good as mine on that score."

"What do you really think?" Ian tried again.

"I don't know Ian, we'd like to see it. They are certainly suited. We'll just see how this develops."

It was not a good night for Fred. He was having a difficult time with his upper leg. He could limp along with a stick, which Mr. Hade had made, but it was not easy on uneven ground. Fiercely independent, he struggled.

At the farm, Jenny had recognised his independence, even encouraged it, to her mother's concern. Now, regardless of his pain, Fred was determined to look after both himself and Ben.

Ben in turn had become close to Jane, who was a better than average portraitist. He had loved watching her concentration with the brush. Jane had a talent for capturing faces in all their moods. Her darning of his shirt was so neat, it was almost unnoticeable. So when Ben heard Mrs. Hade declare she didn't want her daughters marrying Constables, he knew they must leave. Her brother Norm in the police was enough.

"Sam, these are good men, but we need farmers," Mrs. Hade had said.

"Elizabeth, I do see your point…" he shrugged.

Ben was bitter. Would he ever find a girl like Jane again? Unlikely.

*

Next morning, they broke camp long before the sun was even a glow on the eastern horizon. Tom pulled up five hours later to make a fire and boil the quart-pots for tea. They arrived at the barracks after twilight.

Sergeant Green met them near his office and paid Tom for the job.

"Tom, you have somewhere to stay?" Ian asked.

"Yes thanks, Ian. I've a cousin here and can get a bed."

There was no doubt about the welcome from the police in the barracks. The barracks was far happier with several in residence. There was lots of news exchanged and questions asked about their adventures. Not much news had come from the city police, other than Charley who had sent word that he was back in town, where beds were undercover and snakes creeping into his swag were no longer a hazard.

Fred and Ben were taken to the local doctor, as directed by Sergeant Green, keen to know when they would be fit to mount a horse. Having two men on foot could be a problem. They'd almost certainly get up to mischief.

There were new girls in *that* tent, and his two men would be bound to locate them. Then he'd have Mr. Wickham in his office again. The Wickhams of his world were a headache – his boys had to have relaxation and the girls were clean. He left his office and went home.

*

Fred came back from the doctor, who had confessed, "It'll be some time before you can ride a horse. Only when the wound is healed."

"How can I speed up the healing?" Fred was frustrated.

"By walking, keeping the wound clean, and not riding a horse."

Now sitting on his straw mattress, Fred decided to make every effort to improve his leg. He thought of Jenny, and what it would mean to win her hand. Before leaving the farm, he'd asked to speak to her father.

Hade had admitted, "I've been waiting for you to come see me."

"You have?"

"Mr. Hall, I'm not blind. So what are your intentions in regard to Jenny?"

"I'd like to ask her to marry me, Mr. Hade."

"That's what I thought. Now I'd like you to wait a year. If you are still of the same mind, approach me."

"Yes, Mr. Hade. You have my word."

"One other matter, you will no doubt wish to communicate?"

"Yes, Mr. Hade, if you are agreeable?"

"Do it through Mrs. Green for safety."

"I understand, Mr. Hade."

They ended with a firm handshake.

*

As Fred sat on his bed wondering about his next assignment, he heard a call. The Sergeant wanted to see him.

Mrs. Hade had sensed what was "in the wind". She had written to her brother about Fred and Jenny. The note made it clear her daughter would not be marrying a trooper.

"He'd be away for long periods just like our father, and it was hard on mother."

Green remembered, despite the absences, their mother had been happy. Now what to do about Fred? There was a role he needed filled – it would solve a problem for both the Force and the lad. Fred limped into the small room leaning on his stick. The Sergeant waved him to a wooden stool, and he sat and waited.

"I've had the medical report and I've a letter from my sister. I've got a job for you, but you'll have to be walking without the stick. Come back in three weeks."

"Yes, Sir. Does that mean I can visit my parents?"

"Yes. When you return, you'll be trained in stock work, in preparation for an extended undercover role."

Fred looked surprised, "This other job, where is it?"

"North of here, and you'll be under deep cover. You will not acknowledge any police you might know. Only when you are settled in will you be told the problem. Do you understand, Mr. Hall?"

"Yes, Sergeant. Now I see why I'm to write to Jenny through your wife."

"Not frequently. Only rarely we will get word to her – it will be just too dangerous. You're going to be in the company of some lethal characters. The last bloke in the role has vanished. So you will be properly trained."

Fred left the office deep in thought. He couldn't help wondering if the Sergeant was giving him a choice of livelihood, knowing what Mrs. Hade thought. He wanted to talk with Bill and Ian.

*

They had been writing their reports all day, now Ian and Bill squatted in the late afternoon sun outside the barracks.

"Fred has been looking for us, I've been told," Bill remarked.

"Not a surprise, he's been wanting to talk since leaving the farm," Ian replied.

"So you felt it too. Every time, something happened that stopped him," Bill mused.

"Let's go and see what the barrack's meal shed is offering now," Ian laughed.

"Fred's got girl trouble," Bill opined.

"We would've been blind not to have seen it."

At dinner, they were not in the least surprised to be joined by Fred.

"I've got a problem," he blurted.

"Jenny?" Ian wore the smallest smile.

Both his friends burst out laughing. Bill put his arm across his shoulder, "Fred, your friends aren't blind."

Fred blushed. He didn't understand his friends – he was serious. Fred waited patiently for their mirth to subside. "There's another matter that I need advice on," he paused. "I have some money put away and I'd like to increase it. I've heard talk about investing capital."

Both men raised an eyebrow. Ian asking "Please explain, Fred?"

"I've heard you talk of moving money from India to England in trade goods. You did the same coming to Sydney, with goods suitable for mining. And that talk about how well you've done investing in that company of traders. Keeping capital in the bank and using your profit to trade. My money is doing nothing. I want it to grow."

"Fred, you've a sharp ear." Bill was surprised.

"It's my best ability and a useful one," he grinned.

"This is news to us, Fred." Ian scratched his chin thoughtfully.

"We all learn to keep our secrets safe," Fred admitted. "Are you able to help me?"

Ian nodded. "Yes, though you make any investment at your own risk. Understood?"

"I accept the risk, Ian."

"Bill can give you the name of a man in the city, who will assist you – an ex-policeman. He'll look after you."

"How did you make it?" Bill was curious.

"Bits and pieces in the alleyways in the old town. I've always been good at saving. It's the only way out of certain streets."

"Fred, I know what you're hiding. I've been there too, as has Ian. We all had to survive in our youth," Bill spoke quietly. "Is that why you joined the police?"

"I hate those who prey on the weak."

"So where are you now, Fred?'

"On top of the world, now I've met Jenny."

"Whatever your future will be, we're here," Ian assured him. "I've heard you're leaving for the city, to train for an undercover appointment, all hush-hush."

Fred grinned.

Chapter Twenty Seven

Bernie Sharp and Barry Hodge were both unmarried and young. Back from patrol, with reports completed, they wanted to hear what had been happening while they were away.

Near midday, Bernie suggested, "Let's go to Ma Shell's food tent. She always knows what's what!"

They all liked her laugh and her fare – inevitably a pot of stew. No one ever fell ill after eating in her tent. The only trick was never to ask what was in it.

The last time they were in Hill Top, her tent was the last in a row. Now, so many more had been erected that it was closer to the middle.

"Hill Top is a good name," Barry commented.

As they walked four abreast with Bill and Ian, no one spoke to them. Some even crossed the street, or grimaced and muttered. Ian and Bill nodded to a few men. Bernie and Barry only ogled the girls on the street. Most eligible girls were with an older woman who glared, and made her charge turn from any attention. Sometimes words of warning were loud enough to be heard. Bernie generally laughed, Barry just ignored the old biddies.

"Another one making tracks to the Sergeant's office," Ian guessed.

They strolled past Wickham's well-stocked store, but saw no sign of Wickham or his bossy wife. The grog shanty was still beside the tree and a couple of the girls were sitting outside, on wooden barrels. The police received a friendly wave and some words of invitation, much to the disgust of two women walking past.

"Do we know them?" Ian asked.

"Who, those old biddies who have just passed us?"

"No, those on the barrels?"

"Not that I remember!"

"Same here. I don't think so. We'd have to be pretty drunk to think they were pretty."

"Ian, we were very drunk!"

"Perhaps, it's hard to remember."

Bernie and Barry threw insults to the girls about their make-up, receiving in return a mouthful of profanity. These kinds of open-air theatrics delighted locals.

Bill and Ian pulled aside the tent flap of Ma's food tent. There were a few men eating out of bowls on the benches, with mugs of beer beside them. Alcohol dulled the senses, making the meal more enjoyable, especially when unsure what you were consuming!

When sober, most men would pull back in shock at the primitive set-up. Whisky was the glue which kept the food tents successful. Ma was a large woman with a ready tongue, as rough as her timber logs around the benches. She had a kind heart, loved a laugh, mostly at someone else's expense, like her man's. Everyone assumed they were married, though no one was sure given her earlier occupation.

Ma saw the four policemen enter her tent and beckoned them to a bench which they could all sit around.

She grinned, "Well, you're a skinny lot, I must say."

She gave Bill a poke in the ribs. "You ain't put on any fat since I last saw ya."

"No Ma, whereas you're as large as life."

She laughed and patted him on the head. "What'll you have boys?"

"What have you got for hungry men?"

"Stew."

"We'll have a helping, please."

"Coming up, Bill."

She brought bowls of thick stew from a large black bubbling pot hanging from an iron hook over the open fire. It was within view at the back of the tent.

She walked back to their bench, "What does ya want ta drink?"

"Ale please, Ma," Barry said.

"That's what I thought y'd say. I dunna know where it comes from, but it won't kill ya."

This was the age of cast-iron stomach. The stew was going down well. The ale was warm but it helped to settle the stew.

"Doing well, I see?" Bill asked Ma.

"I say to meself, we do well 'ere."

"Your old man behaving himself?"

"'E is, if 'e knows what's good for 'im, 'e's better than no one but only just!" she laughed merrily.

Ian remembered her earlier comments and smiled.

"If I were only a year or two younger, I'd show ya a thing or two!" Ma winked.

"Ma, that'd be before we was born!" Bernie shot back.

She cackled, firing back at him, "Boy, put that stew in ya, drink up and I can still show ya a thing or two!"

Bernie sensed now was the time to retreat.

"I dare say age has nothing to do with knowledge," Barry stood by his friend.

Ma wasn't quite sure what he meant. She'd been listening to men all her life. Barry was a young man with a lot to learn.

She turning to Barry with a smile, "Get on with ya, boy!"

Cackling, she returned to her pot, stirring whatever rose to the surface, keeping it out of sight. No one minded. Ma was a favourite character. In her youth, she'd been a "lady of the night". How she turned up here, no one knew.

The men finished their meal, called out farewell to Ma, and walked back to the barracks.

"Are we going out again tonight?" Bill asked Ian.

"Aren't you too old?" Bernie chipped in.

Ian put a headlock on Bernie. "Who is too old now?"

After a struggle, Ian let him go, though none too gently.

"Bill and I will be going out to a certain tent after we put you to bed," he winked.

Bernie looked shocked, "You aren't serious, are you?"

Bill and Ian guffawed at their own joke.

"I've heard something interesting about that tent," Bill admitted.

"We'll go after a meal at the barracks, I want to know at least once today what I'm eating."

"Ma Shell, I like her. She's rough and tough, but I suspect a different person inside," Bernie mused.

"She's a kind person. There was a problem here when it was small. A family was having a bad time and Ma Shell went to their aid. No one else offered any help. Then she had no tent and was poor, but she had courage. A couple of years later, a member of that family returned and gave her that tent, as well as everything inside it," Bill recalled.

"Are the family still here?" Ian asked.

"No, long gone. Heard they now own a large run out west."

After a meal at the barracks, the four changed out of their uniforms and strolled down to the street-ladies' tent for some fun.

*

It was in the early hours of the next morning that they staggered home, loudly. No one was there to complain, nor could anyone tell if they found their beds. None surfaced until the evening meal – even then they were silent and shaky.

The following morning, there was a note for the men to go to the office.

"Who might have complained this time?" Bill asked no one in particular.

"I don't remember much about the night," Ian worried. "What did we get up to?"

"I don't remember."

Barry cleared his throat. "Ian, you got the girls to act out positions you'd seen in an Indian temple. Caused a few problems. None of us are double jointed!"

All of them decided they remembered nothing. Ian led the way into the Sergeant's office, to see him sitting quietly at his desk – an expression of resignation on his face.

"Mr. Percy, Mr. Todd, Mr. Sharp, and Mr. Hodge. I would have thought the four of you could've had a party, without disrupting one part of the settlement."

Bernie managed to ask, "Which part was that Sergeant?"

Sergeant Green spoke quietly, "Mr. Percy, never before have I had the owner of that particular establishment complain to me. He told me most of his girls wouldn't be able to work for a few days as a result of your visit."

Bernie seemed all at sea. "Sergeant, what's his problem?"

Bernie needed to know when to keep quiet.

"He explained that his girls were not trained to act out certain positions as you, Mr. Percy, had seen in an Indian temple. He also reminded me these 'positions' were not Christian. I'm glad my wife didn't hear."

They trooped out of his office, glaring at Bernie. Some Sergeants would have torn him apart for speaking out of turn. Someone always complained.

Ian wished he had seen the Sergeant's face when the brothel owner paid him a call.

Bill spoke to Ian quietly as they left, "That didn't go too bad, did it?"

"I've got a sore head. What didn't go too bad?"

"You drank more than I did," Bill grinned.

"Not too loud, Bill. I would've loved to have been there when the brothel keeper came in."

"I wonder if this was the first time he's had a complaint from that source?" Bill laughed.

Bernie and Barry caught up with them.

"I've heard Fred and Ben are leaving by coach today," Bernie informed them.

"Where are they now?" Ian asked.

"At the doctor's sick bay."

The sick bay was a small extension to the barracks at the opposite end to the office. No one liked it – a grim little room and not in the least comfortable.

"We'd better go see them now before they leave," Ian suggested.

Both Fred and Ben were dressed and ready to leave, with their bundles packed.

"Remember to ask your father about the Holt family tree," Bill reminded Ben.

"I won't forget."

They reminisced about the valley, until Fred cried, "That's alright for you, Ian, you weren't shot."

"No. It's wise to avoid bullets."

Ben grinned. "Did I hear the brothel keeper came to complain your behaviour wasn't Christian?"

Bernie and Barry chipped in, "Not us! We've never seen the like of what Ian and Bill got up to."

"Ben, these two boys lack the spirit of adventure!" Bill shook his head sadly.

The doctor arrived and the men went silent, as he grumbled at the police.

"I was called this morning to treat some pulled muscles and tendons. I hope you'll not make a habit of such assaults."

"We'll try not to, Doctor," Ian replied meekly.

His friends all grinned with enjoyment. Bill's confused look didn't deceive the doctor for one moment.

Sheepishly, the good doctor was thanked for his troubles.

"I'm going to miss Fred and Ben in the camp," Bill said.

"I've heard Fred is going undercover. We're never to acknowledge him. It'll be hard," Bernie said quietly.

Ian nodded.

"Ben is bound to turn up again over some matter or other," Bill filled the silence.

The remainder of the day was spent checking their equipment, adding rations to their saddle bags, checking the leather straps for wear, and preparation for the next patrol.

Bernie and Barry were called to the office and given their next assignment. They would be leaving the barracks next morning.

Bill and Ian were called in during the late afternoon.

"I've had disturbing reports about a new goldmining area in some steep country. Also a problem in a new diggings on the plains. I want you to scout both places. Send a report back," the Sergeant explained.

"It would be useful to know the source. Time will be important if we are to investigate both," Ian advised.

"The first is from an old friend at school with me. The second is from Cedric Hall, whom I believe you know?" He looked at them carefully.

"Yes – a good, hard-working family."

"Do you want us to contact your friend?" Bill asked.

"Yes – check up on his welfare. His name is Harry Elms."

"How far away is this new field?" Ian asked.

"I'm told two days riding."

"In that case we should leave before sun-up," Ian mused.

They walked down to the stables to check on their horses and talk with the farrier.

"I thought one of the shoes was a bit loose," Bill mentioned.

"Now it is fixed, Mr. Todd."

"My horse?" Ian queried.

"No problem with her, Mr. Percy."

"Thank you."

"Please put them in the night yard. We're off early in the morning," Bill asked.

"Don't let those young police take our mounts. They are also leaving early," Ian warned.

"I'll be up and make sure they take their own horses, never you fear."

With plans for the day ahead made, Bill and Ian returned to the barracks.

"I think we might go out and try that new eating tent?"

"Lead on, Bill."

As they walked past the office, their Sergeant came to the doorway, "Going out again?"

The men nodded.

He sighed, "Do you think you can be careful? I don't want another complaint."

"I'm sure we can, Sergeant!" Bill smiled.

Green had heard a few stories about what regimental officers got up to when fully tanked. His police were mild by comparison. Mr. Percy's army background did make Green worry what else he might try. It did make life interesting.

Walking down the track between rows of tents, a couple of men called out some words about their exploits of two nights before. Stories had already begun to circulate.

The new food tent was opposite the grog tent. It comprised a tent and part slab hut with a fire out back, with black pots hanging from a metal frame. As they entered, a young girl looked up from a back bench. An older lady indicated that the young girl was to stay in her seat.

"What do you want?" the hostess asked.

"What's on the menu?" Ian asked.

"Stew and fresh damper."

Bill watched various emotions cross the woman's face. He could tell they were not welcome. She waited for Ian's response.

"The stew and damper, then."

The bench gave a clear view of the entrance. They ate in silence, until Bill beckoned the woman over. She came reluctantly, and he asked, "The stew is good and the flavour – what is it?"

"Dried rosemary."

Walking back to the barracks, Bill commented, "That young girl was staring at us. I wonder what that old woman's problem was?"

"Probably protecting her daughter from wild men."

"She was pretty," Bill laughed.

"Too young for you, Bill."

"I suppose so."

As they passed the barracks, they noticed a light still burning in Sergeant's office.

"He's never here at this time of the night, something must be wrong." Bill worried.

Ian gently knocked, before entering.

Sergeant Green looked up from his desk. "Just the men I want to see, and are you sober, too?"

"We're sober, what can we do?" Bill assured him.

"I have a job for you. There's been an accident or a hold-up – I don't know which. The coach in which Holt and Hall were travelling has rolled."

Sergeant paused, and Bill asked, "What's the real problem?"

The Sergeant looked hard at Bill. "Mr. Todd, you have just proved your ability. By asking the right question, you have the heart of the problem."

He stopped talking for a moment. "When the ruined coach was examined, there was no one inside it. We don't know where the occupants are."

"What time would you like us to leave?" Ian asked.

"I've already spoken to Sharp and Hodge. They've gone on ahead. Leave in moonlight tomorrow morning."

"When this is settled, do we continue with the other jobs or come back here?"

"Continue with the other jobs – no need to come back here. Just find them safe, please."

"We will, Sergeant," Bill said quietly.

Chapter Twenty Eight

They left the office, followed by the Sergeant, locking the door behind him. Now deeply concerned for their friends, the pair returned to the barracks, deciding to leave before dawn, given there was a full moon.

They rode east. Dawn came and the first shards of sunlight splintered the bush, waking the birdlife. Slowly the sunlight crept down the tree trunks, until their angular forms hardened. Chewing on cooked meat, the riders continued towards the high country.

After midday, they found a roadside hut, set back from the road. There was a hitching rail under a tree – two horses tied to it. They looked familiar.

"Police horses," Ian nodded.

"Does that mean Bernie and Barry?" Bill asked.

There was no one in the hut, and Bill began to look carefully about the ground.

"Ian, there's been a struggle, look. That cloth? I've seen it at the waterfall camp – belongs to Charley."

"Bill, these are city horses – one could have been Charley's?"

They continued to stare at the earth. "Bill, can you follow the tracks?"

"As a boy, a native taught me to hunt game. I'll give it a go."

He made off towards some trees, with Ian leading the two horses plus their own.

"Keep a gun handy," Bill suggested.

"When I have a free hand," Ian shrugged.

The footprints led to a drop in the path, disappearing down into a small valley dense with scrub.

"Let's hide the horses amongst those trees and continue without them," Ian turned to his friend.

They tied the horses, and climbed down to the valley floor. Bill surprised himself – the faint markings were not easy to follow.

"Any horse tracks?" Ian asked.

Indeed Bill made out signs of horses hooves indented in the earth.

"I think we're going to find them." Ian was hopeful.

Patches of green grass now hid the footprints – but they could hear voices. Moving quietly amongst the trees, the pair suddenly came upon Fred and Ben tied to a tree. Tied to a second nearby tree trunk were Bernie, Barry, Alex and Charley. There was no one else in sight.

Charley saw Ian and Bill first, and groaned at the humiliation. These two would never let him forget it.

"What are you doing here?" Bill stared at Charley in bemusement.

"What in the bloody hell do you think?"

"Just untie us," Alex squirmed.

"How'd you end up in this mess?" Bill scratched his head.

"We came around a corner on the road, and found the mail coach being held up. Taken by surprise. There were a lot of them – well organised. One group took the gold box and rode off. The other group divided us, took us down here, tied us up, and vanished," Alex explained, rubbing his now-free hands to get the blood circulating again.

Ian untied Fred and Ben.

"I'd recognise that voice, the ringleader. One day I'll find him," Fred added.

Now the men were all released, they trudged up the hill to where the horses were sheltering with Bernie and Barry.

"How did you two get caught?" Ian asked Bernie.

"We saw the police horses and walked into the hut to enquire. Two men disarmed us."

"Didn't you stop to think it might be dangerous?" Ian asked gently.

"It didn't look dangerous, it was just a hut," Barry protested.

"What would have happened if we hadn't found you?" Ian pointed out.

Barry looked shocked. "They would have told somebody?"

"When?" Ian smiled sadly.

"Do you mean too late?" Bernie said.

"That's exactly what I mean. This is an isolated valley. No one would come here."

Bernie and Barry left for Hill Top to inform their Sergeant that Fred and Ben were safe. The others made camp down near a creek, where Bill obligingly caught a fish of reasonable size.

Bill was curious to know what Alex and Charley were doing so far from their normal habitat.

"What do you think I am, a fuckin' rabbit living in a hole?" Charley exclaimed.

"By habitat, I meant town life," Bill answered meekly.

"Bill, you're an effing liar, you meant nothing of the kind," Charley glared at him.

"Charley, what are you doing so far from the sea? Is that better?" Bill laughed.

"We came to rescue Ben from fuckin' people like you."

Bill tried hard not to smile.

"So that's why you looked daggers at us when you saw Ian," he said.

"Bill, you are a right pain!"

"How far can you take Ben and Fred tomorrow?" Ian leant across offering Charley some more fish.

"Our mounts are strong. We can go to the nearest police barracks and organise another coach," Charley replied.

"Anything we can do to help?" Ian asked.

"Ian, it's a pity you can't have an equally good man as your partner. It's a sad world," Charley grinned.

"Bush police to the rescue," Bill countered.

Next morning, shaking hands cheerfully, they parted, each going their own way. Ian and Bill headed to the goldfields to search for Harry Elms.

*

"What were Charley and Alex really doing this side of the mountains?" Bill asked as they rode along the track.

"They told us?"

"It doesn't hold water."

"What makes you say that?"

"The coach travels faster than they ride – paid to move fast. I can't see Alex or Charley giving the coach an escort."

Ian scratched his head. "What do you think, Bill?"

"There are two things which bother me. How did our Sergeant know about the hold-up and why were those two men at the scene? I suspect it has to do with Fred going undercover."

"You could be right. There are aspects which don't add up. What happened to the coach driver? Was he an undercover cop? He's vanished. Alex is no fool. I think both those city police know a great deal more than we do," Ian mused.

"Are we going to the goldfields or back to Hill Top to get some answers?" Bill asked.

"I think we'll go back to Hill Top tonight."

With this decision made, they rode back and managed to speak to their Sergeant, who reluctantly agreed with their assessment.

"Please don't talk about it to anyone. Lives are at risk. Yes, it seems the crooks and police were in on it. Not quite checkmate. At least no one died," he said.

*

Next day they rode out in search of the Sergeant's friend.

"It's rather pleasant on our own again," Bill winked at Ian.

"Sometimes I could wring John's neck being so cheerful at breakfast," Ian groaned.

Bill laughed, thinking of their friend's irritating humour in the first hours of the morning.

"Friends are good for short periods," he said.

They rode at a steady pace, as if shaking dust from the horses hooves. Leaving the settlement the scent of cesspits receded, replaced by eucalypts. These valleys were mostly free of trees, filled with wildlife. In the early evening, they camped beside a creek. Great flocks of galahs roosted in the trees for the night. They screeched so noisily you might swear their neighbours on the next branch were deaf. Ian was forever asking Bill their names.

Bill wasn't so enamoured. "They shit everywhere. You can't camp anywhere they decide to roost."

Meanwhile, Ian prepared the fire and Bill hobbled the horses. Ian stretched his legs, walking in one direction, and Bill in another.

When the meal was completed, Bill wondered out loud, "I've been thinking all day about what would've happened if those two police horses hadn't been at that hitching rail?"

"Not only the horses. No one knew about the men. It doesn't bear thinking what would have happened if we hadn't come along. They were lucky," Ian added.

"When I was young, I enjoyed time with a native boy. We were good friends," Bill mused.

"You still see him?" Ian asked.

"No, he died a long time ago – venereal disease. I do miss his talk and laughter. I would've been about seven years old. I get a cold shiver down my spine thinking about it. If I hadn't gone on those hunting trips… Some of my mates laughed … but I went with all the same," Bill commented.

"I think the Old Man recognised your knowledge. Have you thought about that?" Ian mused.

"No, and I don't want to."

"You'll always have your friend as a part of you. You loved him."

"Let's get back to the operation. Our Sergeant worried about the unexpected. I wonder how deep he was involved?"

"I'm interested in Barry and Bernie's role. Why didn't they let on about Ben and Fred being police?"

Neither man had a good night's sleep, until in the early morning Ian left his swag, stumbling down to the creek where a water rat swam from one side to the other.

When he returned, it was to find Bill feeding the fire. They fried some leftover fish and ate in silence. Packing up the camp, they unhobbled the horses, mounted and rode away. Neither spoke for several hours.

In the distance, a horseman could be seen coming from the west.

"Who is it?" Ian asked.

"Our silence is about to be shattered," Bill smiled.

"Our talkative friend, John Hale?"

"Yes, indeed. I wonder what he's doing out here?"

"We're about to find out."

They waited as John's horse plodded along, crossing a gully and coming up the other side before riding around some dead logs and on to the bare earth in front of them.

They nodded a greeting. Bill asked, "Didn't know you were out here. What's happening?"

John shrugged.

"Heading north-west?"

John nodded, "Yup. I'll join you for camp tonight. I wasn't looking forward to another night on my own."

"We'll be happy," Ian submitted to the inevitable.

"Hope I'm not too chatty".

Bill laughed, "John, you 'll be talking as soon as the sun's coming up. It's hard not to hear you. The birds are on one scale and you're on another."

Bill groaned, "Some events were meant to happen."

For the next couple of hours, John rode beside them without speaking at all. This was far more daunting than his usual chatter.

"Is everything alright?" Bill asked at last.

"Bill, did you say something?"

"I said are you okay?" Bill was now getting worried.

"Not really, but pleased to see you and Ian."

"John, talk to us?"

John had completed a job and, on his way back, been told about a young married squatter couple who needed help. The directions were clear enough and he found their slab hut nestled in a small valley above a creek. They had a healthy vegetable garden and tidy grounds. He had ridden directly to their front door. After tying up his horse, he had knocked. A young man opened the door relieved at the sight of a policeman.

"You'll know what to do," the bloke had grunted, gesturing towards his wife in labour on the bed behind him. He was begging for help.

John had scratched his head. "I've helped deliver stock. Thought it was pretty much the same."

John stopped talking for a moment. "It was different. She screamed. Difficult. The husband didn't cope with his wife in such pain. A boy and a girl had come – the girl was stillborn. Both parents were emotionally drained."

"What did you do with…?" Ian asked.

"The husband asked me to bury her. I suggested he choose a place at a distance from their hut."

John was silent for some time.

"Chose a lovely place, under some trees in a glade. I suggested he bring his wife, after I'd dug a small grave. I read a burial service, they filled in the soil, in floods of tears. It was tough."

"Was that all?"

"Before leaving I asked what they named their son. Thomas said, 'My wife decided he is to be called John, in your honour. A policeman who came in our time of need'."

John had cried unashamedly as he rode away from that tiny grave.

Chapter Twenty Nine

Telling this tale helped clear his mind. John didn't notice he had fallen behind his friends.

Ian smiled, and Bill asked, "What are you thinking?"

"I wonder if baby John will be talkative?"

They both laughed.

They chose a camp site beside a long waterhole.

"If you don't mind, I'll keep to the shallow end," John said.

"I thought I taught you to swim!" Bill protested.

"But I've forgotten!"

Bill let him off the hook. He stripped and took to the water as if he'd been born in it. John looked at his friends. In the next life, they'd come back as fish.

The heat of the sun soon dried their clothes.

"Where do you go tomorrow?" Bill asked as they sat around the fire.

"There is a small settlement called Arch just ahead. I've been instructed to ride through it, observe anything of interest, then report to Sergeant Green."

The men gazed into the red-hot coals. Bill stirred the fire and sparks flew up like deranged butterflies.

"What about Barry and Bernie? Been subdued – not like them," Bill asked John.

John laughed, "Barry had to go out on a job in a hurry. Spied a lovely mare in the yard and, instead of asking the farrier, saddled up and rode out. On return he found an irate inspector demanding his head."

Bill laughed. "What'd he do?"

"Bernie doesn't like dust – clouds of dust make him very bad-tempered. A couple of days ago, a horseman rode fast through Hill Top. Bernie pulled him from his saddle. Gave him a proper blast."

"What did he say?" Ian asked, fascinated.

"Told the man he ought to be horsewhipped for the total inconsideration of the locals. The bloke was on the way to see a dying man. Bernie told him it was no excuse to leave half the community choking. The man, furious asked, 'Do you know who I am?', and Bernie said, 'I don't bloody well care who you are. Those are damn silly clothes – you look like a clown in a bad show.'"

"Who was he? " Ian held his breath.

John smiled, "The Church of England minister!"

There were peals of laughter around the fire.

"Sergeant told them if they dared to identify Ben or Fred as police, they'd be sacked," John continued.

Bill looked at Ian. "Now we know why they were so good!"

*

At the next tent community, the occupants looked on edge. Older women and young girls were washing. A man stood nearby with a rifle.

"They're washing pottery demijohns," John said quietly.

"So, why?" Bill asked.

"Just ride on as if we've seen nothing of interest," John replied.

They parted, watching John disappear and continued north-west for the remainder of the day, riding into wild looking country. It was steep and rugged, with more trees on the hills and small, sharp valleys. The tracks were not always visible. It was ideal country for roaming bands.

"I wouldn't want to be carrying anything of value," Bill commented.

Ian laughed quietly, "We're under observation."

"I saw a couple of men a mile back. They'll let us pass – they won't want trouble with the police," Bill said.

The hills ahead marked the final barrier before the goldfield just beyond this wild country.

"There's no safe place here to make camp," Bill fretted.

"Let's ride for another hour or two," Ian suggested.

"We must be close to that mining creek?" Bill squinted as he gazed ahead.

"Do you smell any wood smoke?"

"No, nor have I seen any tracks."

They rode on through the trees, around dead undergrowth, large rocks, and impenetrable thickets. Anyone could be lurking amongst the rocks to pounce on an unwary miner.

"Ian, we ought to make the last climb the top of that rise," Bill suggested after looking around.

He pointed at a steep hill on the western side of the track.

"We can fill our water bottles before the climb," he added.

Ian looked at the steep hill shaking his head, "You do choose them, don't you, Bill?"

"We'll have to lead our horses up that bank, more times than we can ride them. But at the top its likely clear of growth – safer to camp."

They filled water flasks and began the ascent close to sunset, leading their horses in the fading light. A few times Ian turned to gaze back at a rather splendid view over a wide range of country.

Bill turned a couple of times wondering why Ian was so slow. Knowing what he was thinking, he smiled and continued to climb. Reaching the summit in late twilight, he was relieved that indeed it was a suitable place to camp, sheltered between rocks. Ian prepared a fire and the quart-pots. They drank mugs of hot tea along with fried meat.

"What was Bernie's problem with the dust?" Ian asked.

"Someone told him that town dust could be dangerous, whereas plains dust is pure. Bernie sometimes has breathing problems."

"Would have thought he knew how the various priests and ministers dress?"

"I don't think Bernie has much respect for the church – not after he witnessed a minister having a man whipped. Colours a boy's outlook," Bill commented.

"Surely he knows not all men are like that?" Ian said.

"I think the victim may have been a member of his own family," Ian explained.

"He has a right to his view. Which reminds me, did you talk with John about the burial?"

"Yes, I did."

"Did he name the infant?"

"Chose his mother's name. You know, Ian, John is remarkable. Did a naming ceremony before the burial."

"Did he now?"

"I asked how come he had a prayer book. His Sergeant told him that on the frontier, he represented civilisation. This meant helping people in dire situations."

"He's doing what we're meant to be doing. Isn't easy. I hope I never have to bury a child again."

"Your own...?" Bill stated softly.

"Rather not go there."

With these words they turned in for the night. In the morning Bill woke up to see Ian had made the fire.

Ian looked at his friend and shook his head. "Virgin country. Magnificent. The views are stunning. Feeds the mind and soul."

Bill replied cheerfully, "If it's all the same to you, I'm interested in food. Then I'll feed my mind."

"Well, at least it's a lovely sunrise."

"Is it?"

"The morning is wasted on you, Bill."

Riding along the crest of the hill, Bill sniffed, "I smell smoke, wood burning. I'd say pine."

On a cold day, it would be bleak up here, but Bill was enjoying being on top of the world.

Bill led the way the way down into a small valley. The valley looked squashed uncomfortably between the tall hills on either side of the creek.

Bill turned in his saddle, "I heard you laugh?"

"Thinking of the Hade boys and their carved faces on the tree trunks. They would suit this place."

Bill smiled, "I don't like this valley – doesn't feel right."

They reached the creek where men were panning for gold – looking for that speck of brilliance amongst the gravel. This was a small goldfield due to its difficult terrain. Bill led the way down, close to the base of the hill. The previous night they had decided their story would be that Harry Elms was Bill's uncle. The first few men they asked had never heard of him. Bill and Ian were more alert than usual. Most wise miners created a circle of friendships nearby. None might be trustworthy, but if one was having problems, it could affect the group. Sometimes this worked well and, at other times, it was a hindrance.

Neither Bill nor Ian wanted to linger any longer than it took to find Harry Elms. There was a silent threat in the air. Men stared, then turned away to their panning, without any interest. There was no laughter – out of character in a place like this. Bill paused beside one man bending over his pan. Beside him was a patch of clear sand. Someone had used a stick to write, "HARRY ELMS HAS GONE".

Bill stared as a man wiped the sand clean with his foot.

"Where can I find my uncle, Harry Elms?"

"Never heard of him, sorry."

The man bent his head over his pan and continued his search for the elusive specks of gold. Almost at the end of the line of miners, one admitted quietly to Bill, "Your uncle left here a week or so ago – heading west."

Bill and Ian turned their horses back along the creek. No other miner appeared to even notice their passing.

"Bill, they are afraid to speak, I can feel it," Ian said quietly.

No one tried to stop them. At the edge of this goldfield, they turned for one last look down the creek, before heading west.

For the next few hours they rode in silence, until Ian remarked, "We're still under observation. Have you seen any tracks?"

"Yes, a couple made after the last rain."

"I don't suppose anyone would tackle those hills, so we'll follow the creek," Ian speculated.

They rode on beside the water. Bill looked across at Ian. "What are you thinking?"

"If I didn't feel under threat, this would be a beautiful ride – tall, graceful trees, the water gurgling over the stones, the swirling of the current through the larger pools."

Bill laughed, "I did ask!"

"I thought you'd found an interest in the landscape. If I'd said I can see a pretty girl, you'd be instantly interested."

"Of course!"

"So what's the difference?"

About mid-afternoon, Bill commented, "I've seen nothing to indicate a camp. If Harry did come this way, he's kept on the move."

"Keep your eyes peeled, he's likely to be on foot. This is about a day's walk from the gold field. If he's being followed, there ought to be a camp near here," Ian added.

As they rode, Ian used his telescope to scan the surrounding hills and was relieved to find no sign of pursuit. All the same, he didn't feel safe, wishing they were in the open valleys again.

Bill began to follow a booted track on open soil. It left the side of the creek, climbed up the side of the hill, and went behind a clump of trees.

Bill remarked, "Someone camped here. No sign of a fire, but you can see where sticks were moved to make a bed, the way we do at our camp. When he left here, he walked along this side of the hill, tree to tree, as if he suspected he was being followed by someone."

Bill continued on foot, and Ian on his horse. The creek was still in sight when Bill spoke. "I think he's returned to the creek. We ought to find a place to camp."

"Let's waiting until twilight – cross the creek here, it's shallow enough with all the stones."

"I'd rather not advertise our presence with a fire tonight. We can make tea somewhere tomorrow," Bill said.

"I agree, these hills are too dark. We'll send a report at the first opportunity on that gold field."

Chapter Thirty

It was not the most cheerful of camps on this summer evening. The men talked quietly. Bill murmured, "Our Sergeant seems to have a large number supplying him with intelligence, don't you think?"

"He's certainly well connected. Who only says what he has to reveal?"

They talked about Harry Elms, speculating on why he had to leave the goldfield.

"And did he leave?" Bill asked.

"If so, whose footprints are we following?" Ian wondered.

Neither man found sleep easy with the dark hills enveloping them.

The next day, they were unable to boil a billy. Doing without tea was hard to bear. Away before sunrise, they crossed the creek in shadow. It would be several hours before the sun penetrated the valley. It would need to be overhead to bath the valley floor in full sunshine.

As they rode west, the open ground between the creek and the hills widened. The grass was better quality. The hills were less overgrown. There was a lightness – more wildlife in evidence. Those hills were lonely without birds and animals. Now the major change was the sunshine – as if they'd come out of a dark cave, into the light.

Riding another hour, the sky and bush brightened.

It was now mid-morning. The fire was burning by the time Bill had caught a fish, which, gutted, was in the pan. Only severe conditions, like escaping an awkward situation, made it necessary to forgo the first meal of the day.

Once the men were on their second mug of tea, Bill announced quietly, "We have a visitor."

"Where?"

"Coming from that hill behind us, on the other side of the creek."

"Continue as if we haven't seen him."

"Doesn't appear to be armed – looks middle-aged," Ian murmured.

Old clothes hung off the man, his beard was untrimmed and none too clean.

"A shepherd?" Bill wondered aloud.

A dog followed him. The man walked to the edge of their camp. "You police?"

Bill stood up. "Yes, we're police."

"I have a message from an old man who stayed with me."

He pointed to the hills behind them and continued talking, "He's gone to another settlement further up."

Again, he stopped and pointed up towards the hills.

"Was the old man okay?" Bill asked.

The man hesitated. "Have you come from that goldfield in the hills?"

"Aye."

"It has a bad reputation, men rarely escape. The old man was nearly caught."

Bill wondered if it was true. Ian decided he had been sent to deceive them. There was something shifty in his face.

The old man shuffled out of earshot.

Bill too was doubtful. "Too well fed for a shepherd. I think he's part of the group running that goldfield."

"In that case, we'll ride into the hills, then once out of sight, return and continue our search."

With this in mind, they relaxed and enjoyed their hot tea before continuing on their way. They were aware the man was watching their departure so crossed a couple of valleys, before doubling back to the creek.

Bill pulled up and looked at the bare ground. "There are men in front of us."

He pointed to the boot marks clearly visible on the dusty ground. A bit further along, he alighted, walked to a recent camp, knelt down to feel the black coals.

He stood up. "They're still warm. Couldn't be far ahead of us."

"We'll ride carefully, until we know who they are."

Keeping well out of sight amongst the trees on the creek, they urged their mounts on at a trot.

"If they're tracking the old man, he's doing well. There aren't many places to hide out here," Bill commented.

"He's lucky they aren't using dogs or he'd have no chance," Ian added.

They rode to the end of the next valley and sat in the quiet of a thicket, looking for movement of birds or kangaroos – anything to indicate humans. Nothing disturbed the valley's tranquility, when suddenly a flock of galahs rose up, towards the end of the valley indicating an alien presence.

The men spurred their horses into a gallop, but this section of the creek wasn't as easy. Several times they had to emerge on to open ground to avoid the steep banks and logs too large to jump. Bill and Ian had their guns close at hand.

Riding in and out of the trees, close to the water, the men lay about a hundred yards ahead, still oblivious to their approach. A cry echoed down the creek.

Bill hissed, "Let's ride straight at them. Be ready to fire at any threat."

With the chatter of the galahs nearby, the police had the benefit of surprise. They burst upon the scene - a wounded and bound man on the ground, surrounded by a number of bandits.

Bill fired, killing one of the bandits. The accomplices scattered in all directions. A couple had guns but were unaccustomed to combat. One fled, and Ian shot the other in the arm, putting him out of action. Still on his horse, Bill rode to near where a wounded man lay.

"Are you Harry Elms?" he asked.

The fellow nodded with relief.

"Can you mount behind him?" Bill pointed to Ian.

"I can if you help me?"

Bill alighted and helped him up behind Ian. Once firmly on the horse, Bill mounted his steed and they left the unarmed group and rode the end of the valley. It was essential to get as far away as possible while they still had light. They would need to push their mounts to keep up a canter for some hours yet.

"Are you okay behind Ian?" Bill asked Harry.

"No problem. I'm a light man."

"We'll be safe in a couple of hours. How badly were you hurt?" Bill asked.

Harry laughed, "I saw you coming up through the trees and cried out so you'd know where I was. I'm a hard man. The last week has been tough. I've slept in dead trees and old logs to keep ahead of them. Only got caught just before you came."

"How?" Bill asked.

"Had to sleep, couldn't keep going. One of them stumbled on top of me. I don't know who got the biggest shock."

"You had a good run to outwit them for a whole week. Good at bushcraft?" Ian mused.

"For a time I lived with the shadow people. Learnt lots of valuable lessons," he admitted, "There's not much of me, and I'd say you, Ian would weigh about the same by the feel of you."

"You could be right," Ian laughed.

It was two hours before Bill suggested, "We can slow down and still keep a steady pace."

But Ian wanted to keep riding to make the pursuit impossible. As they had eaten mid-morning, he was insistent they push on until the night camp.

"Harry, can you last out?" Ian asked.

"I told you, I'm a hard man."

In the late afternoon, they rode out into a valley, clear of trees – a wide spread of grasslands as far as the eye could see, except for a few old trees beside the creek.

They crossed the creek following animal tracks and rode across several low hills. These had long slopes on both sides of the rise, just a steady climb so different from the steep hills, graceful in their structure.

"Looks like we'll have a lovely sunset," Ian nodded at the pink streaks of cloud to the west.

"Is he always like this?" Harry asked.

"Ian would be forever writing about sunsets, if he wasn't a policeman."

"This land grows on you. It's hard and cruel with the bleak winters, droughts, and long hot summers."

"Harry, you are as bad as Ian. It's just land and sky, wet and dry!" Bill laughed.

"I think Bill would rather not spend all his days riding, the way we do," Ian added.

Bill spoke before Harry could say another word.

"I love this bloody country. I was born here – it's giving me a job. It's hard work, but I can't see it the way Ian does."

Finding a camp for the night, Harry was shocked to see the men undress and dive into the long waterhole. Harry stood with an open mouth. Ian and Bill were equally amused at his surprise.

It had never occurred to Harry that two men could strip off and swim up and down at a great pace. They yelled at him to come in. Harry shrugged. His clothes were filthy – it would be a good chance to clean up.

Once Harry was naked, Ian and Bill could see the extent of his injuries. They guessed he was a proud man, reticent to acknowledge pain. Being a man demanded silence.

Well out of Harry's hearing, Ian asked, "What do you think we can do?"

"The same weeds I used on John after his cattle problem?'

"Good idea."

"I see you have a bruise from that fall yesterday?" Ian added.

"What about me giving you a bruise, Ian?"

Ian laughed quietly, while trying to duck Bill's head under the water, "If you really thought you could do that."

Managing to escape a second ducking, Bill spluttered, as water cascaded down his face.

"I don't. I was taught never to hurt an older man!"

With these words still hanging in the air, Bill turned swiftly and swam down the pool to the safety of where Harry was cleaning his clothes. Ian was right behind him and smiled.

"Old man indeed, you're only a couple of years younger!"

These two men were powerful examples of manhood – not an ounce of fat on either. For once Harry was pleased they were on his side.

"Bill, being so young, bruises easily. Not like you and me who have learnt to be tough in the years behind us!" Ian winked at Harry.

"Bill uses a native weed to deal with the bruising. Would you like some?"

"You fellows are surprising, but okay, I'll give it a go."

Ian ducked out of the way as he saw Bill's hand come up out of the water laden with mud.

The mud fell back into the water with a splash. Pulling on their shorts, Bill went searching for the weeds and Ian walked down the creek looking for a couple ducks for their meal. Bill had also located some clay.

When Ian returned to camp soaking wet, he caught Bill's smile.

"Did you say something, Bill?"

"No, not that I can recall."

"Would you like to boil some water?"

"I can do that small job."

The birds were plucked and gutted, to the delight of a family of magpies keenly watching from the branches high above their camp.

Without their help, Harry realised he would be dead now. His gratitude was well hidden, but he would tell his friend, Norm Green.

"What was the problem in that goldfield?" Ian asked Harry.

"I went not long after gold was found. Did well. Managed to send a good quantity out. That field was a happy place for the first six months. Then a group arrived demanding gold for protection from thieves. Some men left but those who stayed had to pay for the protection. But those who tried to leave were brought back. No one escaped. The man you met was one who reported anyone who tried to leave. They would've been shocked to have you ride in. If you'd stayed too long, they would've found a way to stop you leaving." Harry took another mug of tea.

"Who actually runs that group?" Ian asked.

"Dunno. A mate heard one of the men talking about a hold-up in the east, where men were tied to trees. They thought it was a great joke because no one would find them."

Harry was tired, but not unaware of Bill and Ian's sudden alertness.

"What did I say?" Harry raised his eyebrows.

"Nothing, Harry, keep talking," Bill replied.

"We were concerned for our lives and I sent a report out to Norm Green. I suspect someone told the men who Norm represented. Warned they were coming for me, I ran." Harry took a breath of air and continued. "I travelled fast at night without a moon, out of those hills, careful not to leave tracks. Hid away."

"Did you know we were coming?" Bill asked.

"I felt Norm would send someone."

"Harry, we're on our way to another field on the edge of the plains. Would you like to come?" Bill enquired.

"Yes, I like panning for gold."

"We know a family who have recently moved there. Cedric and Nancy Hall and two children, Alice and Alfred. They're trying to make enough to buy a farm," Ian explained.

Harry nodded, "I've always wanted help develop a farm."

They talked about the Hall family until it was time to sleep, Harry was happy with a saddle cloth – using one as a pillow.

"Nothing new in using saddle cloths for me."

*

The next morning, Bill and Ian were delighted to find Harry was silent early in the morning. In fact, no one spoke until the sun was overhead and they were out on the plain country.

"Is it too early to speak?" Harry asked.

Bill laughed, "No, not now, Harry."

"Where's this new field?"

He was damned if he would admit he was looking forward to being off this tandem mount.

"Edge of the plain, I hope it's somewhere along this watercourse?" Bill answered.

"I can see hills on one side and a flat plain over there," Ian added.

"Probably not useful," Bill laughed

"Just thought I'd help, Bill."

They rounded a long bend in the creek. Up ahead on the next bend, tents were visible. Harry gave a sigh of relief. Ian felt the same way. It had been difficult having a man hanging on to him for hours on end.

Their approach was noted long before they were in full sight by the children in the field. Some ran out to meet them. Visitors were rare. Some thought police meant safety. Others took another view.

At the line of tents, Alice and Alfred called out, "Mr. Todd, Mr. Percy, follow us!"

Obediently Bill and Ian followed to where their father was working his pan, sifting for the specks of gold. Cedric stood and came forward to shake hands. He was introduced to Harry Elms who shared something of his goldfields experience.

"Can we leave Harry with you?' Ian asked.

"I'd like a hand with panning. We're doing much better here."

Ian walked beside Cedric to look at his work.

"We've appointed Harry as a Special Constable. We'd like him to make his headquarters with you. I believe that the 'accidents' will stop once it's obvious that the law has arrived and regular reports are made."

"Nancy always said you two men were special men. This is a good solution," Cedric nodded eagerly.

"Please, call me Ian," Ian added.

Nancy returned from teaching her class and was delighted with the news.

The next morning news had spread that they had a Special Constable on the field.

Harry bid the men farewell. "I don't know why I agreed. I must have sunstroke!"

Chapter Thirty-One

As the country awoke and flocks of birds left their night roosts, the silence was shattered by their noisy cries.

As they rode away, Bill asked, "What made you take Harry to the Halls?"

"If Cedric manages to find enough gold to buy land, he'll need a man for security. Females aren't safe on their own when the men are out working."

"Has Harry any family?"

"Sergeant told me he was married a long time ago but she died in childbirth. With nothing to keep him home, he left."

"So that's why you made him a Special Constable. Gives him status."

"Didn't you see his face light up when he saw the twins?"

"That made me to wonder about his earlier life. You sure there were no children?"

"Sergeant said none born alive."

Bill changed tack. "What's our next job?"

"Back to barracks, pick up rations, and new directions from there."

It was near the end of a long hot summer which had extended into autumn. The cold change was late. They rode to the top of a long hill, quite bare of any vegetation, except for one dead tree with most of its limbs still attached to its trunk. The smaller branches had fallen and lay scattered on the grass. The dead tree stood like a silent sentinel of an era long departed since it was a young sapling. Now the dead tree cast a shadow of events yet to come. Ian gazed at the patterns on the tree trunk, thinking about the goldfield lying north. A field of trapped men, a little like this tree, all on their own.

"This tree – it would have been beautiful full of leaves. I wonder how long it's been alone?" Ian commented.

"It's dead, Ian. Quite stark up here all alone."

"See. Even you recognise it as a sole survivor," Ian grinned. "As I stated when we first met, this is a new land for me. I don't take it for granted. It's like a good meal – to be enjoyed slowly."

"I don't see the environment the same way as you."

"Is it so difficult to endure?"

"Not difficult, Ian, just different."

"One day this land will be tamed. Those little enclosures will become much larger. No one will be able to ride across miles of open countryside."

"There you go again into fantasyland. If so, at least the police won't have to endure the winter camps and cold water!" Bill laughed.

"When that time comes, Bill, we'll be snug in the warm earth. That freedom will be gone."

"We're being negative this morning. We have new rations. New orders to join police on another mission," Bill commented slowly.

"I'd be quite happy never to see that gloomy valley again."

"No chance of that coming true, with the message we received yesterday. We are to return to stop any men escaping that way."

"I'm looking forward to seeing George and James arrest that man moonlighting as a shepherd."

Bill summarised the scrawled note from their superior. "Bernie and Barry are back in the Sergeant's good books – leading police up the way we escaped."

"Big operation. Any warning to the miners to lay low?"

Bill checked the details. "An undercover man has gone in as a miner to the field. Been asked to warn the men who helped us. The others are on their own."

"Bill, this is the longest message we have ever received on patrol. S'pose it's important."

"I've been wondering about the report we sent regarding 'the men tied to the trees'. One of the men keeping the miners in check, perhaps?"

"I think you're right. Seems a lot of police have been summoned. Must be more at stake than what we saw?"

They had their new directions clear. This wasn't the time to make detours. By late afternoon, the hills were in full sight, looming large on the horizon.

"We could make camp here and ride up in the early morning?" Bill suggested.

Ian concurred. "We've got company."

"Where?"

"Coming down east. Have they been waiting for us?"

Bill turned and watched the approaching police. "Why are they involved?"

"You don't want to know," Ian chuckled.

"Do you have an answer?"

"No, Bill, I haven't a clue!"

They watched the leading horsemen come into view. It was Charley and Alex.

"I don't know why you fellows can't manage your own damn criminals, without involving hard-working police?" Charley grumbled.

Bill was ready. "Charley, this is the only time we see you working. I do believe you've put on weight!"

"Rubbish! You've got bloody poor eyesight. I'm as fit as ever."

Bill grinned. "That's not very fit, Charley!"

Alex, quite accustomed to these interchanges, intervened. "You camping here tonight?" he asked Ian.

"Yah."

"In that case, I'll tell the others to camp here."

"Who?" Ian asked in surprise.

"Fred, John and Ben."

"They're here?"

"On the other side of that hill," he indicated. "We've been keeping an eye out for you. Thought you might come the other way. We came here to check."

"We were never lost," Bill laughed.

Ian checked Bill. "Let's get on with the details."

"Spoilsport, Ian. Alright, what food are you carrying, Alex?"

"Enough for all of us."

"Good, we're low on our rations. How is Ben?"

"He's been back at work for a bit more than four weeks now. A bit stiff at first, but he's doing well."

"Be good to see him again. Bill and I enjoyed his company."

Charley added cheerfully, "If Ben can keep away from you fellows, he'll remain in good health."

Ian asked Charley, "We need to make prepare the camp. Will you cook?"

"I'd be delighted," he looked pleased.

As Fred appeared, Ian scratched his head. "Why are you here, Fred, I thought you were…?"

"That's a voice I'd recognise again."

"How's the leg?"

"Much better, though I'm a long way from spending all day in the saddle."

"Tough."

"After a couple of hours, I feel it."

"Look after yourself, Fred. It's good to see you."

"Same here, Ian."

It was a happy camp with stories and laughter. But the humour was a distraction. Next day, any one of them could take a bullet.

"Did you find out why the women were washing the pottery demijohns in the creek?" Bill asked.

"Yes, the men were making a lethal form of alcohol. They plied miners with grog. Once drunk, they gave them the bad stuff. While paralytic, the girls remove anything of value, principally gold."

"How were they caught?" Bill enquired.

"Soon after moving camp, they were followed by an undercover policeman. Caught in the act. I was involved. A most satisfactory conclusion."

"A nasty way of stealing. I'm glad that lot are out of action," Ian shook his head.

"Why didn't their neighbours report the thefts?" Alex asked.

"Not so simple, Alex. Most miners don't give a damn about the man next to them. Girls can move around easily. Any neighbour would more likely think he was a lucky bastard and take no notice," John explained.

"You know it. Neighbours in some of our streets have the same attitude. Murder can be committed next door, and they don't hear a thing, even if half the street heard the screaming," Charley agreed.

They settled down around the fire after the meal and Charley told hilarious stories of life in the city. Bill mellowed.

"Charley has a wicked sense of humour," he said quietly to Ian.

"He does have a way of making others the butt of his humour. A little bit of Charley goes a long way."

"John just told me he had to go to Harry Elms' new goldfield ," Bill spoke up.

"Did he now? What did he report?"

"Harry is doing well. The strange accidents have ceased. A couple of men have left. His position has been confirmed, much to his surprise."

"That appointment solved a problem," Ian reflected.

"I couldn't believe it. I had to pretend it was from the Sergeant," Bill laughed quietly.

"He backed up our judgement, Bill."

"I wonder what Harry thought when the confirmation arrived?"

"What else did John say about Harry?"

"Only that Harry had found a large gold nugget and gave it to Cedric and Nancy. Enough value for Cedric to buy a decent chunk of land. Cedric and his family were packing up to leave the field."

"Did John say where they are moving to?"

"Apparently the southern border of Gary and Bessie Holt's property."

"I presume Harry will go with them?"

"Alice and Alfred already treat him like a grandfather. He has become quite attached to the family. That was the impression John received."

Harry had the chance of stability, probably for the first time in years.

"Last one puts the fire out! I'm going to bed!" Charley handed the papers to Alex.

Fred sat at the fire and, by the light of the flames, stared at the map of the approach to the field.

"If he'd been caught with these papers, he'd have been killed on the spot," Fred commented.

The fire was extinguished with a quart-pot of water and they returned to their swags for the last few hours before sunrise. There was a slight chill in the air and those from the city shivered.

"Do you still spend weeks out scouting when the weather turns cold?" Ben asked.

"No, only in extraordinary circumstances are we sent out into the bush."

"When do you retreat to the settlements?"

"When it's too cold to swim, and there's frost on the topside of our swags in the mornings," Bill laughed.

"How is your shoulder healing?" Ian asked Ben.

"Much better now, I've taken up swimming and the exercise is keeping me fit."

Alex leaned across Fred, "He's like a bloody fish."

Ben laughed, "Alex, you ought to come too."

"Not fuckin' likely, a bath once a week does me. Anyway, make sure you don't get eaten by a shark."

"What are they for?" Bill pointed at a pile of white cloth strips.

"Fred. Fred?"

"I'm not here. No one is to see my face outside this camp. I'm here to recognise a voice only," he explained.

"What is it, Fred?" Bill asked.

"Can't say anything."

"After Fred has identified the voice, we're to return to camp, then melt into the landscape. The cloth strips are to cover his head and face, with only the eyes showing. I'll be at his side the whole time." Ben explained.

Alex stood up. "Your attention please?"

The men stopped talking.

"We will cross the hill in front and be on the creek just after sunrise. The Special Constables will make the arrests in the camps. We'll climb the last hill and descend to the goldfield. Any questions?"

"Will there be other police with us?" Bill enquired.

"Yes, they'll arrest any man on the hill. We don't want anyone attacking us from behind our line."

"Where is Sergeant Rich?" Ian enquired.

"He's coming from the north, along the creek. I expect to see him later in the morning," Alex replied.

Chapter Thirty Two

ill and Ian rolled up their swags, attaching them to their saddles. Charley watched them, "Where in the hell are you going?"

"We might be back or we might not," Bill grinned.

"You damned bush police are men of no fixed abode. We always have to come bail you out."

Ian tipped his mug of cold water over Charley's head. "Cool down boy!"

Charley swung a punch in Ian's direction, missed, and hit John on his shoulder.

"What did you hit me for, Charley?" John protested.

"I missed that bastard. You got in the road!" Charley grinning at Ian.

Before anyone could add their penny's worth, Alex interrupted, "Cut it out, Charley, any more of that and I'll put you on report. You too, Ian."

Ian laughed, "Come on, Charley, get on your bloody horse and let's ride."

"For heaven's sake, stop stirring him up, or he'll be grumpy all day. He's bound to continue complaining about us tonight, it gets wearing after a couple of hours."

"We're not returning to the camp tonight," Ian grinned.

"We're not?"

"No, I received a note. When Fred returns to this camp with Ben, we're to escort him to our barracks."

"I thought Ben was to escort Fred?"

"Only as far as this camp. We take over and travel as far away as we can before sunset."

"I like that plan."

"It will be a relief to get away."

They rode out of the camp. Charley rode beside Bill.

"How do you stand that fucker, Percy?" he asked.

"I'm used to him, Charley. He's actually a good companion."

"You're both a little mad."

Bill laughed and lent over, putting a hand on Charley's shoulder. "Charley, we do well together, city and bush."

He grinned, "Damn bush police!"

"That's us!"

The Special Constables had arrested men at both camps. They were now on their way to the nearest magistrate, followed no doubt by time in a road-gang – a hard life for a few years.

Bill and Ian remembered the last time they were on this hill. This time, it was a lot more secure. There were extra police rounding up men who had unmercifully preyed on their victims. There was a tight ring around the hill.

The advancing police heard the shouts from the goldfield as they arrived. Many began to pack up what remained of their property and leave, walking down the creek. There were threats made, though none could be backed up with violence, with the police present.

The police line riding down the hill was a game changer. At last, it dawned upon the ruffians that their control of the field was at an end. The miners who had assisted the coppers on their last visit were packing up and leaving.

A small group of police commandeered a campfire, boiling quart-pots for tea. Bernie, Barry and James prepared damper with wild honey.

Bill and Ian walked up behind them, "The young brigade has arrived!"

To which, a smiling James replied, "We've made tea for you older crew."

Bernie grinned, handing a mug of tea to Ian.

"Any trouble on the creeks?" Bill asked.

"No, not after we arrested the shepherds. One put up a fight, but we downed him before he could do any damage." Bernie gave Bill a mug of tea.

"Bernie has been telling us about Dennis Stone. You remember you arrested him, and we took him to the magistrate?" James reminded Ian.

"Where is he?" Bill asked.

"He's dead according to Bernie!"

"What happened?" Ian asked.

"I became acquainted with the road-gang boss, this side of the mountains. We supply quite a few men. He told me."

"What happened to him?" Bill asked.

"No one knows exactly, some big stones rolled and broke both his legs. He blamed another criminal – Jim Thorne. Said he caused the accident, but he was nowhere near at the time. The gang leader called for someone to look after Dennis once the doctor had seen him. Jim Thorne volunteered, but Dennis didn't want him. He was told to be grateful."

"Did Dennis survive the night?" Bill asked.

"The doctor was surprised. He died during the night. Doc put it down to the shock of losing both legs."

"Is that all he thought?"

"It was the expression on Dennis's face most disturbed the doctor. He must have suffered dreadfully."

"Better off with no legs," Bill mused.

"Jim Thorne told the doctor he'd tried to help him, but he thought Dennis wanted to die," Bernie continued.

"Justice has been served, don't you think, Ian?" Bill commented.

"I do indeed. I wonder what happened during the night?"

"We're never going to know."

Ben arrived with Fred. "We have to go, don't ask any questions. Just get your horses and follow."

Their departure passed almost unnoticed, except Bill noticed Charley. Taking a bag, he walked over. "One of the miners who helped us earlier, gave me these ducks he'd caught last night. You may as well have them. We won't have time to pluck or cook them tonight."

Charley took the bag in surprise. A little colour spread over his cheeks. "Y'know Bill, when I say things, I don't bloody mean them. I just say them because I can."

"Don't worry. We always enjoy seeing you."

Bill nudged Charley and mounted his horse. They waved to Charley before turning and riding up amongst the trees. Out in front, Fred was deeply distressed.

When they could ride two abreast, Ian rode up beside Ben, "What's wrong with Fred?"

"Sergeant Rich wouldn't believe him. Ordered him to leave immediately."

"He identified the voice?"

"Yes, but Sergeant said it couldn't be."

"What?"

They rode in silence, passing groups of Special Constables, some with bound men, beginning the long march to justice.

*

Sergeant Rich was extremely irritated. Fred had identified the wrong man and told him so.

"You have accused a man of the best pedigree. A friend of those who orchestrate the running of the city. He is here with a friend who buys gold".

"Sergeant, it was his voice directing a man to tie us up and leave us to die."

"You are mistaken. Leave now, before you cause any trouble."

"But Sergeant, will you listen?"

"No, you are wrong."

Sergeant Rich was unaware of Fred's escort, or the care taken to protect his identity. So no-one recognisedthe man with the bandaged face.

"I had an accident." Fred explained when Rich had questioned him.

He had tried once more to give a clear picture of the voice he recognised. But, given the political ramifications of such a charge, the Sergeant's mind was closed..

"Leave now or I will charge you for in-subordinance," he barked.

Fred made a sign to Ben that they were leaving. As he mounted his horse, he began to wonder, why was the city Sergeant being kept in the dark? He had not made a mistake, nor did he like having his evidence discarded.

Fred had stormed off. Sergeant Rich was angry at the sheer stubbornness of the policeman. He was still fuming when Alex walked across to him beside the remains of a miner's camp. They talked and the Sergeant shared Fred's accusation.

"Who did he say spoke those words?" Alex asked.

Sergeant Rich spoke quietly.

Alex replied, "A serious mistake, Sergeant."

"Yes, and I commanded him to leave this goldfield or face a charge."

Alex felt a cold shiver down his spine. He was also pleased that Fred, Ben, and his two scouting friends had left. There was no gold-buyer in the camp.

"An appropriate response, Sergeant," Alex replied.

But Alex was not so dismissive of Fred's accusation. He had come to tell his Sergeant that they had found the slab hut, in which they had seized many bags of gold dust – now being loaded onto horses. The man from the city kindly offered to take them on his dray.

"Thank you, Sir, but the correct procedure is a police escort to the nearest bank," Sergeant Rich replied.

This was the Sergeant's operation. When they were all packed up, he gave the command to leave, and stood watching the line make its way up the steep hill.

At last, quite satisfied, he turned to leave. Rich gasped to discover the accused man beside him.

"Don't say my name here," his distinguished visitor murmured.

"There must be a mistake. I will clear it up in no time, Sir," replied Sergeant Rich.

"Who is the man who identified me?"

"No one of any importance. He has been dismissed."

This was a police matter. Rich was not about to betray the name of a fellow policeman. After all, he could be right.

They were on their own, the others having crossed the brow of the hill.

"Do any of your men know who I am?"

"No, Sir."

"How convenient."

Sergeant Rich wasn't an imaginative man. He gazed into the coldest eyes he had ever seen in a human being. It was a moment of complete understanding and horror.

The man smiled, "You're too smart for your own good."

And shot him.

In that brief moment, between life and death, Sergeant Rich smiled. As he dropped the gun into his saddlebag, his killer noticed that smile and wondered what it meant.

*

Three mounted policemen sat on their horses at the top of a steep hill overlooking a densely wooded valley. They had been part of the operation, arresting men during this long day. Bernie and Barry were with Alex, waiting for his Sergeant to ride up from the valley below. They had heard a distant shot but ignored it. After all there had been a lot of shooting all day. Most of the miners had left. They waited and listened carefully for the sounds of horse's hooves on the track.

"I'm going down to see what is keeping Sergeant Rich?" Alex spoke at last.

"We'll go with you."

The bush police followed Alex back down to the valley floor. The silence was confronting after the bedlam of the morning. The last of the miners were walking down the creek, almost out of sight. There was no sign of the Sergeant – his horse still tied to the tree at the base of the hill.

Alex began to feel uneasy in the silence as he trudged up the bank of the creek, followed by his colleagues walking between ancient gum trees, their massive trunks grazing the water. They walked around logs left by a recent flood. Out of sight of the main camp, they spied Sergeant Rich lying perfectly still . Alex walked forward in shock, dropped to one knee, seeing instantly that he was dead. The Sergeant's features were strangely peaceful, satisfied even.

"Bernie, go get his horse. We'll take him to the nearest settlement," Alex stammered.

While Bernie fetched the horse and scouted for rope in the depleted camp, Alex and Barry searched for evidence. It appeared he had been attacked at close range – perhaps someone he knew and trusted.

Alex checked his pockets, removing some papers to examine later. Bernie and Barry tied his corpse to his horse and they rode up out of the valley, without looking back.

"Sergeant Green will need a report," Bernie sighed quietly.

Alex was surprised. "But Sergeant Rich was a city policeman?"

"The event happened on our ground – has to be investigated. You might request to be part of it."

"Alright, I'll ride to the city and make a report with your idea in mind, Bernie."

They found a new cemetery with a couple of recent graves, outside a nearby settlement called Spring and arranged for a burial party to do the job.

"Which Minister do we get?" Bernie asked.

"I don't know, who's available?" Alex shrugged.

"There's a Roman Catholic priest visiting?"

"Ask him?"

Bernie came back and said, "He'll do it."

Alex seemed surprised, until Bernie continued.

"He found a chain around the Sergeant's neck with a religious medal. Told me 'Your Sergeant is probably one of mine'."

"I didn't think to check. Something to remember in the future," Alex mused quietly.

*

The burial was a simple affair at the grave side on a barren patch of land, with just a couple of trees as witnesses. Alex spoke a few words, the Priest blessed the body. An unknown woman dropped some wildflowers into the grave.

Alex stood beside it while two men shovelled the soil into the hole. Once filled in, one of the men stuck a wooden cross at the top end. Bernie and Barry left him alone, to take his leave from his Sergeant, whom he had known since joining.

Alex stood alone with his memories. The sun sank low on the horizon, it was time to leave. He caught the scent of a campfire in his nostrils and turned towards the creek below the hill. Their horses hobbled, his friends were waiting for him.

ACKNOWLEDGEMENTS

I bought my first computer in January 2024; in February my nephew gave me a desk and by March it was set up in my house. Beginning in April my young police friends at the local station – with far more knowledge of technology - taught me how to use it. The first step was to learn to type and become accustomed to a new form of recording. I'm accustomed to writing every day in long hand. This is a new experience.

"It's like going back to kindergarten!" one police colleague told me.

The typing was the birth of this novel, I saw no point in typing without a purpose. Regardless of what Huw says there is something in the computer which takes pages and won't give them back! There were many hours of retyping.

I have thoroughly enjoyed composing the story, it has been fun every day, except when the pages vanished never to be found!

I wish to thank Kayla Arkinstall and Philippa Razey for coming to my house and putting work on USB sticks, before the pages disappeared! I am deeply grateful to Huw who frequently came to my house after work and saved my script onto sticks, at the same time leaving notes, which I followed all the time learning by using one finger to type.

This book wouldn't have seen the light of the day without Wendy Morrow who has acted as secretary and editor of this script. She has worked tirelessly in preparing this work to send to the publisher.

I also wish to thank Sam Everingham for all his assistance in this new adventure.

My computer is about to be connected to the internet, with Huw Moore continuing to teach me in 2025. I wish to thank Ted Lewis for the use of one of his paintings on the cover.